NIGHT HAWK

BEVERLY JENKINS

AVON
An Imprint of HarperCollins*Publishers*

This is a work of fiction. Names, characters, places, and incidents are products of the author's imagination or are used fictitiously and are not to be construed as real. Any resemblance to actual events, locales, organizations, or persons, living or dead, is entirely coincidental.

AVON BOOKS
An Imprint of HarperCollins*Publishers*
10 East 53rd Street
New York, New York 10022-5299

ISBN 978-0-06-203264-5
www.avonromance.com

First Avon Books mass market printing: November 2011

Printed in the U.S.A.

10 9 8 7 6 5 4 3 2 1

This book is dedicated to Maggie Sherman.
May the wind always bring her joy.

NightHawk

Prologue

Coast of Scotland
April 1889

A somber Ian Vance stood over his mother's headstone while a gale blowing in from the North Atlantic raised his black duster like wings. During his life, he'd been blessed with the love of two women, and now both were gone. His wife, Tilda, died at the hands of a murderer named Bivens, and his mother from loneliness and broken dreams.

He gazed ruefully out at the jagged cliffs of Scotland's coast. Angled-winged seabirds called to one another as they dove in and out of the spray. His mother, Colleen, had been like them, rising and falling on the winds of life. No matter the storm, she always had a ready smile and a twinkle in her eye to let him know she'd one last trick up her sleeve, but when her beauty faded, the men who'd eagerly provided for her in exchange for what she provided in bed faded, too. In her world, youth trumped age, and there were no tricks up the sleeve for that.

The sound of carriage wheels traveling over the

cobblestone road that ambled past the small cemetery caused him to glance up. The black coach rolling into view was a lavish one; the red and gold crest emblazoned on the door all too familiar. It belonged to the local laird, Ian's grandfather.

Two decades ago, and with Colleen's blessings, Ian had fled Scotland for a new life in America. He'd vowed never to return to the land of his birth, but the letter he'd received from Colleen's ancient cook about his mother's passing drew him back to pay his respects.

He watched the coach come to a stop. He'd expected his grandfather to get word of his presence; he hadn't expected to be sought out.

The stooped, weathered man who descended the step did so slowly. His hair was snow white and Ian realized he had to be in his late seventies. Colleen had given birth to Ian at a young age and without the benefit of a husband. That sin alone guaranteed her soul a seat in hell, but the revelation that the sire had been a Black seaman with the British Navy so enraged her father that he'd banished her, his only child, from their home.

And now that same man approached. A gnarled cane aided his steps and his sun-lined face held the same green eyes as Ian's. If Colleen's father had been furious about the birth, he'd been doubly so to learn that her half-Black bastard child bore his name.

"I heard you were here," his grandfather offered by way of greeting while critically assessing Ian from head to toe.

"I've no intention of darkening your doorway, if that's your thinking."

"Why are you here?"

Ian let the pun pass without comment. "I only recently found out about her death. Came to pay my respects."

His grandfather turned his eyes to the cliffs and the roaring sea. While the wind whipped at their clothing and the tall grasses covering the treeless plateau, he appeared to be lost in thought or maybe in the past. "I done her wrong," he finally intoned in his thick Scottish burr. "She was me only child."

Ian kept his face void of emotion because the admission had come too late for that only child.

The elder Ian added quietly, "She loved you."

"And I her." But there'd never been so much as a smile from her father for Ian.

"You passed university at Edinburgh."

"Yes sir, in the law."

"That what you do over in the colonies, practice law?"

"A bit, yes."

"Everybody there dress in that fashion?" he asked, pointing the cane disdainfully at Ian's Western-style leather clothing.

"No." Ian supposed he did look out of place in his wide-brimmed hat and the leather duster over his black shirt, leather trousers, and gun belt, but he felt no more out of place than he had growing up. England's vast navy and merchant fleets were made up of men from all over the world, and as a consequence there were mixed-race children throughout the empire's port towns. But in the tiny Scottish coastal village of his birth, there'd never been anything like Ian before, and many of the locals went out of their way to make certain he knew it. As a child, to be singled out and taunted simply for one's parentage had hurt, but he'd used the slurs and bullying to make himself stronger and smarter. To cower and cry would have proven true all the negative things he'd been told about a man with his blood. He'd found prejudice in America, too, but he was no longer a child and could hold his own.

His grandfather reached into a pocket of his worn red waistcoat and withdrew a small leather pouch that he passed to Ian.

"What is this?"

"The dowry I never allowed your mother to have. It's your inheritance now." And apparently he had nothing more to say. Turning away, he began walking to the coach where his driver stood ready and waiting beside its opened door. After taking a few more steps, however, he stopped and glanced back. The aged green eyes that met Ian's held hints of regret. The two men faced each other with only the past and the howling wind between them until his grandfather spoke. "Because she loved you when I could not, go with God, Ian, but never return to my lands again."

Tight-lipped, Ian watched as his grandfather climbed inside and the coach rumbled away.

Ian put the bag of gold into his coat and refocused his attention on his mother's headstone. He offered a few prayers and whispered a final goodbye. "Farewell, my beautiful Colleen. May God love you as much as I. Rest in peace."

He mounted his stallion, Smoke. Taking one last look around at the wildly beautiful place that would hold her, and in many ways himself, for eternity, he reined his mount around and galloped off to meet the ship that would sail him back home to America, where he was known as a bounty hunter named the Preacher.

Chapter 1

The wind gave our children the spirit of Life.
Chief Joseph

Dowd, Kansas
May 1889

Preparing dinner in the kitchen of the whorehouse where she worked as the cook, Maggie Freeman decided she'd had enough. If the owner, Hugh Langley, tried to force himself upon her again, she'd have to give her notice. In truth, such a decision made little sense. In a town as small as Dowd, Kansas, the chances of hiring on somewhere else were slim to none, but she knew she had no other choice.

Maggie's father, Franklin, a Black Civil War veteran and staunch Lincoln Republican, and her mother, Morning Star, a woman of the Kaw tribe, had been killed in a fire when Maggie was twelve. She'd be twenty-five in December and had been on her own since the day they died.

Dowd was a dozen miles south of Kansas City and she'd been employed at Aunt Phoebe's whorehouse for two weeks. Her previous position as a washerwoman in the household of the mayor and his wife in the neighboring town of Madison had been short-lived. Because it was a well-known fact that all Blacks and Natives steal, Maggie had been accused of taking a brooch that belonged to the mayor's wife, and in spite of her fierce claims of innocence she'd been promptly arrested and jailed. The brooch, which had actually been misplaced by its squat, hairy-chinned female owner, was found the next day in the pocket of one of the woman's day gowns. The charges were dropped, but there'd been no apologies forthcoming from the mayor or his wife, nor had they offered to reinstate her. So Maggie'd saddled up her old mare and ridden the six miles west to Dowd where the only job available had been at Aunt Phoebe's whorehouse. She'd taken it gladly.

Now it appeared as if she would have to leave Dowd as well. Two nights ago, Phoebe's business partner, Hugh Langley, had stumbled into Maggie's room smelling of cheap whiskey, and tried to force his way into her bed, again. Showing him the business end of her father's old Colt dampened his enthusiasm, but she'd had to endure his sullen, hate-filled slurs before he finally removed himself and left her in peace. That was the third time she'd had to run him off. After the first incident, she'd tried to talk to Phoebe about his behavior, only to be waved off dismissively and told that Hugh was the scion of a wealthy family, accustomed to getting what he wanted, and that Maggie should be honored by his interest. It became clear that there'd be no help from that quarter so she'd taken to sleeping with the Colt beneath her pillow.

Putting the drunken Langley out of her mind, she concentrated on spooning the biscuit dough into the wooden dough bowl. She'd just picked up the rolling pin when she was suddenly forced against the counter and held there by someone behind her. She felt hands frantically snatching her shirt out of her skirt and forcing her skirt up her legs.

"I got ya now, squaw!" Hugh Langley crowed, his hot, foul breath against her ear.

Fighting to buck off his heavy weight and keep his hands out of her clothing, she cried out and reached for something to arm herself with. He spun her around and tore open her shirt all in one motion. She slapped him hard. In the split second that it took for him to grab his stinging cheek, she swung the heavy rolling pin across his jaw with all the force she had. The blow sent him staggering. His knees buckled. Simultaneously stumbling and falling, he hit his temple hard against the sharp corner of the wooden table in the center of the small kitchen and collapsed in a heap to the floor.

In the silence that followed, she tried to calm her racing heart, hold her torn shirt together, and not cry out from the fear that had flooded her during the attack. Wary, she moved closer to where he lay unmoving. She held the pin high and at the ready in case he tried to grab her again, but she saw blood creeping from beneath his profiled face.

Suddenly Phoebe swooped into the kitchen, asking, "Maggie, are those biscuits—" She glanced first at Maggie standing as she was holding the raised rolling pin, then down at Langley sprawled out on the floor lying in a widening pool of blood, and her overly made up eyes widened. She dropped to her knees beside him and screamed, "Someone run for the sheriff! She's killed him! Oh my Lord! She's killed Hughie."

"He attacked me!"

Phoebe's eyes held fury. "You're going to hang!"

"I didn't kill him! He attacked me and hit his head! Look at my shirt!"

But it didn't matter. The sheriff arrived, and after all the yelling and accusations stopped, Maggie was once again arrested and taken to jail.

Sullen and angry, she paced the small cell like a cat in a cage. No one cared that she'd been trying to protect herself. No one cared that her ripped shirt bore clear evidence of Langley's dastardly intent. The sheriff, a middle-aged man named Wells, seemed to be a reasonable person and had asked that Phoebe find Maggie a shirt to replace the torn one, but he still put the shackles on her wrists and walked her past a crowd of jeering townspeople and down the street to the log building that held his office and the jail.

"Going to be at least two weeks before the circuit judge comes back this way," he told her once she was inside the cell with its straw-covered floor and bare mattress. "But I'll try and make your stay as comfortable as possible." And he departed.

Although she knew crying wouldn't alter her plight, tears of rage and frustration wet her eyes before she angrily dashed them away. It was difficult being a woman alone, having to secure food, shelter, and, most of all, safety. With no family or husband, she was easy prey for thieves and two-legged coyotes like Hugh Langley, but she was determined not to give in to fear. The year after her parents' death, she'd worn fear like a coat. Her parents had loved her, educated her, sheltered her as best they could, and then to find herself suddenly without them had been the most frightening thing she'd ever known. Some of her neighbors had taken her in at first, but in the end she was just another mouth to feed. She'd gone door to door in an attempt to find day work but the roles were already filled by older women who lived nearby. Finally the sisters at a convent outside Lawrence took her. They gave her meals and a place to lay her head at night in exchange for chores like scrubbing floors and working in the kitchen. She stayed for six years.

Although the sisters had been charitable, not a day went by without them reminding her that she would be condemned to hell if she didn't renounce her ties to her Kaw mother and the rest of her *savage* kin, and transform herself into the godly young woman the sisters supposedly personified. It was a constant theme played out all over the country as churches and schools did their best to separate Native children from their tribes, their parents, and the cycles of life that had been practiced long before the landing of the first Europeans. According to the sisters, Maggie's mixed blood presented an even bigger challenge for her immortal soul, seeing as how men and women of African descent were considered inferior in every way, and it didn't matter that her parents had raised her to be proud of her blood, the sisters and the church were right and Maggie's parents wrong.

To stop the daily lecturing, Maggie let them believe she agreed, but in her heart she continued to honor her mother and father and her heritage.

In the jail later that evening, after a dinner of ham and beans, Maggie got her first look at Hugh Langley's daddy, Hank. The big, burly man and six other men rode into town with torches in their hands, firing their guns and circling the jail. She quickly moved away from the window to avoid being seen and prayed the sheriff would stop them before they stormed the jail.

The rapid answering shots of a Winchester sent her hurrying back to the window. A crowd of townspeople had gathered, but it was impossible to tell if they were there to support the riders or just being nosy.

The sheriff's voice rang out, "Hank Langley! Next man to fire is under arrest!"

The steeliness in his tone and raised gun brought the action to a halt. Maggie prayed Langley and his men didn't respond with shots of their own.

Langley called out to the sheriff in a reasonable-sounding voice, "Now, Sheriff, I know you were elected to uphold the law, but that nigger squaw killed my son!"

The crowd reacted with a vocal agreement. From behind his still raised rifle, Sheriff Wells disagreed, "Coroner Potts says differently. Hugh died when he hit his temple against the table just like she claimed, so we'll let the judge sort it out at trial."

"That'll take too long!" Langley shouted back angrily. "I want justice, now! Step aside!"

The sheriff's voice remained firm. "She stays until the judge shows up. Take your men and go before I charge you with interfering with a peace officer."

Maggie didn't know the sheriff personally but she was pleased that he respected the law enough not to hand her over. Vigilante justice was common all over the West, and she had no desire to swing from the end of a rope for something she didn't do.

The sheriff barked again, "Go home! All of you!"

Maggie saw Hugh's father's angry face in the flicking light of the torches. He gave her cell a long, ugly look as if he knew she was in the shadows watching, but he signaled his men and they thundered out of town.

The buzzing crowd dispersed soon after and Maggie finally exhaled her pent-up breath.

For the next three nights, Langley returned, and with each visit the numbers of men riding with him increased. They didn't rush the jail, but were seemingly content to ride back and forth with their torches held high while yelling, calling Maggie nasty names, and threatening her life.

By the fourth morning, the sheriff came to her cell to tell her of the decision he'd made. "I'm taking you up to Kansas City on the afternoon train. You'll be safer waiting on the judge there. I don't think Langley's got the nerve to follow you to a place that has United States marshals."

She hoped he was right. She also hoped she'd be able to get a full night's sleep there instead of tossing and turning and worrying if she'd be dragged out of the jail to her death.

"Got a real dislike for Hank Langley," the sheriff revealed. "He and his money have been running roughshod over folks here for a long time. I ran for sheriff because I was tired of it."

"When do we leave?"

"Train comes in around eleven. Langley's got men watching the place so I'm hoping we can get to the depot and on board before he gets word."

She'd seen the men in question lounging against the doorway of the general store directly across the street. "Will you let me have my Colt in case we're ambushed?"

"No, but I'll do all I can to keep you safe."

Maggie wasn't happy. Her father had taught her to shoot at a young age. Being able to defend oneself was necessary, just as it might be on the way to the depot, but the sheriff had confiscated her ancient Colt and her small cache of personal belongings upon her arrest. The only thing she'd been allowed to keep was her father's old army jacket, which she wore to keep herself warm and the memories of her parents alive.

"You ride?" he asked.

"Yes. My horse's over at the livery. She's old and slow, though. Not a mount I'd want for a dash." Like most farm girls, she started riding before she could walk.

"I'll loan you one. Where'd you get that coat?"

"Belonged to my father. He was with the First Kansas Colored and a sergeant with the Ninth Cavalry. He and my ma are dead now."

"Sorry to hear that. I'd just as soon let you go, but folks here wouldn't like that, so I have to leave it to the judge."

"I understand. Thank you for standing up to Langley."

"You're welcome." He picked up the tray and plate that had held her breakfast of dried fruit and a small piece of bacon, turned the key in the cell door, and returned to his office up front.

The sheriff returned for her later. Maggie had already decided that if she had a chance to escape she would. There would be no justice for a woman with her blood because there never had been, otherwise the Democrats wouldn't be killing her father's people all over the South, and her mother's people would still have their lands, instead of being forced to eke out a living in the dusty poor soil of Indian Territory. She was a descendant of strong men and women on both sides of her family, and she refused to have her fate decided by courts that had proven time and again that people with her ancestry didn't matter.

"I'm going to have to put the bracelets on you again."

"How am I supposed to ride?"

"Very carefully."

By his smile, she assumed he meant that to be a joke but she failed to see the humor. Apparently her cool gaze gave him second thoughts because he cleared his throat and said, "Give me your wrists, miss."

She complied and he clapped on the metal cuffs. He'd cuffed her wrists in front, but in spite of the restraints, she managed to get her foot in the stirrup, and use her immobilized hands to grab the horn of the saddle and pull herself up. Once mounted, she saw that people along the walks had stopped and were staring her way. A man whom she'd seen positioned in front of the general store most of the morning suddenly tossed his toothpick aside and eyed her and the sheriff keenly. She assumed the man to be one of Langley's employees.

"That's one of Langley's men," the sheriff corroborated while lifting himself into the saddle of a big gray stallion.

The Langley hand yelled out, "Mr. Langley ain't gonna like you trying to sneak her out on the train, Sheriff."

Maggie wondered how he'd learned about the sheriff's plan, and from the anger flooding the lawman's face, it appeared he was wondering the same thing. Wells ignored the challenge, however. "Let's go."

Holding on to the reins and the horn as best she could, Maggie rode out of town under the sheriff's escort and the hostile eyes of the people of Dowd. She saw the Langley employee run to his horse and ride hard west. She wondered if she'd make it to Kansas City alive.

The depot was only a few short miles away over wide-open land so she didn't have much time to get herself positioned to make a run for it. It was a struggle for her to get the reins to fit her partially immobilized grip just right and not telegraph her intent to the sheriff riding silently at her side. Unlike her old mare back at the livery, this horse was younger and stronger. She could feel the black stallion's strength and power beneath her and knew that at full gallop the animal would fly like the wind her mother's people, the Kaw, were named for.

A hawk circled lazily overhead and then swooped down after something hidden in the tall grass. While the sheriff's vision followed the bird's flight, Maggie dug her heels hard into the stallion's flank and yelled at the animal to go. The big stallion took off. As it accelerated and adrenaline rushed through Maggie's blood, she leaned low over his neck as if they'd been riding together all their lives. Suddenly she was brought up short. A lariat was imprisoning her arms. Eyes wide, she was yanked backwards out of the saddle and was airborne just long enough to scream with alarm before hitting the ground hard. Then she was being dragged behind the sheriff's galloping horse over the rocky road. Stones scraped her face, dust filled her mouth and lungs. She twisted and cried out but there was no way to escape the sharp stones, sticks, clods of horse manure, and mud from last night's rain. When the ordeal finally ended, she lay there with her lungs pumping like eagle wings. Pain screamed everywhere. She opened her eyes and saw him standing above her glaring down.

"Get up!" he snapped. "Be glad I didn't shoot you."

She wasn't sure she could, but managed somehow and met his angry eyes with her chin raised.

"I've done my best to treat you nice, and this is what I get?"

"The judge isn't going to let me go, and you know it. Once Langley and the others tell their lies, I'm going to hang." Regardless of the extenuating circumstances, she'd caused the death of a White man, and for a person of color punishment would be severe. She could see her words taking effect, but his sworn duty apparently overrode whatever his conscience might have harbored.

"Have to admit, I didn't expect this much spunk."

She took that as a compliment.

"Gotta tie you up for real this time, miss."

Maggie nodded and stood motionlessly while he twined the rope around her torso so that her arms were positioned flat against her sides, and her hands bound uselessly behind her. He cinched the knot tight before helping her back up on the stallion that had been waiting obediently. Trussed and defiant, Maggie rode the rest of the way to the depot trailered behind the lawman like a captured prize of war.

Chapter 2

As the Kansas Pacific slowly wound its way west, Ian gazed out the window at the flat, monotonous plains of Kansas and longed for the rugged mountains of Wyoming and home. After leaving Scotland last month, his ship had docked in Boston and he'd been riding trains across the continent for what felt like an eternity ever since. Jim Crow laws were making it difficult for people of color to travel, and he'd encountered some of the prejudiced attitudes from a few passengers and railroad agents along the way, but his imposing stature and all-black attire seemed to make the bigots think twice about voicing their displeasure at his presence in the main car, so no confrontations had been necessary. That suited him fine because he wasn't looking for a fight. All he wanted was to put the years he'd spent tracking down murderers and bail jumpers as the Preacher behind him so he could reclaim his identity as Ian Vance, return to his ranch, and spend the rest of his life enjoying the mountains, his horses and cattle.

The tall, red-haired conductor walked through

the car to announce the next train stop, a small Kansas town called Dowd. Ian glanced out of the window and was about to return his attention to the *Harper's* magazine he picked up in St. Louis, but was brought up short by the sight of a mounted woman waiting at the Dowd depot. Her arms and hands were bound by a length of rope. She was wearing a battered, blue Union jacket, a long skirt covered with mud, and boots. She appeared to be of mixed race. Black and Native, he thought possibly. There were cuts and scrapes on her autumn-colored face as if she'd been in a fight, and her long black hair hung down her back in an unruly plait. The older man mounted beside her wore a lawman's star, so Ian assumed the woman to be his prisoner and wondered what the story on her was. Was she wanted, or simply under arrest for a recent incident? As if sensing his scrutiny, she glanced up and met his gaze with dark eyes that blazed contempt. The fiery contact lasted just long enough to pierce him before she looked away. For reasons he couldn't explain he wanted her to look up at him again, but she'd apparently given him all the attention she intended to spare. The lawman was conversing with the conductor, who seemed to be gauging the female prisoner warily.

His curiosity high, Ian watched the lawman lead her and her mount towards the back of the train. The sound of gunshots startled him. Through the window he saw five riders racing hell-bent for leather towards the depot. The other passengers crowded around the windows and panic swept through the car. Women began pulling off their jewelry and hiding it in their bosoms. The men quickly opened the windows closest to where they sat and waited to see if they'd be adding themselves to the fight. Ian cursed inwardly and got to his feet. In the same motion he reached into the inner pocket of his duster and smoothly withdrew the sawed-off pump action rifle he always carried. He set off to find the conductor. Even though train robberies were declining near the larger cities, out on the plains lawmen were stretched so thin there were still outlaws looking to prey on trains and help themselves to whatever valuables it or the passengers carried. He knew this to be true because at one point in his life, he'd been one of them.

Angry that his peaceful ride home was being delayed by men bent on who knew what, Ian heard the train's whistle blow. When he felt the cars begin to move he hoped the engine would be able to get up to full speed before the riders caught them.

The harried-looking conductor was so distracted he ran right into Ian's chest. Before the man could begin apologizing, Ian cut him off. "Are you carrying gold?"

"No. The sheriff says they're after his prisoner."

"The woman?"

He nodded hastily. "I need to get to the front."

But before he could depart, Ian stayed him. "Where is he?"

"Cattle car."

Ian headed for the end of the train.

Inside the cattle car, he found the tense-looking

sheriff feeding shells into his Colt while keeping an eye on the approaching riders through the opened door of the car. Ian surveyed the woman. The rope was no longer binding her but her hands were cuffed.

The sheriff looked up and scanned him silently before saying, "You're Vance Bigelow, the Preacher."

Ian adopted the Bigelow name when he became an outlaw in order to hide his true identity, and continued to use it when the death of his wife, Tilda, turned him into a bounty hunter. He acknowledged the sheriff's words with a nod. "Came to see if you needed my gun."

"Heard Judge Parker made you a deputy marshal."

It was true, and although Ian still had the star, the appointment wasn't something he crowed about.

"My name's Wells, by the way. I'm the sheriff over in Dowd. The riders belong to Hank Langley. He's holding her responsible for his son's death."

The sound of gunfire was steady and close.

"I didn't kill him," the woman said hotly, "but Langley wants me to hang anyway. Give me my gun, Sheriff, so I can defend myself."

"And have you maybe shoot me and the marshal and make a run for it? No, miss."

Ian studied her while loading his gun. Was she a deadly beauty? The sultry set of her mouth alone could set brother against brother, and even with the fresh-looking scars and scrapes marring her skin, she was stunning.

He was about to ask for more details on the

riders when the scream of the emergency brakes filled the air and they were thrown off balance as the train screeched to a halt.

"Now what?" Ian grumbled. "Stay with her, Sheriff. I'll be back soon as I can."

There were three mounted men in the middle of the track. The brakes had been applied to keep the train from mowing them down. Surveying them from the engineers' station at the front of the train, Ian sighed. At this rate, he wasn't ever going to get home.

One of the men yelled, "Send out the squaw and we'll let you pass!"

Ian assumed they meant Wells's prisoner. To hear her called a word as demeaning as the ugly word *nigger* didn't improve his mood.

The scared-looking conductor whined, "I have a schedule to keep and lives in my hands. Tell the sheriff to send her out."

"How about we send you out instead?"

The man drew back.

Ian stepped out of the car and down onto the track. As he did, he noticed that the five riders had caught up with the back of the train. They had their guns leveled on the sheriff and the woman and were forcing them to walk up the tracks while the wide-eyed train passengers looked on.

Ian added the number of men with the sheriff to the three waiting on the track. Eight against one, or maybe two, if the sheriff was able to wade in. Still, Ian liked the odds.

When he reached the three riders on the tracks, the big bearded man positioned in the middle, who appeared to be too heavy for such a small mount, asked disdainfully, "And who are you?"

Ian ignored the derisive tone and held up his star. "United States deputy marshal. You?"

The man quickly covered his shock with bluster. "Hank Langley. That squaw murdered my son."

"And what are you going to do with her?"

Wells and the woman arrived. Wells looked angry. The woman did, too, and Ian saw her meet Langley's mocking eyes with disgust.

"Gonna teach her about justice."

"Justice doesn't need a mob."

Langley turned red as the conductor's hair. "You calling me a coward?"

"Sure am. Also advising you and your boys to head home before you get hurt. I've been on a train for weeks and my temper's not real good. I'm liable to shoot you just for making us late."

Langley stared at his fellows as if he couldn't believe what he was hearing.

Ian quoted, " 'There is a way that seemeth right unto a man, but the end thereof are the ways of death.' Proverbs 16:25."

Out of the corner of his eye, he saw one of the men by the sheriff raise his gun. Ian whirled and fired. Horses reared, men cried out, and when the quiet resettled three of the five were on the ground writhing in pain from the bullets in their shoulders and arms. The two wide-eyed men still mounted slapped the reins across their horses and hightailed it out of there.

Ian watched them riding hard across the plains. The three he'd shot slowly clambered to their feet. From the pain and fear on their faces, it was apparent they hadn't been expecting resistance when they joined Langley's merry band of vigilantes.

Ian announced to them, "Boys, you have one minute to hand the sheriff your guns, mount up, and ride away."

They needed only a portion of the allotted time, and escaped on their mounts.

Ian was liking the odds more and more. He turned a wintry gaze on the wide-eyed Langley. "Are you going to let the train pass or do I shoot you three, too?"

The two men flanking Langley didn't need the question repeated. One rode off without a word, while the other, eyeing Ian warily, stayed just long enough to say to his boss, "Sorry, Mr. Langley," before wheeling his horse around and riding after the others.

"Need your answer right now," Ian told Langley.

Sheriff Wells declared, "I'll answer for him." Irritation filled his face. A big Colt filled his hand. "Langley, you're under arrest."

"The hell I am!"

Wells shot him in the leg. The big man yelled out in pain as he tumbled from the horse. While he lay writhing and cursing, Wells walked over to his female prisoner. "Miss, if you'd hold out your arms, I need my bracelets back."

She obliged and while she massaged her freed wrists, Wells snapped the cuffs on Langley and hauled him to his feet.

With a bullet wound in his leg, standing appeared to be difficult for Langley, but it wasn't Ian's concern. None of it was. He'd neutralized the situation and could now return to his seat. He gave the woman a passing glance and started back to the train.

The sheriff's voice followed his steps. "Bigelow, I'm going to take this vermin back to Dowd. Need you to take my prisoner to the sheriff in Kansas City."

Thinking he must have misheard him, Ian stopped and turned back. "Excuse me?"

"Langley's going to jail for impeding a train, assault on peace officers, and anything else I can come up with, but I can't be in two places at once."

Ian stared between the watching woman, the mutinous-looking Langley, and the sheriff. "Who says I'm going to Kansas City?"

"The train schedule says Kansas City is the next stop, and you are a peace officer."

Ian sighed. He'd taken the oath a few years back to help out a friend, nothing more. He didn't even know if the appointment was still valid.

"And make sure you keep a tight rein on her. She's already tried to escape once."

Wonderful, he thought and glanced over at the dirty-faced woman. "Tell me what happened between you and his son."

She calmly detailed the times Hugh Langley attempted to force his way into her bed, and the sequence of events that led to his death. Having met Hugh's father, Ian was inclined to believe every word, but he wasn't the judge.

"Bitch is lying!" Langley snarled.

Wells glared. "Coroner says she's telling the truth. I'd've already dropped the charges, but knew I'd have to deal with this one," and he indicated Langley, "so I wanted to wait and have the judge rule."

"I need a doc, dammit!" Langley bellowed. Blood was beginning to seep through the hole in his trousers, but his demands were ignored as Ian mulled over the sheriff's words. He could either argue with the sheriff and further delay his journey home or he could agree and get the train moving again. "All right," he said to her. "Come on."

It was easy to see from her tightly set features that she'd rather not, but she had no choice and so fell in beside him for the walk back to the train.

Once aboard, the conductor said breathlessly, "Thank you! Are you taking her back to the cattle car?"

"No, she'll be in the seat by me." He pulled a pair of cuffs from his coat and clapped one ring on her wrist and the other on his.

The startled man looked at her mud-stained skirt and boots. "But she can't ride in the main car."

Ian shot him a dark look.

"Um, well maybe she can, as long as you take full responsibility for the safety of the other passengers."

"Isn't that what just happened?"

The man cleared his throat. "I, um, I'll have the engineer get us under way."

"You do that."

So the female prisoner now under his care took Ian's seat by the window. Ignoring the outraged faces of the other passengers, he settled into the aisle beside her and the train resumed its journey to the next stop. Kansas City.

Maggie didn't know what to make of the marshal seated beside her, but she did know that she'd never witnessed anyone take down three men in the space of a breath the way he'd done back there. If Sheriff Wells had his way and all the charges against Langley stood, she'd never have to worry about Langley threatening her life ever again. But that left the problem of how to escape from Bigelow, or better still, convince him to let her go. After the astounding display of his gun prowess an escape attempt didn't seem real smart. Convincing him to let her go might prove the better idea, but in truth, she was stuck with him, at least for the present.

The train got under way and she was glad to be away from Dowd. She could see only a portion of Bigelow's face because of the brim of his black hat, but the green eyes were memorable. He had a faded scar that ran vertically down his unshaven cheek. She looked around the car and found herself being scrutinized by the other well-dressed passengers. There wasn't a friendly face in the bunch. Admittedly she looked like something the cat dragged in because she had been dragged through mud and manure and heaven only knew what else. Her hair had come loose of its single plait and was wild as an eagle's nest, and she was so dirty she could smell herself from a mile away. Like the conductor, the paying customers probably wanted her in the cattle car, but she had the marshal to thank for not agreeing. He could have just as easily retied her, tossed her in with the cows and horses, and fetched her when they reached Kansas City. That he hadn't made her wonder what kind of man he was.

Something else that caught her attention was the tone of voice he'd used during the confrontation with Langley and his men. He hadn't yelled or shouted. In fact, he had a way of speaking that might be considered soft-spoken until you heard the deadly power behind the words. Watching him scare the bejesus out of them, he'd reminded her of a coiled snake. You knew it would strike, just not when.

She hazarded a glance his way and found him reading a *Harper's Weekly*. That surprised her as well. Not many people in the West were literate enough to read just for the sake of reading, so she assumed him to be an educated man. She added that kernel of information to the pot and wondered what else she might learn about Deputy Marshal Vance Bigelow before he handed her over to the authorities in Kansas City.

"What's your name?"

"Maggie Freeman."

"Bigelow," he said by way of introduction, and returned to his *Harper's*. She gave him another discreet glance and wondered how he'd gotten the scar. Not that it mattered. She was facing larger issues, and musing over the sheriff's past would not save her from what lay ahead. People like her had been hanged for much less than what happened to Hugh Langley, and that scared her. No, her life wasn't the best; she'd been living hand to mouth since the death of her parents, but it was her life, and she didn't want it to end swinging from a scaffold.

Chapter 3

As the train rolled into Kansas City, Maggie stared out the window at the largest depot she'd ever seen. There appeared to be more people milling around it than there were living in Dowd and Madison combined. She saw women wearing fancy traveling ensembles and carrying parasols. The gentlemen were decked out in cutaway suits of all colors and patterns and wore smart-looking derby hats. In her present filthy condition she knew she'd draw the eye of everyone within ten miles. She wanted to ask the marshal if she could get a bath before he turned her in but doubted he'd afford her such a luxury.

As it stood, all she could do to try and make herself presentable was attempt to tame her hair with her hands, but that was difficult because of the cuff on her right wrist attached to his left. Raising her arm garnered a stare from him, so she explained, "I just want to try and plait my hair before we go out into the streets."

"I don't think it'll much matter."

Her lips thinned. Ignoring him, she raised her

hands to her hair again. She expected him to protest but he didn't, so she did what she could while his arm moved in tandem like a puppet. When she was finished, she watched him slowly survey the results. Before he turned away, she thought she caught a ghost of a smile cross his unshaven face. That didn't help her mood, but there was nothing to be done about it.

The train slowed to a stop. The other passengers grabbed the handles on their valises and carpetbags and prepared to depart.

"We'll wait until everybody else gets off," he told her, and placed his magazine into his saddlebag.

Maggie tersely nodded a reply while doing her best to ignore the disgusted looks the other passengers threw her way as they passed by. She knew what she looked like. She didn't need reminding.

"Okay. Our turn."

Maggie scooted across the seat. He led her off the train and out into the busy depot.

As she and the marshal made their way, some of the travelers stopped and stared slack jawed. A buzz went through the place. Mothers grabbed their children as if the handcuffed Maggie or the tall man in black might do them harm. One woman, wearing an expensive, bustled traveling costume, looked so terrified, Maggie snarled at her like an angry puma. The woman screamed and swooned.

As people rushed to her side, the marshal didn't break stride, but he glanced back at her satisfied face. "Stop that."

"I couldn't resist."

"Try harder."

"Yes, Marshal."

That earned her another look, which she met unflinchingly.

While people continued to give them a wide berth, he headed to the end of the train to retrieve his horse.

"I'm going to undo the cuffs. If you run, I will find you."

She believed him.

It was a magnificent smoke gray animal, even larger and more powerful-looking than the one she'd ridden on her futile escape attempt from the sheriff. Bigelow led it down the plank and she watched as he greeted the animal with an affectionate voice. "We'll be home soon, old boy. Promise."

He handed her her old saddlebag that had been left behind in the straw when she and Sheriff Wells were ordered off the train at gunpoint by Langley's vigilantes. She opened it and checked the contents. Her precious red dress and shoes were inside but not her weapon. "Wells still has my Colt."

"You're under arrest, you aren't allowed firearms."

"But it belonged to my father," she protested. "That and this coat are all I have left of him."

"Take it up with Wells next time you see him."

"Please don't patronize me."

He viewed her silently for a moment.

She asked coolly, "Am I not supposed to know the meaning of the word *patronize*, Marshal?"

"Not sure." There was muted humor in his eyes.

"Something amusing?"

"Where'd you learn to speak so properly?"

"My father was an Oberlin graduate, and a schoolteacher before and after the war."

"That explains it." He mounted his horse and offered her a hand up. She accepted the help, and although the palm that closed over hers was rough and calloused, the grip was gentler than she'd assumed it would be.

"Hold on."

She wrapped her arms around the leather duster, and he reined the horse out into the streets of Kansas City.

Maggie had never been to Kansas City before, so she was impressed by the modern brick buildings and all the people. She had no idea if Bigelow knew where he was going, but she stared longingly at the public bathhouse they rode past.

After another few minutes of picking their way through the thick traffic of wagons, carriages, buckboards, and riders, he stopped. "We're here."

Maggie read "Sheriff's Office" on the hand-painted sign above the building's door, and sighed resignedly. She dismounted and waited while he tied the horse's reins to the post.

Inside, a young man wearing a star on his red plaid flannel shirt was seated behind a desk. He eyed them curiously for a moment. "How can I help you folks?"

"Got a prisoner for the sheriff. You him?"

"No, sir. I'm Deputy Peterson. Sheriff Nash is out with a posse. Bank was robbed this morning." The kid's eyes slowly widened. "Why you're the Preacher! I've seen your picture in the newspapers!"

Maggie glanced up at the marshal. Was he a famous lawman then? And why was he called Preacher? She remembered him quoting Scripture before opening fire on Langley but she didn't know any men of God who could wield a firearm the way he had.

He didn't speak to any of that, however. "Dowd's Sheriff Wells wants her kept here until the circuit judge comes around. Vigilantes are giving him problems."

"Sheriff's going to be real upset that he didn't get to meet you."

From the marshal's stony set features, the deputy seemed to understand that Bigelow was there on business and nothing more. "Um, what's she charged with?"

"Accidental death."

"Can't take her."

"Why not?"

"Under instructions not to put anybody in the jail. Sheriff wants the cell empty so he can throw the bank robbers in when he gets back."

"And that'll be?"

The deputy shrugged. "The men he's after are supposed to be heading to Indian Territory, so maybe be a week, two, maybe three." His eyes brushed Maggie. "Besides, we don't have any place to put a woman. Try the sheriff in Abilene. Maybe he can take her."

The deputy paused and grinned. "I can't believe I'm talking to one of the most famous bounty hunters in the West. Heard Hanging Judge Parker down at Fort Smith made you a marshal, too."

He didn't speak to that, either. "Wells wanted me to leave her here."

"I understand that, sir, but you can't."

"Is there a marshal in town?"

"Yep. He's with the posse."

Maggie wanted to cheer, but kept her face impassive as stone.

"Try Abilene," the deputy repeated. "Sorry."

Bigelow turned to go. "Thanks."

Maggie followed him back out to the street. She waited to see what he might propose next, but before he could, they heard a woman shout accusingly, "You!"

Maggie's eyes widened at the sight of Minerva Quigley barreling down the walk towards them.

"I want that heathen arrested!" Minerva demanded angrily.

Ian sighed. *Now what?* "Afternoon, ma'am. Is there a problem?" She was glaring at his prisoner with such vehemence he was surprised there wasn't steam pouring out from beneath her ugly straw bonnet. His prisoner appeared calm, but there was a hint of icy humor in her gaze.

"Somebody get the sheriff! I want her arrested!"

"She's in custody, ma'am."

"You're a lawman?"

"United States deputy marshal," he said hoping that would deflate whatever this might be about.

The doubt on her face was plain. In many areas of the country, men of color were not allowed to wear a star, and those that did were sometimes forbidden to arrest Whites. Judge Isaac Parker didn't follow the practice.

By then a number of people on the walks had stopped to see what was occurring, including the young deputy who'd stepped outside to investigate the commotion.

"Why's she in custody?" Minerva demanded to know.

"None of your damn business!" the Freeman woman responded.

Hearing that, Minerva puffed up like an outraged hen. "Don't you dare talk to your betters that way." She raised her parasol as if to strike her for her insolence, only to have the parasol snatched from her hands and thrown forcefully out into the street, where it promptly struck the head of a teamster innocently driving by. The unexpected blow caught him so by surprise he lost control of his four-horse team. They reared and spooked another team pulling a load of wagon wheels, which ran into a team of bays hooked to a fancy coach that careened directly into the path of an ice wagon, which lost its load and sent a buckboard skittering up onto the crowded walk, where people scrambled to get out the way. Arguments broke out as drivers confronted one another over their wrecked vehicles, spilled cargos, and runaway horses, and then fisticuffs commenced. The young deputy tried to instill order by firing his gun in the air, which of course only caused more horses to rear in fear and more collisions to ensue.

A speechless Ian stared down at the woman who'd caused it all. She met his gaze with a raised eyebrow.

A short while later when things began to settle down, Minerva Quigley turned to accuse Maggie Freeman of starting the disaster, but she and the marshal were no longer there.

As Ian and Maggie rode slowly across the open countryside outside the city limits she was glad to be rid of Minerva Quigley. At the height of the disturbance the marshal had taken Maggie's hand, and under the cover of the chaos, they'd mounted up and ridden away.

Now with his horse reined to a walk, he asked, "So who was that woman?"

"Minerva Quigley. Owner of Miss Minerva's School for Quality Girls. It's a boarding school for incorrigible young females. I worked there for a while."

"Until what happened?"

"Until I woke up one morning and found my plait had been snipped off while I was asleep and tossed into my chamber pot." And she had never known such fury.

"Who did it?"

"Belinda Carrington, a fifteen-year-old, spoiled little hussy who'd been sent to the school by her parents in Boston."

"Did you talk to Quigley about it?"

"Of course, but I was told to get back to work. Same story when I complained about their slurs, their tripping me when I carried in dinner, and the day they smeared mud all over the floors I'd spent hours mopping and waxing."

"Sounds like a nice bunch. When was this?"

"A few months back."

"So after your talk with her, you returned to your duties?"

"I did, but I knew Belinda was the ringleader so I confronted her and told her plainly how I felt about having my hair cut. She laughed, called me a squaw, and walked away." And what happened next was something she'd never forget. "Later that morning, I was called down to Miss Quigley's office and told that Belinda had accused me of slapping her. Quigley didn't believe my denials, so to punish me for assaulting my betters, as she put it, all the girls were lined up and allowed to slap me in the face as hard as they could."

She felt his back stiffen in reaction.

"How many were there?"

"Eight." Maggie's rage rose all over again. Quigley's charges took great pleasure in striking her, especially the hateful Belinda, but Maggie refused to react to the blows, even though by the time they were done, her face was swollen, black and blue.

"Was that the end of it?"

"No. I was then informed I'd been let go, and that I wouldn't be receiving the month's wages I was owed due to my inappropriate actions, so I gathered my personal belongings and left." Being denied the wages she'd worked so hard for only added more salt to an already blood-raw wound.

"If she let you go, why's she still mad?"

"Because when I left the house I hid in the woods nearby. I knew it was the day they went into town to visit the lending library, so when they all piled into the wagon and drove away I went back into the house." She didn't tell him about the furious tears she'd shed while waiting for them to leave. "Since Quigley had fired me before I could empty the chamber pots, they were still in the upstairs hallway. I took them back into the rooms and poured the contents onto the beds. When I was done, I went out to the barn, saddled up the old mare they'd left behind, and rode away."

"Adding horse theft to her list of your sins."

"I didn't care. She should be glad I didn't burn the house to the ground, that was how enraged I was. My jaw was so swollen I couldn't eat for over a week." There were no words for how she felt having to stand there and be slapped like an uppity slave, but as she calmly moved from room to room exacting her revenge it gave her some measure of satisfaction imagining the looks on the faces of Miss Quigley and her charges when they returned. "I suppose you think I should have just licked my wounds and turned tail."

"Didn't say that." What she didn't know was that he'd had similar experiences at some of the schools he'd attended during his youth, and like her he'd had to mete out some hard lessons to make the daily torture and harassment cease. "You said your pa was dead. Is your mother living?"

"No, they were both killed in a fire."

"How old were you?"

"Twelve. Been on my own since. What about your parents?"

"Mother died last year. Never knew my father."

Maggie had adored her father and wondered how it had been for the marshal growing up without one, but she thought that too personal a question to ask. "The deputy in town made a real fuss over you. Are you famous?"

"I just do what I'm paid to do."

The deputy said the marshal was a bounty hunter, too. She wondered what kind of life men like him led. Did he have a family, a wife? Maggie yawned. She couldn't remember the last time she'd had a full night's sleep. Her stomach reminded her it had been almost five days since she'd had a decent meal, too. The ham and beans at the Dowd jail had been just enough to keep her alive. According to Sheriff Wells, usually one or two of the town's women volunteered to provide meals for his prisoners, but there'd been no such offers while she'd been there. He didn't know if they'd been influenced by threats from Langley, so he was forced to share his own humble meals with her. As a result she was hungry enough to eat a saddle boiled in witch hazel.

Because of her weariness, the lulling motion of the slow-moving horse was making it difficult for her to stay alert and awake. "So where are we going?" she asked through another yawn.

"The farm of some friends of mine. We'll stay there for the night and get back on the train in the morning. That is unless the deputy comes after you for causing that ruckus."

"It wasn't my fault. She was going to hit me. You saw her."

"Mayhem like that follow you around often?"

"No." Or at least she didn't think so, but at the moment she was too weary to be absolutely positive. The leather of his coat was soft and smooth against her face and her next thought never materialized because she was asleep.

Chapter 4

Ian didn't realize she had fallen asleep until her body slumped against his back. When he turned around to see about her, she would have tumbled to the ground had he not reacted quickly to keep her upright. Still, her snoring resembled the sound of a fast-moving train. Deciding she was turning out be more faceted than he'd envisioned, he roused her gently. Her eyes popped open and fear flashed in them before she awakened enough to get her bearings.

"You should ride up here in front of me before you fall off."

She dragged her hand across her face and straightened her shoulders. "No. I'm fine."

He wondered about the source of the fear she'd masked so quickly.

"How much longer until we get there?"

"Hour or so."

"Oh." Her disappointment was plain. "Let's just go on then. I know how badly I smell, and if I sit in front of you, we'll both stink to high heaven."

"Smelled worse." Most of the outlaws and bail

jumpers he'd dealt with hadn't placed a priority on personal hygiene, and neither had he when he'd lived on the wrong side of the law.

"Nice of you to say so, even if you are lying, but I'm all right here. I'll stay awake."

He could see both determination and embarrassment in her manner. He also wondered about all the nicks and cuts on her face.

She placed her arms around his waist again and he set the horse back on pace.

After a silence she asked, "Why don't you just let me go? You heard Sheriff Wells say Hugh Langley's death was an accident."

"Can't."

"You mean, won't."

"No, can't. I told the sheriff I would drop you off. I'd like to think I'm a man of my word, even if I don't think you should be here."

"The judge isn't going to see things my way and we both know it."

"Depends on the judge."

He heard her sigh in what might have been frustration or anger, but he had no way of knowing. What he did know was that he wasn't going to spend the next hour arguing with her over something he wasn't going to allow, at least not until he could come up with a way to circumvent her legal dilemma that wouldn't have him hauled before a judge, too.

When they rode up, Rand Tanner was out in the field feeding slop to his hogs. He was shaped like a cracker barrel, and the smile that creased his features when he saw Ian showed a few missing teeth within the graying beard that covered his cheeks and chin. His eyes were still as blue and as sharp as they'd always been, however. "I'll be dammed, if it ain't the Preacher man."

Ian's face broke into a rare smile. "I'da thought Betsy would've gotten herself somebody younger and better-looking by now."

Rand had retired from the outlaw business about the same time Ian had. Since those days he'd taken up farming and wound up married to the youngest daughter of a Baptist preacher, a feat much talked about in outlaw circles when word got around. Rand and Betsy had been together over a decade.

"Ain't a young stud within five hundred miles can replace this old stallion. Who you got there with you?"

"Prisoner." Ian dismounted.

Rand seemed surprised by the gender. "Well, come on in. Betsy's got supper almost ready." He looked the woman over. "She okay to be in the house?"

Before Ian could respond, she slid from the horse and said, "No, and not because I'm a danger to you or your wife, but because I am far too filthy." She turned on Ian. "And contrary to what the marshal says, my name is not prisoner. I'm Maggie Freeman. Pleased to meet you."

Rand appeared flummoxed.

Ian took in her cool fire and wondered why she was so puffed up. She was a prisoner.

Rand had a distinct twinkle in the old blue eyes when he turned back to Ian, but he kept his thoughts to himself, which Ian appreciated because Rand usually had more opinions than the Book of Kings had names.

"Come on in, Miss Freeman. We'll see what Betsy can do to help you clean up." He asked Ian, "She is allowed a bath, ain't she?"

"Yes."

"Good."

Why Rand made it sound as if Ian was playing the role of villain he didn't know but followed them into the house.

His mood lightened when Betsy hurried over to give him a hug that he returned genuinely.

"Oh, Preacher, it's so good to see you again. Been too long."

He agreed, and when she stepped back he felt warmed by her smile. The feeling brought to mind his late wife, Tilda, and he immediately buried the thought. "Told Rand, I was surprised you still keep him around."

She glanced her husband's way and her eyes shone with deep affection. "I could do much worse."

Rand grinned.

Only then did Betsy seem to notice his prisoner. "I'm so sorry. I'm Betsy Tanner, and you are?"

"Maggie Freeman. The marshal's prisoner."

Betsy's surprise was as plain as her husband's had been. She turned to Ian for an explanation, to which he responded, "Tell them why you're under arrest."

"For defending myself against an attacker. I walloped him across the face with a rolling pin.

He fell, hit his temple against the corner of a table, and died."

"Good for him," Betsy declared. She then peered at the cuts and scrapes covering Maggie's face. "He do that to your face?"

"No, the sheriff."

Ian's eyes spun to hers.

"I tried to escape. He lassoed me and dragged me behind his horse. Teaching me a lesson, I suppose."

Betsy gasped, "My heavens, that couldn't have been necessary."

Ian expected Freeman to agree but to his surprise she said, "He's a lawman, ma'am, and I was trying to get away."

Betsy didn't look as if she agreed. "First thing we need to do is get you a bath. You smell terrible, honey."

"I know, my apologies. There was no place to bathe at the Dowd jail and I was dragged through quite a bit of manure."

"How long were you there?" Rand asked.

"Four days."

Betsy shook her head as if she found the entire episode disturbing. "Why on earth would the sheriff lock up a woman for defending herself? Probably for the same reason half the population of this country can't vote," she added pointedly.

Ian and Rand kept their mouths shut. They knew what a crusader she was, and they didn't want to get her started.

"Come on, Maggie." She turned to the men. "You

two make yourselves useful and heat up some water. Once she's had her bath, then we'll eat."

"Mrs. Tanner, please don't delay your supper for me. I can sit outside until you all are done."

"Nonsense. I'm not letting you spend another minute smelling or looking this way."

So Ian watched his tight-lipped prisoner be led down the hall. She glanced back at him for a second and then refocused her attention on whatever Betsy was saying.

Rand's voice made him look up. "Let's get the water started and we can sit and talk."

Ian followed him out to the pump.

Once Maggie and Betsy were alone in Betsy's bedroom, Maggie discreetly studied the room. It looked so normal and lived in, with its patchwork quilt covering the big bed. An upholstered wing-back chair had a crocheted doily spread over the back and there were framed pictures of painted birds on the white plaster walls. Maggie couldn't remember the last time she'd been in a real home where a person could sense the love within its walls. She corrected herself. She'd been twelve years old and living with her parents. She buried those thoughts and concentrated on what Betsy was saying while looking through a large wooden armoire. "You and I are about the same size, so here's a shift, a blouse, and a skirt."

"I can't take your things, Mrs. Tanner."

"Sure you can, and call me Betsy."

"But—"

"No buts, Maggie Freeman," she countered with a look that was both stern and gentle. "I may not know you, but you're in this mess because you defended yourself, and the least I can do is offer you a bath, supper, and clean clothing before you move on to wherever you're going."

"I think Abilene. The marshal was supposed to bring me here and leave me with the sheriff but the deputy wouldn't take me." Maggie told her about Hank Langley and the vigilantes and what happened when Langley met the marshal.

"Leave it to the Preacher to scare the pants off someone. He's good at that from what I hear."

"You heard right." The shock on the faces of the men he'd shot would have been comical had the situation not been so serious. "He wasn't pleased when Sheriff Wells gave me over to him, though."

"That's okay. Sheriff Wells put you in good hands."

Maggie scratched at what were probably the fleas she'd picked up from the straw-filled mattress in the Dowd jail, and was immediately embarrassed.

"Let's get you in some water."

Maggie had no idea what kind of bathing room the house had but finding herself outside was unexpected.

"Rand likes to tinker, and this is one of his contraptions."

It was built like a tall, closed-in horse stall. Betsy opened the door. "The water is placed in that barrel up top there."

Maggie looked up at the barrel curiously. The

base of it was attached to a short piece of wood. Connected to the wood were two long lengths of rope.

"You pull this rope to tip the barrel so that water comes down like a rain shower. Then pull this one to return the barrel to an upright position."

Maggie had never seen anything like it before.

"The ground can get kind of muddy so he built that short platform of slats to stand on. It keeps your feet out of the muck."

"This is very ingenious."

"Works like a charm, too."

Betsy gave her soap and a washrag, some towels, and a robe to put on once she was finished. "I'll get them to start filling the bucket. They'll have to climb up there to fill it each time, so make sure you cover yourself until they're done. And we have plenty of water, so don't worry over how much you're using. You get as clean as you need."

"Thank you."

"You're welcome. I'll send them right out."

Shortly after Betsy's departure, Maggie heard Rand calling, "You ready, Miss Maggie?"

"Yes." She was as giddy as a child.

"Okay. Coming up the ladder out here to fill you up."

"This is a wonderful invention, Mr. Tanner."

Next she knew he was at the top of the stall and looking down. They both grinned.

He filled the barrel from another barrel of water about the same size.

"All done. Betsy show you how to work the ropes?"

"Yes, she did."

"Then happy washing. Yell if you want more. Preacher man and I'll hear you." He offered a parting nod and disappeared back down the ladder.

Maggie quickly undressed and placed her dirty clothes on the ground in a corner. She tugged on the rope and sure enough, the barrel tipped and the water began to cascade down. It took her a moment to get the flow right, but the idea was to get wet, soap up, and rinse off. The rope didn't allow for the water to flow in a continuous steady stream but she imagined Mr. Tanner would figure out a way to perfect that before long.

All in all it was wonderful. Even though she could only douse herself a portion at a time, the water was hot and glorious. She used the first two barrels on her hair. Because of her mixed heritage it was thick and long. And filthy, having not been washed in weeks. When she was done soaping and rinsing it, her head felt ten pounds lighter and her jet black hair was sleek and running down her back like an African stream.

Ian and Rand were seated on the back porch within shouting distance of what Rand called his washing tower. Tired and worn out from all the traveling, Ian hadn't protested when Rand took it upon himself to be the Freeman woman's water bearer. So far, he'd delivered four barrels.

"You get the next two. I'm old and getting tired."

"Sure."

Settling himself back into his seat, Rand picked up the conversation where they'd left it before he'd gone to deliver more water. "So, tell me about this marshal business I've been hearing about. Is Judge Parker getting feebleminded?"

"No," Ian replied while slowly savoring the cigar Rand offered him when they first sat down. "I was really sworn in by Griffin Blake."

"Oklahoma Red? Who in the hell was crazy enough to make him a marshal?"

Griffin Blake was a good friend. At one time he'd been one of the most notorious outlaws west of the Mississippi, and like many in the profession answered to various names, most of which had the word *red* in them due to his coloring and hair. "He was in a Kansas jail when Seminole Marshal Dixon Wildhorse got him freed in exchange for help with an investigation Wildhorse and Judge Parker were working on down in Texas last year."

"Blake as a lawman. If I was dead, I'd be spinning in my grave."

"Gets worse. The other two deputies he swore in were the Twins."

Rand choked on his whiskey. In a strangled voice he asked, "Neil and Shafts?"

Ian nodded. "And believe it or not, we got the job done. Griff even wound up marrying the lady rancher we were there to help."

"You're pulling my leg. Blake? Married? Is the woman blind?"

"Nope. Name's Jessi Rose. She's a pistol."

Rand shook his head. "Will wonders never cease."

Silence crept between them for a moment as they both thought back on the past.

"Once I get back to Wyoming, I'm going to put the Preacher to rest."

Rand studied him and then nodded as if he understood. "Preacher was a force to be reckoned with, but there comes a time when who we were no longer fits who we've become."

"Amen. And I'm hoping I've balanced the scales enough to make the man upstairs forgive me for my earlier sins." In the years since coming to the States, he'd been an outlaw, a hired gun, and had ridden with gangs that robbed trains and banks. In one of those banks he'd met Matilda Lawson and his entire world shifted.

"You need another woman," Rand offered sagely, as if he knew Ian had been thinking about Tilda.

"No, I don't. Never letting that happen to anybody I love ever again." Tilda was killed by a member of a gang Ian had been riding with. It took him a year to track down Bivens, the man responsible. The bounty on Bivens said dead or alive, so Ian sent him to hell.

"Another woman will heal you just like Betsy healed me."

"You're awfully philosophical these days."

"Betsy says the same thing."

The two friends shared a smile, and a past few could imagine.

"We had some fun, didn't we?" Rand asked in a wistful tone.

"That we did."

"Bet you never thought an Edinburgh-educated lawyer would wind up robbing banks just so he could eat." Rand was one of the few people who knew Ian's life story.

"Not in a hundred years." But the prejudice in places like the large cities on the East Coast had let him know early on that making his living as a lawyer would rarely be allowed. Within six months he'd used up nearly all the funds he'd brought with him from Scotland, so he took the last bit of it and purchased a train ticket west. As luck would have it, he found himself on a train to Denver sitting next to a man of color who introduced himself as Neil. They struck up a conversation, and over the course of the next few hours, Ian told him his tale of woe. Neil was easy to talk to and listened well. Ian had been enjoying his company when all of a sudden Neil stood up and announced a robbery. In reality he was Neil July, one half of the outlaw siblings known as the Terrible Twins. In fact, the twins had members of their gang positioned in seats throughout the train. After they finished relieving the passengers of their valuables and the train of its gold, the smiling Neil asked Ian if he wanted to join them. A lover of adventure his entire life, Ian didn't hesitate. He rode with the twins and their lawless associates on and off for the next five years. "The law degree came in handy when I represented Neil in his fight against the railroad last fall."

"Heard about that, too."

"May I have more water please, Mr. Tanner!"

Rand called back to her. "Sure can!" He looked over at Ian. "Your turn."

Ian stuck the cigar in the corner of his mouth and got to his feet.

When he reached the top of the ladder, she was standing below him looking up. He sensed she'd been expecting Rand because her eyes widened with surprise for a moment and she put a firmer grip on the towel she had wrapped around her body. Her transformation from filthy to fresh was so dramatic, the cigar fell from his lips. He saw her hop out of the way so she wouldn't be burned by the glowing tip and then look up at him as if he'd lost his mind.

"Sorry." But he couldn't stop staring.

"Something wrong?" she asked tightly.

Realizing his eyes were stuck on the smooth tops of her breasts rising discreetly above the towel, he shook himself free and looked away. "No. How does this contraption work?"

"Pour the water in the barrel."

He complied.

"Thank you," she said. "That should be the last barrel. I don't think I'll be needing any more water."

Ian knew he'd been dismissed but he couldn't seem to move. She was so clean that her bared shoulders and arms outside of the towel glowed like newly minted copper, as did her face. When he first saw her back at the Dowd depot, he'd sensed the beauty beneath the dirty coating, but he had no idea she was beautiful enough to turn a man into stone. And below his belt he was just that—stone hard.

"You leaving or not?"

"Sorry," he mumbled. He climbed back down the ladder and beat a hasty retreat.

Later, when Ian availed himself of Rand's tower, all he could think about was the woman who'd bathed in the space before him.

Chapter 5

The others were already at the table when Maggie came in. Rand took one look at her all cleaned up and declared, "Maggie Freeman, the only woman lovelier than you is my own Betsy."

Betsy gave her husband a nod of thanks, then gestured for Maggie to take her seat. "You look wonderful, my dear."

Maggie felt wonderful. Her borrowed white blouse and plain brown skirt fit well. She'd braided her freshly washed hair into its signature single plait, and for the first time in a long time was clean from head to toe. She glanced the marshal's way. It appeared that he'd washed up as well. The hat was gone and she got her first unencumbered look at his features. The emerald green eyes staring back at her were set in a pale gold face that remained unshaven. His hair was brown with a texture that gave a nod to his mixed-race blood. He was arrestingly handsome and the faded scar only added to his dangerous air. For a moment she watched him watching her until she finally severed the contact and turned her attention to the gathering.

Betsy brought out platters of chicken, potatoes, and collards along with fat hot biscuits running with freshly churned butter. The sight of so much food almost made Maggie swoon, while her stomach growled approvingly at the prospect of a meal that consisted of something other than the bits of ham and beans she'd been given at the Dowd jail.

Rand said the grace and they dug in. Maggie didn't realize she was attacking her food like a starving dog until she looked up from her plate and found the marshal and the Tanners staring her way. Self-conscious and embarrassed, she sat back and used her napkin to wipe her mouth. "Been a while since I had a true meal," she confessed quietly. She sensed tears forming. "And I do have manners, just haven't had to use them much . . . Excuse me." She rose from the table and hurried from the room.

Outside on the porch she gazed up at the moon and tried mightily to ignore the sting of the tears clouding her eyes. Her behavior at the table left her appalled. The sight of the moon made painful memories stir and she unconsciously found herself singing the traditional Kaw chant to greet the rising moon that she'd learned as a child. For as far back as she could remember, her mother and grandmother had honored the old ways and made sure Maggie did as well, so each evening as dusk turned into night, they sang. Moving into the second verse, she vocally greeted the wind and the night sky. The familiar words gave her comfort while the tears ran unchecked down her cheeks. Spirits knew she needed comfort because she'd had so little of it since her parents' deaths. The well-loved and well-brought-up girl child who'd had aspirations of attending Oberlin, or one of the new Negro colleges in the South, to become a teacher was now so hungry, she'd fallen on the food at the Tanners' table like something feral and wild. She'd spent the last thirteen years on her knees scrubbing other people's floors, or standing over vats of hot, lye-laced water washing other people's clothes. She'd been beaten, slapped, and called names no one had a right to be known by, and she'd been paid insufficiently and sometimes not at all. She'd also done things no woman should have to do in order to survive, but she had, so that she could.

And now, as if her burdens weren't weighty enough, she was facing incarceration and maybe an appointment with the hangman. She didn't expect a judge to show her mercy because she'd had so little of that in her life, too.

After singing the last few notes, she quieted. Feeling a presence behind her in the shadows, she turned and saw the marshal. She didn't speak and neither did he. They seemed content to silently study each other while the insects and owls chanted their own greetings to the night. "Did you come to make sure I hadn't run off," she finally asked before turning back to the darkness spread out over the Tanners' land. She wiped at her eyes, not wanting him to see her tears.

"That was one of the reasons."

"And the other?"

"We all know how it feels to be hungry. No one thinks less of you."

She tightened her lips as the shame rose again. "I owe them an apology for my rudeness."

"They weren't offended. Betsy wants you to come back in and finish your meal. Said she'd even let you have your pie first if you'd like."

A small smile showed. "She's very kind." Kindness was lacking in her life, too. In the years that she'd been on her own, no one had given her anything that hadn't come with strings or a price attached.

"What were you singing?"

"It's an evening song I learned from my mother."

"What nation?"

"Kaw. The trappers called us Kanza. She and my grandmother were members of the Wind Clan. Our lands were where the Blue Earth and Kansas rivers meet." Her people had lost so much. The reality that it might never be reclaimed added yet another layer to the melancholy she'd fallen into. Only rarely did she allow the circumstances of her existence to overwhelm her as it had inside. To give in to the loneliness and despair would be to descend into a kind of madness that would paralyze her; she'd seen it in the blank eyes of whores and saloon girls, and in the sadness of women trapped in marriages with no love. They moved through life like puppets in a show, as if all of their hopes and dreams had been stripped away. Hers had been as well, but melancholy be damned, she was still standing, and still fighting to hold on to who she was in her heart and mind.

As if he somehow sensed the shift in her emotions, he asked quietly, "Ready to go back in?"

She turned to him. "Yes."

Ian watched her for the rest of the evening. Although she'd seemed genuinely appalled by her earlier behavior, he'd been more appalled by the reason for the ravenous hunger she'd displayed. Had Wells not fed her, or had the portions been so small that she'd never gotten her fill? How long had it been since she'd had a full meal? Obviously some time. When she ran from the table earlier, he hadn't expected to find her crying. Granted, he didn't know anything about her, but she hadn't impressed him as being prone to weeping, so it gave him pause. He took a sip of whiskey from his shot glass and continued to view her while Betsy talked about a rally the local suffragettes were holding later in the month. Having enjoyed Betsy's apple pie, Maggie looked content as she sat at the table listening to Betsy, who was now on her soapbox. She was still thin, however, and he doubted one meal would restore her entirely, but at least tonight she'd go to bed on a full belly. He knew it was unusual for him to muse over a prisoner. Usually his only concern lay with transporting them and himself to the appointed jail or courthouse and getting there in one piece, but for some reason she was different. From the moment he saw her at the Dowd depot sitting on that mount, looking all the world like a conquered but still defiant queen, his curiosity had been piqued. Her outstanding beauty was also having an effect. He ran his eyes over her full lips, the smoke black eyes, and relived how she'd looked standing below him glowing with dew in Rand's washing tower.

Ian took another sip. He prided himself on his self-control, especially where females were concerned, but the sight of her had left him as hard as a virgin cowboy with his first whore. Just looking at her made him aware of how long it had been since he'd last let desire have its head, and that was out of character for him as well.

When the women rose from the table to begin the after-dinner cleanup, he glanced up to find Rand observing him. As if his old friend had been reading Ian's thoughts, Rand smiled and raised his whiskey in silent salute. Ian chose to ignore him. The only thing he was concerned with was finding a solution to her dilemma so he could go home. He knew she was right to be concerned about seeing a judge. Depending upon who it might be, she could face serious consequences, and no part of him wanted to be responsible for her being incarcerated or worse, hanged. Were it up to him, he'd cut her loose, especially since Wells admitted the only reason he'd arrested her was because of Langley's father. He sighed. He'd figure it out.

By bedtime, a weary Maggie was dead on her feet. Betsy showed her into the small, cozy spare room where she'd be sleeping. The sight of the large, comfortable-looking bed would have made Maggie weep with joy had she not been so exhausted. Sleeping in a bed for the first time in days was going to be heavenly.

Betsy loaned her a long-sleeved nightgown and a robe. After she departed with a friendly "I'll see you in the morning, rest well," Maggie removed the borrowed blouse and skirt, left them nicely folded on the floor by the bed, and donned the gown. She wanted to think about a plan for escaping the marshal, but as she sank into the arms of the soft, down-filled pillow, she was asleep before she could finish her contented sigh.

Rand and Ian sat out on the back porch and watched the night. Rand said, "That Maggie Freeman is a pretty little thing. What are you going to do about her? She shouldn't be going before a judge for defending herself."

"I know. The sheriff said he would've let her go free if the vigilantes hadn't gotten involved. Times being the way they are, who knows what a judge might do."

"You got a law education, you ought to be able to figure out a way for her to wiggle loose."

"I've been thinking about it. Maybe I'll wire Sheriff Wells. Now that's he got the father in jail, maybe he'll go ahead and drop the charges against her." He told Rand about the confrontation with Langley on the train track.

Rand shook his head in disgust. "Eight men against just a slip of a girl. Good thing you were there. What about Judge Parker, didn't you give him and Blake a hand down in Texas?"

"I did."

"So, he owes you."

"Parker doesn't owe anybody, you know that. Ask Grover Cleveland." While president, Cleveland had tried to get one of Parker's verdicts overturned, but in the end, the president was the one who backed down. "I'll hold off on Parker until I hear from Wells. Where's the train stop after Kansas City?"

"Bradley. It's about a half day's ride."

"Okay, I'll wire Wells and go from there."

He and Rand spent a few more minutes catching up on their friendship, then they agreed it was time to turn in.

Carrying a lamp to light the way, Ian could hear her snores even before reaching their room. Opening the door, he stepped inside. She was cocooned under a pile of bedding. The wavering light showed a comfortable-looking wingback that he could sleep in, but first he wanted to start a fire in the stone grate to take the chill off the air. He set the lamp down and as quietly as he could went about the task. Once he was satisfied that the flames would hold he stood and glanced down at his sleeping prisoner. She hadn't moved, and from the volume of her snoring, he doubted she would before sunrise. She was obviously weary. Because she'd already tried to escape once, he would be sharing the room just to make sure she was still around come morning.

Maggie awakened to a semidark room. Groggy and disoriented, she glanced around at the unfamiliar surroundings. Seeing the marshal seated in a chair in the shadows brought everything rushing back. Calming her racing heart, she wondered how long he'd been there. "What time is it?"

"Almost four."

The flickering light from an oil lamp on a small table beside him was just strong enough to pierce the darkness. Near her bed was a fireplace that she'd apparently been too tired to notice earlier. Its heat warmed the air, and the dancing flames added their light to the shadows. She didn't question his presence; she was his prisoner after all, but the sight of him left her rattled. That her body was calling did not. "I need to use the facilities." From her visits earlier in the evening she knew it was outside.

Swinging her legs from beneath the warm bedding showed that the gown had hiked up during her sleep and that her copper legs were on full display in the soft glow. Refusing to look his way to gauge his reaction, she set the garment to rights and got to her feet. "I suppose you'll be going with me." She pushed bare feet into her old boots and donned the pink robe Betsy had left.

He answered by rising from the chair.

On the short walk there, she shivered in the cold.

"Should've brought your coat."

"I've been out in worse, in less." When she lived with the sisters, it was her job to chop the morning wood while wearing only a thin jacket as protection against the frosty air.

When they reached the door, she asked, "You're not coming in with me, are you?"

"No."

Thankful for that at least, she went inside.

On the return trip, he maintained his silence but his presence loomed as vividly as the star-studded sky stretched above her head. She was still tired and wanted to go back to sleep, but wasn't sure how difficult that might be knowing he'd be seated only a few feet away.

Back inside the Tanners' spare room again, she climbed beneath the bedding and felt the shivers coursing over her as her body tried to warm up again after the brief sojourn outside.

"If you're worried about me bothering you, don't."

She paused and sought to make out his features in the wavering darkness. From any other man those words might have left her skeptical, but him she believed, even if she didn't know why, and even though she remembered those smoldering emerald eyes looking down on her from atop the washing tower. "I appreciate that."

"Go back to sleep. Train to catch in the morning."

Ian knew she'd drifted off when the soft sounds of her snores rose against the silence. He pulled the lamp a bit closer and went back to reading his Bible. After Tilda's death, pain and grief waged a war for his soul. The night he found her body, he'd screamed at every god he knew and in every language he spoke. *Why?* Why did a woman as sweet and innocent as his Tilda have to die so horrifically? For weeks after her funeral, rage and revenge consumed every moment of every day and he neither slept nor ate. In spite of all his inner turmoil he continued to ask why. Tilda had been a churchgoer and always believed the Bible held the answers, so he picked it up one night. Having been raised by his Catholic mother, Ian was familiar with the holy book but hadn't opened one in decades.

The New Testament had been Tilda's favorite, and as he read a bit each night, he learned why. She'd tried to live her life by the Son's teaching by being charitable and forgiving to everyone she knew. He, on the other hand, found the Old Testament more to his liking. Yahweh gave no quarter, and after tracking down Tilda's killer, Ian spent his years as a bounty hunter doing the same.

He stretched his arms and shoulders in his chair. The few hours of sleep he'd snatched right after midnight had been more than enough. He'd slept confident that he'd hear her if she awakened and made an attempt to sneak away under the cover of darkness.

Looking over at her, he found himself wondering what she'd do if Wells granted her her freedom. She'd given him the impression that she'd been living pretty much hand to mouth since being on her own and finding employment when and where she could. It was not the life a woman should have to lead, no matter who she was, but it wasn't his concern. Once he heard from Wells and everything was cleared up, he'd go his way and she'd go hers.

He read the last few verses of Kings and in spite of his claims of being rested, his lids slid closed and after a few more ticks of the clock on the wall, he was asleep.

Maggie had been feigning sleep, so as soon as his snores reached her ears, she stayed motionless for another minute just to make sure he wasn't pretending as well before she sat up slowly. Silent as a shadow she left the bed. Having lived in a convent, she knew how to move like a whisper. Gathering up the borrowed clothing, her boots, and her pack, she kept one eye on his sleeping form while she covered the short distance to the door. Hands on the latch, she worked it slowly until the door opened. She shot one last look back his way. Noticing no discernible change in his position or measured breathing, she slipped out and gently shut the door. The sisters at the convent would've praised her stealth; Maggie'd only had to be beaten twice to realize that when the nuns said quiet, they meant it.

She assumed the Tanners were early risers like most farm people, but it was still dark, so she hoped they were asleep. Her heart pounding, she crept by their room as silently as she could. The thought of all the food in the Tanners' kitchen drew her there. If she succeeded in her escape, food would be needed. She had no money to leave in payment and felt bad about stealing from them after their many kindnesses. Maybe one day in the future she'd be able to return and make amends, but presently she had no time to chide herself about fractured morals. Getting away from the marshal and finding a place to hide until the law forgot about her was her only concern.

Problem was, she couldn't see a thing in the small kitchen. Although she'd helped Betsy clean up after dinner, this was not Maggie's home and therefore she didn't know what was where in the dark. She sort of knew where the cold box stood, but could she get to it without tripping over something or knocking against something that might be heard and bring attention to herself? She could still taste the succulent chicken Betsy had served for dinner and she knew there'd been a good portion of it stowed away, but decided she'd have to leave without it. Too chancy.

And just as she turned to head out of the door that led from the kitchen to the outdoors, she saw the light of a candle, followed by Betsy's soft voice. "Are you leaving us?"

Startled and guilty, Maggie froze. Taking in a deep breath and knowing the marshal was probably standing behind her as well, she braced herself and turned. "Yes."

But Betsy was alone. "Then take these and I'll get you some food." She handed Maggie some folded garments. "They're an old pair of trousers I use in the field, and a man's shirt."

While the speechless Maggie stared agape, Betsy and her candle moved quickly to the cold box, now visible in the small glow.

"Why are you helping me?"

Betsy responded with a shrug and whispered, "You shouldn't be punished for defending your honor, and the color of your skin shouldn't be a factor, either."

Maggie knew Betsy was a female crusader, but

also knew that many times crusaders like her were only interested in their own personal equality. At that moment Maggie wished she could remain and enjoy the friendship of such a remarkable woman, but that couldn't be, either.

Betsy quickly placed a variety of food items in a tea towel. Tying the edges tight, she passed Maggie the small bundle. "Godspeed."

Once again Maggie wanted to linger but knew she could not. "Thank you." She hurried out into the night.

Chapter 6

Ian awakened to a sun-filled room. Head fuzzy with sleep, it took a few seconds for the empty bed to register and when it did, he jumped up and rushed out to the main section of the house. He found Betsy in the kitchen frying bacon. "Where's my prisoner?"

"She isn't in the room?"

Ian hurried outside to the facilities. On the way, he spotted Rand pouring water into the pig's trough. "You seen the Freeman woman?"

Rand stopped. "No. She missing?"

Ian pounded on the door of the facilities. Receiving no response, he gingerly opened the door and found it as empty as the bed had been. He cursed and took a slow survey of the countryside. It'd been just before dawn when he saw her last, which meant she had a good two-hour start on him. *Dammit!* "Any horses missing?"

Rand went to see. Ian hurried to join him. She'd already confessed to having stolen a horse in the past. If she'd ridden off on Smoke, he'd skin her alive.

The stallion was in his stall, however, and so were all of Rand's animals. Ian let out a sigh of relief that only marginally tempered his stormy mood. Seeing the knowing smile on Rand's face didn't help matters.

"Weren't you two in the same room?" Rand asked. "How'd she get by you?"

Ian had no idea.

"Aren't you supposed to be the best in the West?"

The emeralds glared. Rand's grin widened. "Being on foot is going to slow her down, so that should help you out."

Ian agreed. Unless she'd sprouted wings, he should be able to find her easily enough.

"I'll tell Betsy you'll be taking your breakfast with you. Go ahead and saddle up." But Rand had one more dig. "Who'd've thought that little girl would outfox the famous Preacher."

Still chuckling, he exited the barn and left the tight-lipped Ian to his task.

Once Smoke was readied, Ian walked around the property looking for tracks. Luckily for him, either she didn't know how, or had been in too much of a hurry to cover her escape because it took him only a short while to discover her boot print tracks on the edge of Rand's recently plowed fields. She was headed east. The bounty hunter in him wondered, Why east? Had she chosen that direction purposefully or was she just running?

He began the walk back to the Tanners' house. His offer to do a good deed for Sheriff Wells had delayed his trip home and now had him chasing across the countryside after a woman who'd had no business being placed under arrest in the first place, and that didn't help his mood, either.

He was mounted and eager to depart when Betsy came out and handed him some food tied up in a tea towel and a canteen of coffee. "Please, if you find her, don't be too harsh. I'm sure she only did what she thought best."

"I'll keep that in mind."

Rand offered up a parting handshake. "Come back and see us when you can."

Ian nodded, reined his horse around, and set out east.

Maggie had no idea how far she'd walked since leaving the Tanners' farm, but it was presently midday and she was pretty sure she'd put a fair amount of distance between herself and the marshal, or at least she hoped so. More than likely he hadn't been happy to wake up and find her gone. With any luck, he'd just forget about her, but she doubted he'd choose that option. He apparently had a reputation for being very skilled at his occupation, and having her disappear the way she had sullied that. In the end, her only option was to keep moving and pray she got away.

She decided she was going to Oberlin, Ohio. Its college had been the nation's first institution of higher learning to offer advanced education to men and women of color. Attending had always been one of her dreams. Her father was a graduate, and although that wouldn't gain her entrance, especially with her being penniless, she was determined to find employment and save up enough money so she could finish her schooling. Afterwards, maybe she'd head to one of the big cities like Detroit or Philadelphia. Both had sizable Black populations established well before the war; surely in such progressive environments she'd be able to fulfill her other dream of being a teacher just like her father. She'd always had an appetite for knowledge, no matter the subject, and her parents fed that need by providing her access to books, newspapers, and broadsides. Her father jokingly called her a funnel because everything he poured into her head went straight in. That memory made her smile, and for a moment she wondered what he'd think of her now, on the run from a United States deputy marshal. Having been a soldier, he'd probably be appalled, but he'd been a realist, too. He'd've understood the rationale behind her flight.

Maggie pushed the thoughts of her past out of her mind and kept walking. She was following what appeared to be a cow path through a large stand of trees. She kept her eyes out for wildlife. A short while ago, she'd had the life scared out of her by a deer darting across the path. Deer were harmless. Bears were not. The weather was warm but the leafy green canopy overhead screened out much of the sun. The trousers were a godsend. In a skirt she would have been snagged by branches and brambles and wasted precious time working herself free. Betsy Tanner's assistance still touched her, and she dearly hoped the woman hadn't gotten into trouble with the marshal for her role.

Up ahead the trees opened into a wide swath of cleared land. Pausing at the edge of the trees, Maggie saw a lone cabin a few hundred feet away. By the fenced-in livestock and freshly plowed fields, she assumed the dwelling to be occupied. She didn't want to expose herself to whoever lived there so she glanced around to make certain no one was about before moving quickly across the open land to the next stand of trees.

By early afternoon, she was tired and hungry and sorely in need of food and a short rest. She also needed to search out a safe place to spend the night, provided the marshal didn't appear and make that unnecessary. Once again she wondered if he was on her trail. Deciding not to think about it, she kept walking.

The woods now skirted a shallow but pristine stream. Ducks and geese were on the surface, and she could hear songbirds offering up their melodies. Before the Europeans, the Wind Clan lived from the Solomon River to the Neosho River encompassing most of what was now called the state of Kansas. She doubted this little piece had changed much since that time even though the Kaws' way of life had been all but obliterated.

The pastoral setting seemed a good place to stop and take her well-earned rest. To make sure she was alone, she peered at the opposite bank and up and downstream. Feeling safe, she sat at the base of a tree and removed the food from her pack. As she bit into the slices of seasoned chicken nestled between two fat pieces of bread she again sang Betsy Tanner's praises. She was far hungrier than she'd initially realized, and it wasn't long before the sandwich was gone, along with a few bites of the cake and some wedges of dried apples.

Her canteen was dry, so after taking another cautious look around she made her way down to the bank to fill it. The water was sweet and cold. Smiling, she dipped her cupped hands into the stream again. In the process of bringing the water to her mouth, her eyes widened at the sight of Marshal Bigelow mounted on his big stallion on the opposite bank. In the moment that her surprised eyes met his, he was already wading the horse into the water. Maggie ran. Bolting up the bank, she grabbed her pack and fled back into the trees. The retrieval cost her a few precious seconds of escape time but she couldn't afford to leave it behind. How had he found her so quickly! Dappled light played over her as she dashed through the maze of trunks and grasses. She prayed he'd have a difficult time riding her down in such close quarters so she ran as dizzying a path as she could manage. Crashing through the carpet of dead leaves and other vegetation, she could hear the sounds of her own breathing and her heart pounded in her chest. The echoes of the galloping hooves behind her were just as loud. She let out an involuntary moan of distress and ran faster.

Next she was off her feet and held tight by an iron arm snaked around her waist. She fought as fiercely as she could, but when you're being carried like a rug curled under someone's arm, you look comical at best.

"You through?" he asked.

She snarled and kicked and twisted some more, but she wasn't going anywhere and they both knew it. The horse kept up the slow pace and Bigelow rode as casually as if he was accustomed to holding irate females clamped against his side all the time.

"Put me down!"

"How'd you get past me?"

"Quite easily, obviously!"

The ghost of a smile curving his lips beneath his shadowy brim only made her madder. "Put me down!" Bobbing along like a length of female bedroll was not endearing him to her in the least.

"Back in Kansas City you cause the biggest street ruckus I've ever seen. Pour commodes on beds to get even, and now you're the first prisoner who's ever escaped me. I'm impressed."

"Then put me the hell down!"

"Cursing woman, too." He moved his attention to her face. "Certainly didn't expect all this."

Flush against his side, she looked up into his unshaven face, intending to give him what for, only to have those exotic eyes steal her breath. The power in them pulsed through her, quickening something inside she'd never experienced. Her heart pounded and her lips parted unconsciously. Then he dropped the reins and with two hands lifted her as effortlessly as if she weighed less than a dozen eggs and set her behind him on the stallion's back. "Hold on."

Shaken, she complied. She had no name for what had passed between them, but that was fine because it made no sense to explore something connected to a man she'd never see again once they went their separate ways.

Leaving the trees, they rode south. When they reached a road that led west, Maggie sighed softly with resignation. Her escape attempt hadn't borne fruit, but at least she'd tried. Given the opportunity, she'd do it again. If she had her way, he'd eventually get so tired of chasing after her, he'd throw up his hands and say good riddance. Presently, however, that outcome existed only in her imagination. In reality, she was his prisoner once more. "Where are we going?"

"Town called Bradley."

Ian knew that it would be quicker to go back to Kansas City and use the telegraph there, but he didn't want take the chance of their being seen and have her hauled in by the young deputy and questioned about all the commotion she'd caused yesterday with the Quigley woman's parasol. The owners of the damaged vehicles were probably looking for someone to point the finger at for compensation, and he didn't have time for that. Rand said Bradley was a half-day's ride away. If they didn't run into any problems along the way they'd arrive by evening. He had no idea how large the town might be but hoped they had a telegraph and a place to get a room for the night, otherwise he and Little Miss Escape would have to sleep under the stars.

With the logistics for the next day firmed in his mind, he turned his thoughts to the woman. To be truthful he'd lost her trail about an hour ago and just happened to be at the stream. He'd been about to let Smoke drink and rest up while he decided what to do next when she suddenly appeared on the other side. Admittedly he could have shown himself at that point, but for some reason he held back. Grabbing his spyglass he watched her instead, noting the wariness on her face and that she was wearing blue denim trousers, of all things. When she reached into her pack and pulled out something tied up in a towel that matched the towel Betsy had given him, he wondered if someone in the Rand house had assisted her escape. He'd lowered the glass and mulled that over for a moment. It had been dark when she took flight. Had she hidden the food somewhere ahead of time? But that wasn't likely because she hadn't been out of his sight. She also wouldn't have been able to make her way around a dark kitchen she was unfamiliar with, not without making a racket that would have brought him running. Which meant she'd had an ally, and he'd bet his best hat that ally had been Betsy. "Betsy helped you?"

"Did she say that?"

"No."

"Then I'm not, either."

Her spunk reminded him of the wives of his friends Griffin Blake and Neil July. Jessi Rose Blake and Olivia July were both women to be reckoned with, and the small, angry hornet riding behind him seemed cut from similar cloth. "Where'd you get the denims?"

"Had them in my pack."

He wasn't sure he believed her, but in truth, it didn't much matter. All that mattered was getting the mess she was in straightened out so they could part ways. For reasons he couldn't name, that thought made him frown.

It was early evening when they rode into Bradley, but the sun had yet to set. Maggie saw just a handful of businesses fronting the main street, one of which was a dentist's office that had a large white tooth mounted on a sign above the door. As she and the marshal rode slowly down the middle of the street, the few people on the walks paused to watch them pass by. From the expressions on their faces, they didn't get many visitors wearing all black, or women dressed in denims, but no one commented.

He stopped Smoke in front of the telegraph office. "I'm going to wire Sheriff Wells to see if I can let you go, now that he's got Langley under arrest."

Why the look of joy spreading across her face seemed to fill his insides with sunshine was something he couldn't explain, either.

"How long do you think it'll be before he wires back?"

"Probably not until the morning."

"Thank you, Marshal," she gushed.

"You're welcome."

Inside, they found a wizened old man whose bald head shone like a billiard ball. "What can I do for you folks?"

"I want to send a telegram."

"I can do that, but equipment's busted up so bad, I can't receive anything back. I'm sorry. Been waiting weeks for new parts."

Ian saw the crestfallen look on her face. "Where's the next closest working telegraph?"

"Topeka hasn't been working for the past couple of days because of a bad storm that went through. Poles down and everything, according to the railroad conductors, so probably Abilene."

Abilene was a good two days away. Ian sighed. "Okay. Let me send the message. Have the operator on the other end send the reply to Abilene and I'll pick it up there. Tell them to send it care of the town's sheriff." Ian didn't know anyone in Abilene, so having it sent to the sheriff's office would keep it from being lost or misplaced. He'd used the method successfully in the past, especially on occasions when he was unsure about the day of his arrival. Usually the local lawman didn't mind.

Ian wrote out the message he wanted sent and handed it to the clerk.

The old man read what he'd written and his eyes rounded. "You're Vance Bigelow? The Preacher?"

Ian held on to his irritation. "Yes."

"I'll send this off first thing in the morning," he promised, eyeing Ian with awe. "Wait till I tell the missus I met the Preacher."

"What time does the westbound train come through tomorrow?"

"Around nine."

"Any place in town where we can get a room for the night?"

"Try Wilma's down the street."

The disappointment on Maggie's face made Ian wish he'd come into the office alone and saved her hopes from being dashed. "We'll get this straight, if we have to go all the way to Denver to do it."

"Let's go find Wilma's."

Just as the old telegraph operator promised, just up the street they found a small whitewashed house with a hand-painted sign that read: "Wilma's Emporium—Eats, Drinks, Rooms."

Inside, it was more saloon than emporium. There was a bar with a huge cracked mirror behind it. There was an old man in a threadbare white shirt banging out an unrecognizable ditty on a piano badly in need of tuning. At one of the place's three tables were a couple of men drinking. Seated with them were two rouged-up, past-their-prime women in skimpy, well-worn dresses, one red, the other green. The one in the green got up and came over to greet them. On the way, she sized up the marshal and apparently liked what she saw. "Name's Wilma. Can I help you?"

"Bigelow. Pleased to meet you. Looking for a room."

"Don't usually take coloreds but I'll make an exception for you." She gave him a winsome smile that might have been effective had she not been missing her two front teeth. Still grinning, she appeared to see Maggie for the first time. The smile faded. "One room for the both of you?" she asked him.

"Yes."

"Too bad. You look like you'd give a girl a good time."

Maggie stood silent.

"How much?" he asked.

She quoted a price, and after the coins disappeared down into the bosom of her dress, she led them down a narrow hallway to a small room in the back. "Clean sheets is extra."

Maggie had never heard anything so outrageous in her life, but he handed over the amount without complaint, asking, "Meals come with the price of the room?"

"Nope. That's extra, too."

Maggie knew that beggars couldn't be choosey but at the rate he was being charged, he would be beggared by the time the woman was through, but he didn't complain.

Wilma immediately sent the handful of coins down into her bosom with the rest. "Your sheets and food'll be here directly."

Before she could leave, Maggie asked, "Where are the facilities?"

"Back down the hall. First door," Wilma replied while visually feasting on the marshal again. "You sure you don't want to put her in a room of her own? I can give it to you at half rate."

"One will do."

She sighed her disappointment and left them alone.

The room's furnishings consisted of a large four-poster brass bed, and a nightstand topped with an old oil lamp. The shutters were open on the one unscreened window. The frayed wallpaper sported bright pink cabbage roses on a field of green. She could feel his silent scrutiny. She hazarded a glance over her shoulder and was again captured by the intensity in his eyes. Looking away, she set her pack on the floor. "I need the facilities."

He gestured her towards the door.

"You're going with me?"

"Just to make sure there's only one way in and out."

"Scared I might run off again?"

He stood over her, arms folded, silent.

"It's nice to know I've gained your respect, so let me lead the way. Wouldn't want you to lose me on the walk down the hallway."

She swore he smiled, but as always it was gone so fast she wasn't sure. When he stepped aside she led him out.

After his inspection of the facilities, Ian walked back into the room and stood in front of the window. He couldn't believe her sassiness. She was obviously unaware of his outstanding reputation or how legendary he was. To her he was merely someone she'd outwitted, which apparently earned her the right to crow. Maggie Freeman was neither mild nor meek, and the longer he was around her the more his curiosity about her rose. What kinds of things had she done since the death of her parents? How had she survived? Her singing last night still resonated. Who was she really?

He heard a commotion out in the hallway. A

man was yelling at someone heatedly. A female yelled right back. Realizing the voice belonged to Maggie, he hurried from the room.

He stopped at the sight of her arguing nose to nose with a short Black man in a checkered suit. She was grabbed by her arm and before Ian could bellow challenge, the stranger hauled off and struck her across the face with the back of his hand. She went flying and Ian did, too.

In the next breath he'd grabbed the little man by his fancy starched collar, raised him up, and slammed him against the wall so forcefully the plaster split. The man whimpered in shock, and his eyes widened to find himself within an eyelash of Ian's glacial fury. "You okay, Maggie?"

"No. Damn that hurt." She had her hand against her jaw as she struggled to her feet.

Ian locked eyes with his prey, he growled, "Who is this?"

She gingerly worked her jaw as if to make sure it was in one piece. "Carson Epps. Kill him, please."

"No!" Epps cried out in terror.

"Better yet," she added, eyes blazing, "just hold him there a moment." Hand still cradling her jaw she walked over. "Can you move to your left, just a bit, Marshal?"

Confusion on his face, Ian moved the lower portion of his body a step to the left but kept the squirming Epps pinned.

Suddenly she pointed at the ceiling. "Oh my goodness! Look at that!"

When both men looked to see, Maggie punched

Epps hard in the groin. His mouth opened in a silent scream and his eyes bulged.

Ian was so stunned and surprised, he turned Epps loose, not caring that the man slid to the floor, where he immediately curled up and began rolling back and forth. Studying the lightning in her eyes, Ian folded his arms and didn't know what to make of her, or what to say. Instead he gently moved her hand aside so he could assess her injury. The jaw and eye were already swelling. "You need a steak."

Epps was rocking back and forth. He seemed to have regained his voice because he was moaning softly in rhythm with his writhing.

By then, Wilma and some of her male patrons had come to investigate all the commotion.

Utterly fascinated by the small woman before him, Ian glanced away for a moment. "The lady needs a steak for her eye."

Wilma surveyed Maggie, then took in the man rolling on the floor. "What happened to him?"

Still contemplating the hellion that was Maggie Freeman, Ian replied uncaringly, "He fell. He'll live. About that steak?"

She appeared genuinely confused by the scene, but when Ian showed her another silver dollar, she snatched it from his fingers. "I'll see to that steak." Still eyeing Epps curiously, she hurried off, and the men followed.

Ian finally tore his attention away from Maggie and walked over to where Epps lay on the floor still in the throes of distress. Ian hunkered down beside him and Epps let out a moan of fear. When Ian placed his star on the floor where Epps could get a good look at it, the whimper rose an octave.

Ian's voice was soft but clear. "Name's Preacher. I'm a bounty hunter. I'm also a deputy U.S. marshal. Here's some advice. The next time you see that lady over there, go the other way. If I find out you even tipped your hat, I'm going to hunt you down and make you have the worst day of your life. Do we have an understanding?"

Epps nodded hastily.

Ian picked up the star and rejoined Maggie, who was still simmering and had every right to be. Only a coward would hit a woman. "Come on. Let's find Wilma and get that steak."

He saw her shoot Epps one last furious glance before they left him where he lay.

Chapter 7

"So how do you know him?"

Maggie was seated on the top step on Wilma's back porch, holding a steak on her eye and cheek. The sun was going down and the marshal was above her braced against the post. "I worked for him about six years ago."

"When'd you see him last?"

"Six years ago." Maggie wondered how long she was supposed to keep the clammy meat against her skin. It had been in place for only a few minutes, but the feel of it was most unpleasant. Shelving talk of Epps for a moment, she asked, "Who came up with the idea that placing a piece of uncooked meat on a black eye was beneficial?"

"Can't answer the first part, but it's supposed to take down the swelling."

"Does it work?"

"Seems to. Why's Epps still so mad if it's been six years?" Last they'd seen of him, he'd been half limping, half crawling his way out of Wilma's establishment under the derisive laughter of her customers. He eyed her closely. "This isn't like that business with the Quigley woman, is it?"

Maggie thought back on the root of Epps's anger and allowed herself a bittersweet smile. "I suppose it could be viewed that way." For a moment she lost herself in the memories. "I was nineteen, and he was the first man who ever paid attention to me, you know." She glanced his way to see if he understood her meaning. "Sitting here now, I can't believe how naive I was, but I thought he loved me. He'd declared it to me often enough."

She was having a bit of difficulty speaking with her painful jaw but she wanted to explain.

"How'd you meet him?"

"At church. I was singing in the choir at a little Baptist church down near Council Grove where I grew up and he was the nephew of the pastor. He'd come to visit, and after church asked me if I'd like to join a traveling troupe he managed because he was impressed by my voice. Said his troupe was going to be more heralded than the famous Fisk Jubilee Singers. I had no ties to bind me in Council Grove, and I was impressed by his speech, his dreams, and ultimately him."

She set the steak aside and gazed out at the slowly dying sun. "It took only a few days to realize he wasn't the man I thought. He did have a troupe. There were four other girls, but we were never given any of the money he was paid for our performances. He always had a ready excuse to explain why there wasn't any left: he'd spent it on our rooms, or train tickets or meals. In the meantime, I also learned that I wasn't his only true love. He had a woman in nearly every town we visited. I'd given him my virginity because he told me I was special, but apparently I was simply a new link in a very long chain."

"So what did you do?"

"I went to his room while he was out having dinner with his lady du jour—"

"And stole the money?"

"No, Marshal. He always kept his money on him."

"So what did you do?"

"Put red pepper sauce in his rubbers." Maggie watched the marshal's eyes widen and then his laugh split the evening air. He laughed so hard, she thought he was going to fall from the porch. She liked his laugh, it was full and deep. She wanted to join in but couldn't. "Stop laughing," she scolded. "You make me want to laugh, too, and I can't because it hurts."

"You put pepper in his rubbers?"

"What better revenge for a man like him. And after he and his woman returned and went to his room, it wasn't long before the agonized screaming began. That was the last time I saw him."

The marshal's chest was heaving up and down. "Woman, you are something."

"Thank you." She decided she liked his smile as well.

"Surely he hasn't been after you all this time?"

"No, he said he just happened to be in town. He's a salesman of some sort now. Apparently he saw us ride in."

"And he couldn't resist coming by to pay his respects."

"Yes."

"Bad choice on his part."

"Only because you were around. I'd probably be needing an entire cow to heal me up if you hadn't been, so thank you."

"You're welcome. He got what he deserved. No honor in manhandling a woman."

"I agree. Next time he wants to assault someone, I hope he'll remember what happened to him today." From the degree of difficulty he had in making his exit, she thought he just might. He also might be a soprano for the rest of his life, too, but she didn't care about that. In truth he'd gotten off lightly; she'd wanted to geld him. Thinking about her time with him, and that one awful night she'd endured in order to prove she loved him, made her angry all over again, so she drew in a deep calming breath. "My life has not gone well since my parents died. I've spent years on my knees, either scrubbing or begging. I've been beaten, slapped and accused of theft. Now I might still be facing a judge for something I didn't do, and today, Carson Epps reenters from the wings to assault me. You wouldn't happen to have a magic lamp on you so I could wish this life away and be given a new one, would you, Marshal?"

He held her gaze steadily. "Is that what you'd do? Wish for a new life?"

He seemed to be peering into her soul, so she turned away. "Yes. I'm tired of being a tumbleweed and having no permanence in anything, not employment or steady meals or a place to lay my head." She paused for a moment and looked over at him. "I'd prefer not to be poorer than a church mouse, as well, since you're asking."

Silence floated between them until she added softly. "I'd like to be able to read books again and wear a nice dress. I'd like to look out the window of my own kitchen and watch my flowers and gardens grow. I want to teach school." Hearing herself, Maggie stopped. "My apologies. I rarely let myself sink into despair this way, but I've done it twice now in the past twenty-four hours and you've been witness to both. You must think I'm trolling for sympathy, but I'm not. I know you don't care about my dreams. After we part in Abilene, you'll go back to your life and I'll continue to be mired in mine. Thank you again for aiding me with Epps, though."

"Again. You're welcome. Nothing wrong with having dreams."

"True, but how do you face the possibility that they'll never bear fruit?"

"Bible says, God will bless you with all abundance."

"Have a little faith, is that your meaning?"

"Sometimes, that's all we have."

"So you really are a preacher."

"No, I'm a man who used the Bible to overcome the murder of my wife."

Maggie's heart stopped. Dusk had risen so it was difficult to see his expression clearly, but she didn't need full light to sense his pain. She also sensed that this wasn't a subject he discussed freely or often, so why now and with her, was curious. "I'm sorry for your loss," she responded softly. "May I ask how long ago you lost her?"

"Eight years. We were married for two."

Maggie wondered what she'd been like. Would a man with his strength be pledged to a woman of equal substance, or less?

He turned the tables on her. "Ever been married?"

She scoffed, "Me, no, and not likely to be, either."

"Why not?"

"The few men who've called on me were uncomfortable with my education. One went so far as to declare he would never marry a woman who had more schooling. His loss, I say."

Wilma stepped out to interrupt them. "You done with that steak?"

The question caught Maggie off guard. "I suppose so."

"Need it for one of the diners."

The marshal straightened. "I already paid you for it, remember?"

"You paid to use it. Got somebody inside paying to eat it."

Maggie shook her head with amusement. "You'll be returning some of his money, correct?"

The firm tone got Wilma's attention. She fished down into her bosom for some coins. After grudgingly making the exchange she and the steak returned inside.

Maggie cracked, "Quite the businesswoman, isn't she?"

"Makes the capitalists back East look like rubes."

The silence rose again. Maggie found her mind drifting over the past events in her life like a canoe set adrift. The faces of people she'd known were followed by experiences she'd had. And now in the present, she wondered what the future would hold. "How long will it take us to get to Abilene?"

"Couple of days."

And once there they'd separate. A part of herself was disappointed at the prospect because she wouldn't be able to learn more about him. "Where will you go after?"

"Home to my ranch in the Wyoming mountains."

"I've never seen mountains."

"Some of God's prettiest work."

"Do you farm?"

"A little, but mostly raise cattle and round up wild horses."

"You sell them, the horses?"

"Yeah."

A rugged man for a rugged land, came the thought. Maggie looked out at the now-darkening countryside. She had a natural curiosity for everything, it seemed, so she wanted to ask him a dozen questions about Wyoming, his life, his wife, but didn't because the answers didn't matter. As she had mused earlier, once they parted, she'd never see him again.

"How's your jaw feeling?"

"Been better, but like Epps, I'll live. Planning to stay away from mirrors for the next few days, though. I'm sure I'll be rather frightening come morning."

"Maybe not."

She wanted to believe him but doubted he'd be

right. Instead she concentrated on the beautiful night. She hadn't been able to sit under the stars since being jailed back in Dowd. The twin pleasures of hearing the wind spirits whispering in the grasses and feeling the kiss of the breeze grace her cheek were something she'd always taken for granted, but not anymore.

"Did your mother's people have a name for the wind?"

"*Waucondah,*" she replied, and stared up at him with mild astonishment. "Few people would know to ask such a question."

"I have friends among the Arapaho. They've taught me a great deal."

She found that astonishing as well. Once again, there were a hundred questions she wanted him to answer. She settled for one. "Are they still on their land?"

"No, they're on the Wind River Reservation."

"The Kaw were forced into Indian Territory in '73. When they were removed there were less than five hundred members of a tribe that once numbered in the thousands." They were decimated by disease, poverty, and the theft of their lands and way of life by a government whose word held no honor. "We should probably go inside. I'd like to wash my face so I don't draw flies while I'm sleeping."

He stood. "After you."

Once inside the rented room, Maggie walked over to the bed and pulled back the bed quilt to make sure they'd gotten the clean sheets Wilma had charged the marshal extra for, and was pleased to see that they had. Her jaw throbbed much less. Maybe the steak had done the trick. It was still sore, however.

"Sheets clean?" he asked while removing his gun belt.

"They appear to be."

Watching him place the folded leather on the nightstand, she wondered what type of sleeping arrangements he might propose. She dearly wanted to sleep in the bed because there was no guarantee she'd get another opportunity anytime soon, but his weariness probably equaled her own and he undoubtedly wished to sleep in the bed as well. "Do you mind sharing the bed so that neither of us has to sleep on the floor?"

His compelling gaze captured her from across the room. She'd never been more aware of a man in her life. "Um, just for sleeping. Nothing else. Did your mother have green eyes?"

"No, my grandfather."

"Is he still alive?"

"I believe so. I saw him a few months ago."

"Where does he live?"

"Coast of Scotland."

She went still. "Why Scotland?"

" 'Tis where he was born," he told her in a thick Scottish accent.

Her eyes widened and her hand flew to her mouth.

A smile teased his lips. "I was born there as well." That time he used the voice she was more accustomed to hearing.

Both confusion and awe claimed her. "You're Scottish?"

"And Black."

She remembered him saying he hadn't known his father but it never occurred to her that he might be foreign born. "How long have you lived in America?"

"Since I was twenty, so eighteen years."

That made him thirty-eight, thirteen years her senior. She found him to be so very interesting she sensed she could question him about himself from now until sunrise and still need days more to ask the rest. *Scotland.* She'd never met a person of color who hadn't been born in the United States. How in the world had he gone from being a Scot to a bounty hunter and to a marshal? Sadly, it was yet another question that would go unanswered once they separated. She refocused on the situation at hand. "Are the sleeping arrangements agreeable?"

"Yes."

She wondered if she should be the first to move to the bed or wait and let him take the lead.

"I'll sleep closest to the door," he said to her. He sat down on the edge of the bed and removed his boots.

She walked over to the side he'd designated as hers and sat to remove her boots as well. When she finished, she turned to him and went still at the sight of the handcuffs he held. His green eyes held no hints of amusement, just purpose.

She blew out a short exasperated breath and extended her left wrist. He locked the bracelet around it and attached the ring's twin to his right wrist.

"No need in getting mad," he said, leaning over to douse the lamp. They were lying side by side. The chain linking the bracelets was long enough for them both to move comfortably.

"Who says I'm mad?" she responded crisply.

"Your eyes do. Even in the dark they're spitting like summer lightning. Can't have you running loose terrorizing the countryside."

"I'm not a terror."

"Tell that to Epps."

"He deserved what he got."

"Amen, and I deserve to get some sleep and not have to worry about you sneaking past me again."

She turned over to face him. "Am I really the first to escape you?"

"Yes."

"Will that ruin your reputation somehow?"

"I'm sure it'll make a few people laugh, especially after Rand's done with the telling."

"I'm not going to apologize."

"Don't expect you to. Just like I don't expect you to apologize for slugging Epps the way you did."

"When I came out of the facility I was dumbfounded to find him standing there, but when he began yelling and threatening to kill me, all I could think about was how much I detested him, and that I should have been threatening him."

"He threatened your life?"

"Oh yes. Apparently his soldier has had difficulty saluting since being introduced to Lady Pepper Sauce, and he—"

She didn't get to finish her words because the marshal was laughing to high heaven. She let the pleasurable sound fill her before mockingly scolding him once more. "You're laughing again, Marshal."

After a few more moments of amusement he quieted. She could see him eyeing her as closely as the darkness would allow. Finally she asked, "Yes?"

"You're a wonder, Maggie Freeman."

"You're a wonder yourself. I'd love to be able to wield a gun the way you do."

"Why?" He sounded surprised, appalled, she couldn't tell which.

"So I could protect myself. I can shoot but not as well as I'd like. Having to protect myself is how I got in this mess in the first place." She thought back on what he'd said to her at the telegraph office. "Do you think Wells will really let me go free?"

"I don't see why not, but the law can be complicated sometimes."

"I just want to know one way or the other."

"That's understandable."

She yawned. "It's been a long day."

"Yes, it has."

"I think I'm going to go to sleep now, Marshal."

She could feel his eyes moving over her in the darkness as if he were still caught by the wonder he'd just referenced, but eventually he said, "That's fine. I'll see you in the morning."

It took her a moment to get comfortable, but once that was accomplished she closed her eyes.

Lying beside her, Ian heard her slip into sleep but didn't know whether she was playing possum or not. She'd tricked him before. She lay facing him. He glanced over and wished there was light enough to see her face, not just because he wanted to see if she was awake but so he could feast his eyes on her countenance. He'd called her a wonder but that didn't begin to describe the woman she was turning out to be. Poor Epps. Ian almost felt sorry for the man. Almost. Hearing that he'd threatened her life made him want to get up and go find the salesman. He buried the idea, however. They had more pressing things on their agenda, and besides, she'd already given Epps more than he could handle; the man would have to be a fool to seek her out again. She was a firecracker. Were she living in Wyoming, her spirited nature would have every eligible male from Laramie to the Tetons lined up at her door. That thought didn't sit well. He mulled over why and honestly admitted that were circumstances different, he might be one of those men, but she wasn't fated for him. If everything worked in her favor, more than likely they'd never see each other again, and that bothered him as well.

Chapter 8

When Ian opened his eyes, it was still dark. Sometime during the night, Maggie had curled closer and was lying half sprawled atop him. Her head was resting just beneath his chin. Her right arm was across his chest and one leg rode his. Her soft weight felt so good he wanted to pull her even closer, but he was already fully aroused, so he didn't think that a good idea. A true gentleman would move her back to her side of the bed, but she seemed to be sleeping so peacefully he didn't have the heart to wake her up. Or at least that's what he told himself. His physical reaction also brought home how long it had been since he'd awakened next to a woman. She was his prisoner, so he wasn't supposed to be musing on her warmth, her scent, or the sensual pressure of her leg resting lightly against his groin, but he was fighting a losing battle. He and his late wife, Tilda, had never slept in the same bed. She, like many woman of the era, believed that the only time a husband and wife came together in bed was for marital relations. Tilda hadn't cared much for the act, so out of respect for her sensibilities he hadn't approached her very often. Yet and still she'd been the sweetest, most loving person he'd ever met, and because of her he'd given up his outlaw ways in order to win her hand. After her death, he'd shed the easygoing lover of life he'd once been, and a more dour, humorless man had taken his place. He'd become easily irritated, arrogant, and so joyless he rarely laughed, but he had laughed with Maggie, more than he ever remembered doing before. No way would Tilda have punished Epps the way Maggie had, and Tilda would have cut her tongue out before mockingly referring to a man's "soldier," let alone recounting the difficulties it was having saluting. Just thinking back on the remark brought on a smile. Although Maggie'd voiced her doubts about ever becoming married, he was certain there was a man somewhere who'd appreciate all that spirit, especially if she proved to be as spirited in bed as she was in life. The thought of her lying beneath him while he made slow, sweet love to her sleep-warmed skin caused his own soldier to rise up again, forcing him to gently shift her clear so he could breathe. He ran his unfettered hand down his face and fought to shake himself free of Maggie Freeman's powerful spell. In a few days they'd be taking separate paths. He needed to keep that in mind.

When Maggie opened her eyes, he was lying beside her. Meeting his gaze, she smiled sleepily. "Morning, Marshal."

"Morning. How'd you sleep?"

"Fine, I guess." She sat up and rubbed at her eyes. "How about you?"

"Slept well."

"I need to go to the facilities."

He unlocked the bracelets and she left the room. When she returned he had his boots on and was brushing his hair. She'd taken a look at herself in the washroom's mirror and had been correct about how frightening her appearance would be as a result of her encounter with Epps. Her jaw was still slightly bruised and the eye above it was a riot of purples, blacks, and blues. It would be days before her skin and vision cleared up. Her hair was a fright as well. She watched him place his brush back into his saddlebag and wished she had one of her own, but contented herself with trying to tame it with her hands as best she could.

"Do you want to borrow my brush?"

His offer made her both embarrassed and grateful. "If you don't mind?"

"Here." And he handed it over.

A bit self-conscious, she combed her fingers through the braid to free it and applied the brush, while trying not to acknowledge her burgeoning attraction to him. He reached over and gently raised her face so he could assess her eye. "One quick look in the mirror was all I could take," she admitted with a self-deprecating smile.

"You'll heal up."

"I hope so."

Maggie held his green eyes and began drowning in them again. She took a hesitant step back.

"Um. Let me finish so you can have your brush back."

"No rush."

She did it quickly anyway and once she was done, she handed it to him. "Thank you."

He returned it to the saddlebag and she let out the pent-up breath she'd been holding in response to his nearness. With her hair righted, she then wished she had some clean clothing to change into, but since she didn't, she'd have to make do with the wrinkled shirt and trousers she'd slept in and been wearing since leaving the Tanner farm.

He asked, "Ready to see about some breakfast before we head to the train station?"

"I am. I wonder how much extra we'll be charged for it?"

Wearing smiles, they left the room.

Sitting in the smoking car of the still idling train that was scheduled to stop in Topeka before taking them on to Abilene, Maggie tried not to think about what lay ahead. It wasn't as if she could simply wave her hand and make all her problems magically disappear. In truth the only option she had was to wait and see what the response to the telegram would be, otherwise she'd drive herself insane worrying. She sighed. Because of her bruised face and eye, she'd drawn stares from the other passengers when she and the marshal boarded the train. Some of the women drew back in shock and glared his way as if holding him responsible for the damage.

Maggie'd wanted to come to his defense but he never slowed on his way to the smoking car, so she'd hurried to keep up.

They were seated at a table near the rear of the car, and like everyone else they were waiting for the train to get under way. There weren't many others in the car and the atmosphere was subdued, but the layout with its long bar reminded Maggie of a few saloons she'd sung in while working for Epps. At one of the tables a card game was under way. Playing were two dandied-up men she pegged as gamblers, and two nondescript cowboys who were probably going to lose more than they could afford. Sidled up against the gamblers and looking on were a couple of tarted-up women who might or might not be ladies of the night. The train's whistle blew, signaling departure, and just as the wheels began to move the door to the car opened and a harried-looking Carson Epps rushed inside lugging a large black display case. The marshal was reading his *Harper's*. When he glanced up and spied Epps, he turned to Maggie with cool eyes and declared, "If he causes any trouble I'll be throwing him off the train."

She didn't actually believe that, but she appreciated the thought.

Epps had no difficulty spotting them in the sparsely occupied space. When his eyes brushed hers, his anger was obvious, as was the contempt he threw at the reading marshal. Maggie didn't care. Even though she'd come away from their confrontation with a black eye, she'd won the hand and they both knew it.

But no sooner had the train left the station than Epps began to speak. Maggie wasn't sure if the blow to his privates had loosened his brain or if he was too mad to remember the marshal's warning. "Hey, Maggie. You tell your marshal friend that you used to whore for me?"

She froze.

Everyone in the car turned his way, including the marshal.

Epps gave an ugly-sounding laugh. "Bet you didn't. Did you?"

Fury and embarrassment made her storm to her feet. "It was one night, Carson. One! And don't you dare lie and say it was more. Better yet, tell everyone why. Tell them how you took advantage of a nineteen-year-old girl who was addled enough to think you actually loved her. Tell them how you said we needed the money to eat, and that it would be just that one time. Tell them how I put pepper sauce in your rubbers and made you scream like a burned sow! Tell them that, damn you!"

Hearing her response, the gamblers' eyes went wide and then they began laughing at Epps. The girls clapped.

Maggie was so angry she was shaking. Tears of rage stood in her eyes. She hadn't wanted Bigelow to know about that night, and she wanted to flee because of how he probably viewed her, but to her surprise, he covered her hand for a calming moment and then got to his feet. As he focused attention on the still sneering Epps, the deadly air he exuded soon plunged the car into tense silence.

"Do you remember the agreement we had, Mr. Epps?"

"Go to hell Padre or Preacher, or whatever your damn name is, and take that phony badge with you. Nobody believes you're a marshal except that ignorant squaw. Touch me and I'll have the conductor put you off. See if I don't."

One of the gamblers, a White man with a razor-thin mustache said to his companions in a voice just loud enough to be heard, "That's the Preacher. Vance Bigelow! I thought I recognized him when he came in here." He turned to Epps. "Mister, if I were you, I'd fall to my knees right now and start apologizing to the little lady. His name is real, and so is his Bible, but it's his gun you have to worry about."

Maggie could see the others at the table viewing the marshal in a new light.

Epps was trying to conceal his own reaction but the fear on his face was there for all to see. "Now look, Marshal, uh, sir."

By then Bigelow was looming over him, and Epps pleaded, "If you want me to apologize—"

"Nope. Want you off the train."

"Okay, okay," he said hastily. "At the next stop. I'll speak to the conductor."

"No. Now."

Epps stared.

Bigelow said in a quiet voice, "Maggie, would you open that door behind you, please."

Now it was her turn to stare, but she quickly moved to comply. As the rhythmic sounds of the wheels filled the car via the now opened door, the marshal grabbed Epps by the front of his checkered suit coat and dragged him across the space.

"No!" Epps tried to forestall his fate by setting his feet, but Bigelow was much taller and stronger. The other passengers in the car looked on gleefully as the marshal hustled the twisting, squirming, and cursing Epps out to the platform, picked him up, and tossed him over the rail. Epps's fading scream could he heard as the marshal returned to grab Epps's salesman's case. Once that followed its owner over the side, he closed the door again and sat. Giving Maggie a small smile, he returned to his reading.

Stunned, she glanced over at the gambler. He touched his hat and commenced dealing out the next hand to his chuckling companions.

Keeping her voice low, she said, "Thank you."

"You're welcome."

Again, she could only imagine what he must think of her. "I want to explain what happened that night."

"You just did." And there was no judgment in his eyes. "Sometimes life makes us do things we don't want to. You were young."

She thought back on that awful night and confessed softly, "I cried the entire time."

His lips tightened. "You don't have to explain, Maggie. Not to me."

She wiped at the tears threatening to fall. "I'm not a whore," she whispered fiercely.

"Only person accusing you of that is Epps, and everybody saw what happened to him, so no more worrying." He reached down to his saddlebag and brought out a well-read newspaper. "Here. Read."

Maggie took the offering and did as he asked.

For the next hour, Maggie pored over the Boston paper. She wondered how a paper from Boston had come to be in his possession, but she felt she'd bothered him enough for the present, so she didn't ask. Instead she read about a country in Africa called the Ivory Coast being declared a protectorate of France, and she wondered if the African people who lived there had had any say in the matter. On the next page was a notice about the Pemberton Medicine Company down in Georgia changing its name to the Coca Cola Company and she wondered what kind of medicine Coca Cola could be. Reading on, she glanced at a different article about an archduke in Austria found dead with his mistress, a baroness named Mary Vetsera. Below that was a story about the first trainload of oranges from Los Angeles to make its way east by rail. Closer to her heart was reading about the ongoing controversy surrounding the opening up of Indian Territory to White settlers. She shook her head sadly. First the politicians in Washington confiscate all the land belonging to the Native tribes, force the tribes to live in the dusty dry environs of Indian Territory, and now that same government planned to allow settlers to claim that land from the Natives, too. She wondered if it would ever end, and if there would be any tribal members left when it was all said and done. From what she'd heard of the five hundred members of the Kaw tribe sent to Oklahoma back in '73, presently less than two hundred remained. Her heart ached knowing the tribes would be facing more problems once Indian Territory's borders were opened, but seemingly none of the rich and powerful cared.

The newspaper did have something inspiring to report, though. A small article on the bottom of the last page chronicled the efforts of a Black physician named Dr. Daniel Hale Williams who was raising funds to construct a hospital in Chicago that would treat all races. One of his goals was to offer Black nurses the opportunities denied them by other hospitals because of their race. Maggie hoped his dreams would bear fruit.

After making a stop to take on water and more fuel, the train was about five miles outside Topeka when the emergency brake screamed and they were all tossed about in reaction. Everyone hurried to the windows expecting to see outlaws, but from their vantage point at the rear of the train they couldn't see anything but the open plains.

The conductor entered a few moments later. "We just hit a cow. There's going to be a big delay while we try and get it off the track and assess the damage. Sorry folks."

Ian shook his head. The railroads were hated in the West for all the livestock that were killed and for all the land it had swindled away from farmers so track could be laid. Somewhere a farmer would be adding his curses to all the rest once he found about his dead cow.

The conductor returned about thirty minutes later with more bad news. "The collision damaged the brakes, and we can't move without repairs. Hate to say this, but we're going to have to ask all passengers to walk into Topeka. We should be squared away by morning and you can reboard at that time."

Exclamations of disappointment and disbelief greeted the announcement. Ian began gathering his gear. "Let's go, Maggie."

Most of the passengers were gathered outside for the walk to Topeka. Ian and Maggie saw what was left of the poor cow beneath the train's wheels. Fortunately for them because Smoke was in the cattle car, they wouldn't have to make the long walk to Topeka. Once Ian got the stallion saddled up, they mounted and rode towards town.

"Do you know anyone in Topeka?" Maggie asked them as they made their way.

"Used to and if she still has her boardinghouse we can sleep there tonight. We'll check on the telegraph while we're there, too."

Maggie dearly hoped it had been fixed, but the way her life had been going lately, she doubted it would be.

And she was correct. A sign in the window stated that the office was closed until further notice. She sighed her frustration.

Ian didn't want to admit it, but in a way he was pleased to find the telegraph office closed. One part of him was disappointed of course due to the continuation of her unresolved problem, but other parts of him didn't want to turn her loose. The episode with Epps had revealed more about her past life, and what he learned not only angered him but made him want to protect her as well. The anger stemmed from the position Epps had put her in. She said she'd cried the entire time during the night with the man, and she had to have been scared as well. He wanted to find Epps and beat the tar out of him. It was a common ploy by pimps and other nefarious men who preyed on susceptible young woman. Yet in response to Epps's slurs she'd stood up and defended herself with courage and a spirit that made him want to cheer. Her past meant nothing to him. Granted there were men who'd hold what she'd done against her, and the fact that she wasn't a virgin, but he wasn't among them; not with his past. What he saw when he looked at her was a woman who'd done the best she could with the hand life dealt her, and in spite of it all was still standing. In that, she was a lot like his mother. Colleen had done whatever was necessary to keep him clothed and fed, even if it meant sneaking away in the middle of the night to avoid paying a landlord the money she owed due to a lack of funds, or stealing bread and teaching him how to do the same so they could eat. Life changed for the better once she caught the eye of a certain English earl, but he clearly remembered the hunger, the ill-fitting, hand-me-down clothing, and all the men who traipsed through her bedroom door before that. He knew firsthand how hard life could be, and that taking steps to keep living wasn't something to be ashamed of.

The streets of Topeka were fairly crowded. Ian spotted an old man sweeping the walk in front of a barbershop and asked after his old friend Lola.

"Does she still have her place over on Century Street?"

The man looked him up and down as if trying to discern his ties to the gregarious boardinghouse owner before replying, "Yep."

"Thanks."

"You're welcome. Have Miss Lola get that young lady something for her eye."

"Yes, sir." Ian clicked at Smoke and they slowly galloped up the street.

On the way, Maggie asked, "Who's Lola?"

Trying to ignore the heat of her softness against his back, Ian replied, "Runs a boardinghouse. Used to be the only place between Kansas City and Denver where a man of color could get a decent meal and a clean bed just for the asking." What he didn't say was that Lola prided herself on having the prettiest and cleanest girls, too, and the men loved her for it. "We'll sleep there tonight and reboard the train for Abilene in the morning."

"Okay"

When they reached their destination, Maggie slid off the horse and looked at the neat little green house with a matching green sign out front that read simply: "Lola's." She waited for him to tie the stallion's reins to the post and followed him inside.

He opened the screened door to let her enter first and it took Maggie's eyes a moment to adjust to the dim interior. There was a bar on one side of the room, but unlike at Wilma's no one was beating on an out-of-tune piano.

"Preacher! You just march your bounty-hunting arse right on out of my place!"

Maggie turned to see a short, well-endowed, curvy woman dressed in a low-cut blue gown bearing down on them with stormy eyes. Her red wig had seen better days.

"Now, Lola," he said quietly.

"Don't you now Lola me, you traitor," she tossed back as she planted herself before him, glaring the entire time. Tight lipped, she beckoned him with a long, red-nailed finger. He bent down and to Maggie's surprise, Lola kissed him on the cheek. "Good to see you."

He straightened silently but Maggie could see the light of humor in his green eyes.

Lola declared dismissively, "You were a lot more fun when you were an outlaw."

Maggie stared agape. *Outlaw.*

"Who's this?" Lola asked him.

"Maggie Freeman. Officially she's a prisoner."

"So now you're arresting young women? I know you aren't the one who gave her that black eye, so who did, and is that why she's in your custody? Did she shoot the man responsible I hope?"

Maggie liked her instantly. Next she knew, Lola's red-nailed, flamboyantly ringed fingers had her by the jaw and were gently turning her face so Lola could get a better look.

"I have something that'll help with the bruising and those scrapes. Did Preacher find you in a briar patch, honey?"

"No, ma'am."

For the first time, Maggie noticed that they

were not alone. There were a few men seated at some of the tables sipping drinks and playing cards. All eyes were trained on the marshal and he seemed to be evaluating them from beneath the wide brim of his black hat.

"None of them are wanted, so put away your interest." She turned back to Maggie. "You look like you could use a hot bath and a warm meal."

"I could."

"Then come with me." She had a final warning for the marshal, though. "And don't you dare arrest anyone while I'm gone. You hear me!"

He gave her a nod. As Maggie followed Lola out of the room, she looked back and saw him watching her. *Outlaw!*

"Was he really an outlaw?" Maggie asked once she and Lola were alone.

"Yep, then he got married, lost her to that hell spawn Bivens, and turned into something straight out of the Old Testament. Lots of fire and brimstone. Even had a shoot-out here a few years back trying to collect a bounty. Cost me customers and plenty in renovations. Cursed him for months." She then eyed Maggie. "Has he been fair to you?"

"So far."

"Even as an outlaw he was always a gentleman. So what's your story?"

Maggie explained, and when she was done with the telling, Lola shook her head sadly. "Judge could go either way on that one."

"I know. The marshal said he thinks Sheriff Wells may okay him letting me go."

"Well, we'll hope for the best, but in the meantime, let's see what we can do to get you spruced up a bit. It'll make you feel better all the way around."

They were in a large room that held a big white bathing tub with claw feet. Fancy red drapes lined the walls and gave one the impression of being in a velvet cave. Because of the drapes she couldn't tell whether the room had windows, but it was softly lit by two gas lamps. Each had a coyly smiling nude woman painted on the base, which when coupled with the draping made Maggie wonder if Lola's place doubled as a cathouse.

Lola pulled some drying sheets from a white-washed armoire beside the door. "I'll have water brought in. You take as long as you like. My girls won't be needing the room unless they snag somebody special tonight."

Maggie had her answer. Lola turned a critical eye on Maggie's clothing. "You want a set of clean clothes?"

"Yes, but I don't have any funds to pay for them."

She waved a ringed hand. "Don't worry. I'll add it to Bigelow's bill. He owes me anyway."

Maggie wasn't sure about that, but Lola didn't impress her as being one to argue with, so she offered up a simple, "Thanks."

"You're welcome. Once you're clean we'll get that face of yours fixed up. I do most of the doctoring for the race around here, deliver all the babies, too. Learned my doctoring during the war."

"Where are you from?"

"South Carolina. Trained under Susie King Taylor."

Maggie was unfamiliar with the name and it must have shown on her face because Lola explained. "Susie helped nurse the Black troops of South Carolina's Thirty-third Regiment. She was fairly well known back during those days."

Lola stopped a moment as if reflecting on those times, and as Maggie listened she told how Susie's family, including her brothers, father, and uncles escaped slavery on a Union gunboat and joined the Union Army. "She was about fifteen when the Yankee officers came to St. Simon Island to recruit soldiers. She was hired to be a laundress at first, but when they found out she could read and had been teaching school, they realized she was a very smart young woman. Before you knew it, she was doing everything from writing letters for the men, to clerking for the officers, to nursing. Followed the men into battle a few times and could even take a rifle apart, clean it, and put it back together. She was something." She went on to tell Maggie about Susie's nursing of the troops afflicted with smallpox and how the young woman married one of the soldiers, a man named Edward King.

"Where'd you meet her?"

"On that same gunboat she and her family were on. I'd gotten on a few days earlier with my husband and mother. Lost them both by the time emancipation was declared, but that little Susie taught me everything I know about nursing. And the salve I have should make short work of all those cuts and scrapes you're sporting."

Maggie truly hoped so.

"So, I'll send in the water and bring you some clothes. They won't be new though."

"Doesn't matter. I'll be appreciative of whatever you can spare."

"Good girl."

And with that, she sailed from the room and Maggie was alone.

Chapter 9

Ian settled into the hot water, glad that Lola was still in business. The tub, one of two in the house, if his memory served him correctly, was large enough to accommodate two people if need be. Even though it had been years since he'd last seen her, he'd expected to be railed at. After all, the fight that highlighted his last visit had reduced her place to shambles. Matt Stapleton had been wanted for killing a man in Denver and decided not to go quietly when Ian hunted him down to take him back to Fort Smith for trial. Lola's place had always been a haven, and lawmen usually respected that, but Stapleton's crime had been especially heinous because he'd shot the victim in front of his wife and children. During the initial fight with him, Ian proved to be better with his fists. As a result, Stapleton drew his gun, but soon learned that Ian was the superior in that category as well. When the dust settled, Lola had been as mad as the proverbial wet hen. While patching up the bullet holes in Stapleton's shoulder and leg she'd told Ian he was banned from her place for life. Apparently she'd changed her mind after Ian wired her the bounty money he'd collected for bringing Stapleton in. She was a businesswoman, after all.

A soft knock on the door interrupted his musings, and before he could ask who was there, the door opened and Cleo, one of Lola's girls, slipped in.

"I heard you were here. Been a long time."

"Yes it has." But not long enough for him to forget the nights they'd shared. "How've you been?"

She shrugged. She was still a good-looking woman even though the passage of time had softened both her face and what he could see of her body in the thin red wrapper she had on over her obviously nude frame. She came over to the tub and sat down on the edge. "You miss me?" she asked sultrily, and slid her hand into the water. Before she could reach her target he gently but firmly locked onto her wrist. She paused with mild surprise. "No?"

He shook his head.

"You married again?"

"No."

"Then what's wrong?"

"Nothing."

She sat back, folded her arms across her ample breasts, and viewed him as if trying to determine the reason for his response.

"Nothing to do with you," he offered.

"But you're not interested." It was more statement than question.

"No."

She sighed with what sounded like resignation and stood. "Suit yourself."

As the door closed softly on her exit, Ian sighed and wondered if he'd lost his mind. Cleo was a sorceress in bed and would have been the perfect solution to the pangs he'd been suffering since waking up that morning with Maggie's sweet little body sprawled atop him so intimately. Yet he'd turned her down and didn't know why until the voice inside tossed back, *Because you want Maggie.* Not wanting to give the voice any credence, he cursed and got out of the tub.

Stepping out of the warm, scented water, Maggie wrapped herself in the bathing sheet and dried off. The marshal had been on her mind the entire time because after hearing about his past life, she now had more questions to add to all the previous ones. What made him turn outlaw and how long after his arrival in America had it taken place? Had he been a desperado in the country of his birth? She knew next to nothing about Scotland so had no idea if there were outlaws there or not. What she did know was that the marshal was a walking, talking conundrum. He was a bounty hunter, a marshal, and an outlaw all wrapped up in one. It was enough to make her head spin. It appeared as if the people who knew him, like Rand and Betsy Tanner and Miss Lola, were aware of some of his many sides, but she wondered how true that was. Although she had nothing solid to go on, she sensed that there were aspects of him no one knew. So many questions, so few answers and so little time, she thought.

She put on the plain skirt, underslip, and blouse Lola had brought in while she was bathing and used the borrowed comb and brush on her hair. Lola had been in and out, bringing this and that and making good on her promise to help Maggie look and feel brand-new from head to toe. The orange oil she'd provided restored the shine and luster Maggie's tresses had been lacking because of her inability to afford any in the recent past. After braiding it into one long plait, coiling it, and pinning it low on her neck, she faced herself in the mirror. The small scrapes and cuts from being dragged behind the sheriff's horse were healing well. The moist, warm tea towels Lola had insisted she hold against her face while she bathed had indeed reduced the swelling. The color seemed to be lighter, too, but she wasn't sure if that was the truth or just wishful thinking. As she turned from the mirror and left the red velvet bathing room, even though her eye felt better she silently cursed Carson Epps and hoped he was somewhere still walking.

Night had fallen in the lengthy time she'd been gone, and the main room was now lively with piano music, men of all races, and Lola's four girls wearing low-cut gowns and face paint. There were card games being played, a buffet at the back of the room, and lots of noise and drinking. She glanced around the dimly lit room for the marshal and found his eyes waiting for her. The spark that flowed between them flared again and she found herself unable to look away. He seemed to be all she could see or wanted to see. Were the circumstances of their meeting different, where might that spark lead? she wondered. He was certainly a formidable and handsome man, but for the moment, he was on one side and she was on the other.

"Wish he looked at me that way."

The female voice broke the spell and Maggie turned to see one of Lola's girls standing at her side. "Pardon?"

"Bigelow. The way he's looking at you. Wish it were me. I'm Cleo by the way."

"Maggie Freeman."

"Yeah, I know. Lola said you're his prisoner. You sharing his bed?"

The query caught Maggie off guard. "Yes, I mean, no."

The tall, sable-skinned Cleo raised an eyebrow. "So which is it?"

Maggie was put off by the rude questioning. "Why?"

"I see the hunger, and was just wondering."

"Hunger?" She turned back to Bigelow. He hadn't moved.

"Yes. The hunger a man has for a woman."

Maggie wondered if the woman had had too much whiskey. "You must be mistaken. All he wants is to be rid of me."

"What a man says and what he wants are often two different things."

"I haven't known the marshal very long but I'm certain he knows his own mind."

"I agree, and you're what's on it."

"Only as someone in his custody."

Cleo smiled. "Whatever you say, honey. I'll see you later. Go get you something to eat."

She left Maggie's side to greet a rotund man in a nice suit who had the bearing of someone important and a light in his blue eyes that shone brightly at the sight of her coming his way. She hooked her arm in his and they walked to one of the tables in the shadows on the far side of the room.

Maggie turned back to the marshal and found him still watching her with the same veiled intensity. She doubted the hunger referenced by Cleo had anything to do with her personally. More than likely the only hunger he had was for the food on the buffet.

"Can I buy you a drink?"

The question was from a man who was tall, brown-skinned, and nice-looking. His plain shirt and trousers pegged him as an ordinary citizen of the plains. She guessed him to be a few years older than she.

"Pretty girl like you shouldn't be alone." His smile was engaging.

She sent a quick glance the marshal's way and saw him approaching. "Thank you, but no thank you."

"You're new here."

"Um, yes, but I'm just visiting."

"Oh, I see. Married?"

She shook her head.

"Looking to be?"

She grinned. "Not at the moment, no."

"Well, if you change your mind, I'm available. Name's Tate Greer. Own a ranch not far from here."

"I'll keep that in mind."

He winked and departed just as the marshal walked up. "What did he want?"

"To buy me a drink and to marry me."

She liked the surprise that grabbed him. "Think I'll get something to eat." Walking away, she felt his eyes but didn't look back.

Ian studied the man she'd been talking with. He'd retreated to the bar but his attention was focused solely on Maggie, now filling her plate with samplings from the buffet. He doubted the man had been serious about marriage, but due to the paltry number of good women on this side of the Mississippi, Ian couldn't be sure. That same dearth was one of the reasons Wyoming allowed women of all races to vote when no other state did. The unconventional legislation had less to do with suffrage than with trying to entice Eastern women to move to the rugged, mountainous territory and bolster a female population that was nearly nonexistent. Intelligent, literate women were hard to find, and were as valuable to the ranchers and farmers of the West as water rights.

While Ian watched and sipped his watered-down whiskey, more than a few of the men enjoying Lola's hospitality came over to the table where Maggie was sitting and began chatting. To her credit she rebuffed them all with a pleasant smile, but he knew she might have responded differently had she been free to do so. As it stood, she wasn't, and when the man who'd wanted to marry her came over and slid into one of the empty chairs at her table, Ian thought it time to let everyone know he had prior claim, even if it wasn't formal or binding.

"Evening," Ian said to the man as he sat down at the table, too. "Name's Preacher."

"Tate Greer," came the reply, along with a look of annoyance. "The lady and I are having a private conversation, if you don't mind."

"I do, seeing as how she's with me."

Greer stilled and turned to Maggie in confusion.

Ian received a look from her that should have set his hat on fire before she made the introductions. "Mr. Greer, this is U.S. Deputy Marshal Bigelow. I'm in his custody at the moment."

"Custody? You're under arrest?"

"Afraid so." She gave him a weak smile and Greer looked her up and down as if it might help determine what she'd been arrested for. She must have sensed the same, and so explained, "I inadvertently caused a man's death."

"I see." He slowly rose to his feet. "I'll be moving on then. Nice meeting you."

"Same here," she said softly.

As he walked away, Ian saw her shoulders sag, and when she looked up she was full of quiet anger. "I was just having a conversation. It wasn't as if I was going to elope with him."

"You're under arrest. You can't be keeping company."

"Thank you for the reminder. Shall I stand on

the table and make an announcement to that fact? Lord help us if I try and enjoy myself while I'm with you."

"We're not here to have fun."

"Thanks for that reminder, as well."

Ian wanted to smile but was afraid she'd turn her cutlery on him. "You're probably way too spirited for him anyway."

"So now you're a prognosticator."

He did smile then.

"He's the first nice man I've had the pleasure of meeting in quite some time, and it isn't funny."

"I'm not laughing."

She snarled quietly and went back to her food.

Ian tried to make amends. "Man like him just wants to put you behind a plow, give you a bunch of babies, and work you to death."

"And what will you give me besides a date with the judge?"

"If things were different, books."

Her mouth dropped. He rose to his feet and walked over to the exit and out into the coolness of the night.

Outside, he lit a cheroot and blew the smoke at the moon. A puff later, Lola was beside him.

"Saw you running off Maggie's men."

"She's a prisoner, not a dance hall girl."

"Saw the way you been watching her, too. Like a stallion eyeing a mare."

He didn't respond.

"What are you going to do about her?"

He told her of the wire he'd sent. "I'll pick up

the reply in Abilene since the telegraph office here is closed."

"Why not just let her go?"

"I'd like to. Thus the wire."

"She should be somewhere in a man's arms making him smile. I believe she and Tate would do good together. He's got some schooling, owns his own land—a lot like you."

Ian blew out another stream of smoke.

"Of course, his past doesn't include train robbing, gunslinging or bounty hunting, but I'm sure Maggie would be willing to overlook that."

"You're having fun, aren't you?"

"Sure am. How about you?"

"No."

"A good woman can cure that." She patted his shoulder consolingly. "See you back inside."

Ian stared out at the night and mulled over Lola's words. Apparently he'd been wrong about Greer, but if the rancher was as good a catch as she'd claimed, he shouldn't have any trouble finding a suitable wife, even if it meant advertising back East for one. Had he really been interested in marrying Maggie or just pulling her leg? He remembered the talk they'd had about her dreams: wearing a nice dress, being able to sit and read a book, having her own place where she could watch her garden grow. With a husband she might be able to attain those things. He turned his mind away from thoughts of her with another man. Since Tilda's death he'd been insistent upon not taking another wife, but because of Maggie and her feisty spirit he was sensing cracks in the foundation of that stance. Could the light of a woman dissolve the darkness inside him? Could it soften the years of being in the saddle day and night in all kinds of weather? Would it reinvigorate a heart that had to grow callous in order to arrest a man at his mother's funeral or on his wedding day, and then turn to stone from having to face the keening grief of the mother of a seventeen-year-old boy who'd drawn on Ian in effort to get his picture in the paper—and he had, lying in a coffin. The boy's death was regrettable, but he felt nothing for the others. Every man he'd brought in dead or alive had been a murderer, rapist, or coward who'd used his fists on women and children. The world was a better place with them either behind bars or dead and in hell, but in doing his job, Ian had paid the price in terms of who he'd become.

Ideally if he was to pursue a wife, he'd want her to be made in Maggie's image. Back home in Wyoming there were women who'd gladly volunteer for the role, but compared to their sweet milk ways, Maggie was like a kick of raw tequila At one time in his life, he'd craved the innocence of a Tilda to counteract the wild and wooly man he'd evolved into since meeting Neil July on the train those many years ago, but Ian was older now. He'd tasted life in all its many forms and flavors, and all he wanted now was to heal, and to let the accumulated darkness and death bleed out of him so he could enjoy the years that remained in peace.

So where did that leave him and Maggie. Right where they were, he supposed. After they went their separate ways, he'd keep an eye out for a woman whose beauty, wit, and inner strength mirrored hers. It occurred to him that it might be easier to find a nugget of gold on the streets of Topeka, but life had always been hard.

Chapter 10

Maggie was lying on a bed in one of Lola's bedrooms with a warm, moist tea towel over her black eye. She had no idea where the marshal had gotten himself to and in truth, she didn't care. Being the center of all that male attention down in the main room had been nice, mainly because they'd been so nice and polite—for the most part. There had been one indecent proposal but that was because he thought she was one of Lola's girls.

She'd especially enjoyed Tate Greer and got the impression that had they been allowed to speak longer than thirty seconds she might have learned more about him, but Bigelow had put the brakes on that. No one had ever proposed marriage to her before, and it wasn't as if she'd been in a position to say yes, but that she hadn't even been allowed to enjoy imagining such a scenario was what irked her.

But even as she grumbled about the marshal's interference, in the back of her mind his parting words continued to resonate. *If things were different, books.* What type of man promised a woman books? He'd left her speechless and her heart pounding. She remembered telling him her dreams, but didn't think he'd paid her words much mind. Apparently he had, and she wondered what his dreams were. Did they revolve around how he made his living, or were they more intangible? She knew he'd loved his wife, so did he dream of having another, or was he one of those men who lived only for her memory? *More questions.* She imagined that if he did take someone else into his heart, the woman he chose would need to be strong and patient and have the ability to make him laugh. He seemed to take life far too seriously, but then again, she'd never walked in his boots, just as he'd never walked in hers.

Hearing the door open and someone walk into the room, Maggie assumed it was Lola. "This is making my eye feel better."

"Good" came a familiar low-toned voice. It wasn't Lola.

She eased the folded towel aside, surveyed him with her good eye, and closed off her vision again. Next she knew he was beside the bed.

"Let me see."

"I'm fine."

"You are such a pigheaded woman."

She removed the cloth and glared up to find a smile playing across his full lips. "You've been finding an awful lot to smile at these past couple of days."

"I'm blaming it on you. Didn't used to."

He touched the bruised skin lightly, and her blood shimmered in response.

"Does it hurt?"

"Not as much as yesterday." She was held captive by all that he was. There was a heat burning within him that was palpable enough to reach out and hold in her hand. She didn't know how she knew, but the woman inside her was certain that when he loved, he loved passionately and well, and Lord help her, she wanted to be that woman, because she'd never experienced that, either.

Hearing herself, she shook herself loose and replaced the towel. It had cooled though and needed reheating, so she sat up. Ignoring him, she walked over to the small brazier burning below a small pot of water in the fireplace. After soaking the end of the towel in the hot water and wringing it out, she refolded it, placed the warmth against her eye, and resumed her position on the bed.

"I could've done that for you."

"My eye hurts, Marshal. Not my feet."

Ian's eyes traveled innocently down to the aforementioned appendages, and the erotic sight of her bare, ruby-tipped toes hardened him so swiftly and completely he fell into a coughing fit.

She moved the towel aside and looked down at her feet, turning them back and forth as if admiring them. "Pretty, aren't they?"

Ian was fighting to breathe.

"Lola fixed them up. It's oil mixed with crushed rose petals. You put it on and then buff the toes with a chamois until they shine. Smells heavenly, too."

She held out her foot. He stepped back.

"Something the matter, Marshal?"

Ian headed towards the door. "I told Lola I'd help her with something. I'll be back later."

In the silence after his departure, Maggie looked up at the ceiling and chuckled softly. She couldn't predict her future but she was sure he'd remember her for a long time to come.

Ian took a seat at a table in a shadowy corner at the back of Lola's main room and tried to slow his breathing. As he sipped on a shot of the house's watered-down whiskey, noise, music and the high-pitched squeals of the girls echoed around him but he barely heard it. He'd never been one to drink to excess, even in his outlaw days; drink dulled the mind and reflexes. In his line of work he'd needed both to stay sharp, so he usually appreciated her doctored spirits. Not tonight. Tonight he needed something stronger, say a bottle of raw tequila, to rid himself of an overpowering hankering for a bruised-faced, one-eyed woman with rose petal toes. Thinking back on the arousing display made his manhood surge again. He tossed back the drink and set the glass down on the tabletop. From the moment they met she'd done nothing but surprise him, and now the toes . . . It had taken all his discipline not to fall on her and slowly kiss, touch, and suck his way from the toes to her sassy mouth. He ran an amazed hand down his unshaven face. This was supposed to be a simple transfer of a prisoner to the proper authorities, nothing more, yet here he sat throbbing and pulsing like a stallion in heat.

His attention settled on Lola pouring drinks behind the bar. This was all her fault and whether she was aware of it or not, the turmoil plaguing him from Maggie's toes was more than an apt revenge for all the damage he'd caused during the fight with Stapleton. He got up to fetch another drink.

Lola splashed more whiskey in his glass. "Doing pretty good business tonight. How's Maggie? She show you her toes?"

His hard-eyed glare made her howl.

"Got you going, didn't they. Figured they would. The queens of Egypt favored ruby red. Cleopatra preferred crimson."

Ian didn't know if any of that was true, or how she'd come to possess such knowledge. It made him wonder if madams were given some kind of secret schooling in man pleasing. He tossed back the whiskey and set the glass down. "Why are you doing this?"

"Because you need prodding. You've been stuck in your grief like a calf in mud since your Tilda was killed. I'm just trying to make you climb back onto solid ground. Remember, I knew the man you used to be."

Ian gazed unseeingly out into the crowded boisterous room while considering her words, and admitted that they were in line with his earlier thoughts of wanting to shake free of Vance Bigelow and reclaim Ian. "She's not for me."

"Sure she is. Have you met a better candidate?"

In truth he hadn't. He was just about to admit that when he heard a loud male voice shout, "Bigelow! You got five seconds to get your gun 'fore I send you to the devil."

He spun and met the angry drunken eyes of a man he didn't know. The grizzled gray hair on his face showed his age but Ian couldn't attach a memory to it. Two younger men flanking him couldn't have been older than sixteen. Both were armed. Both looked scared. Ian immediately flashed back to another kid holding a gun on him and slapped the image away. "Who is this?" he asked Lola almost impatiently.

She sighed. "Matt Stapleton's daddy, Dale. The two boys are his sons, Dale Jr. and Billy. They must've heard you were in town."

While the patrons scrambled to get out of the line of fire, Ian cursed silently and drew both guns so quickly the gaping crowd swore later it was like magic. "Boys, take your daddy home."

Lola added to the warning. "Go home, Dale. You don't want those boys to have to bury you, too."

Keeping his eyes on his adversaries, Ian asked her, "Who else they bury?"

"Matt. Killed in a prison escape last winter."

Ian didn't understand why Stapleton was holding him accountable. "I'm not responsible for your son's death, Mr. Stapleton."

"Yeah you are! You brought him in! Hadn't been for you, Matt be still here."

"Your son killed a man in front of his wife and children. If I hadn't brought him in, some other bounty hunter would've." Ian watched one of the sons touch his daddy's arm with what appeared to be concern.

Stapleton snarled, "Get your hands off me! You ready, Bigelow?"

Ian cocked both pistols. In the thick silence it sounded like cannon shot.

Stapleton fired. Ian unleashed his own guns, dropped to the floor, and rolled. Dale Jr. screamed as hot lead tore through his shoulder. Brother Billy followed with a piercing cry as his bullet-shattered knee gave way and the leg folded beneath his weight. The elder Stapleton kept firing. Ian managed to pull a table down in front of him while counting how many shots he'd heard Stapleton use. The sons hadn't gotten off any before being taken out of the fight, and didn't seem inclined to reenlist. In fact, the one who'd been shot in the leg reached over and tried to grab the Colt from his father's hand. "Stop it, Pa! I ain't dying for Matt's memory!"

But the wiry old man fought to keep possession. The second son joined the fray on the side of his brother and for the first few seconds it was impossible to determine who might gain the upper hand. A shot rang out. The father's eyes widened in disbelief and he clutched his chest as he fell against his son before slowly crumpling to the floor. The front of his blue cotton shirt showed an ever-widening stain of his life's blood as it soaked through the fabric. The sons dropped to his side. Ian's calculation had been correct. Stapleton's gun had had one bullet left.

Lola ran out from behind the bar with a handful of towels and pressed them to the wound hoping it might stop the flow, but the effort was futile. Stapleton looked at Billy and then at Dale Jr. He cursed them both, and died.

Still holding the gun, Billy Stapleton looked over to where Ian stood waiting in the now silent room. He asked in a grief thickened voice, "Are you going to arrest us?"

Ian shook his head. *Another useless death.*

"Thanks," Billy whispered softly. "We'll be taking our daddy home. That all right?"

"Yes."

Billy turned to Lola. "Sorry for all the commotion, Miss Lola."

"Sorry for your loss, Billy. You too, Dale Jr."

Dale nodded while holding the towel she'd given him to the wound in his shoulder.

Ian wondered if they had a mother or other family to help them with the burial. "You boys have a way to get him home?"

"Just over his saddle."

Ian glanced at Lola. "Do you have a wagon we can use?"

She nodded.

"Have it brought around. I'll drive. Let me speak with Maggie and I'll ride home with them."

Ian headed down the hallway and found her standing in the faint light cast by the oil lamp sconces. He stopped. The sight of her seemed to melt the frost encasing his heart. He was so weary of death.

Her voice was soft with concern. "I saw what happened. Are you all right?"

"No, but I want to help them get their father home."

"That's very noble."

"You'll be here when I return? You won't run?"

She shook her head. "I won't run."

As time stretched between them in the silence, she placed her hand gently against his scarred cheek. The balm of her touch flooded him with so much sweetness he ached. He covered her hand with his, then eased it away so he could press his lips against the center of her small palm. "Thank you."

"You're welcome."

Holding on to the sweetness she'd placed inside, Ian strode away.

The Stapletons lived on a small piece of land not far from the town of Topeka in a crumbling, dilapidated structure that was little more than a shack. Not even the dark could mask the family's poverty. Ian saw the black outline of a lean-to that might have doubled as a barn or the place where the boys slept. From what he could see of the interior in the light held high by the tired-looking woman who answered the door, the house wasn't large enough to hold four people.

The woman was their mother. Dale Jr. made the introductions and told the story of how his father died. Pearl was her name and she met the news of her husband's demise with a dry-eyed silence and instructed the boys to "Leave him out in the yard. We'll bury him in the morning."

She faced Ian. "Thank you."

She and the light disappeared back inside. Only then did her wails of sorrow and grief pierce the night.

Weary in mind and spirit, Ian made the solitary trip back to Topeka. He drove the wagon to the livery and walked through the darkness back to Lola's place.

The interior was quiet. Order had been restored to the room and the place didn't look too much worse for wear considering all the shooting. She was alone washing glasses and stacking them on the sideboard behind the bar.

She smiled sadly when he walked over. "Everybody left after all the excitement. Thanks for what you did—taking him home and all. How'd Pearl take the news?"

Remembering the sounds, he shook his head soberly.

"Such a waste, but he brought it on himself so don't go blaming yourself."

"I won't," or at least that's what he told her. "Maggie still here?"

She nodded. "You go get some rest."

"We'll be leaving in the morning."

"Why not stay a few more days, put your feet up."

"Can't. I have to get to that wire in Abilene." And he headed for the hallway.

"Good night, Ian."

Surprised to hear her use his true name, he stopped and turned back.

She smiled. "Have known it since you rode with the Twins. Neil and his brother are lousy secret keepers."

He could only smile. "Night, Lola."

The darkness in the room he'd be sharing with Maggie was lightened by pearly moonlight streaming in through the partially opened shutters. She was asleep, so he removed his gun belt as quietly as possible and used the same care in taking off his boots. He eased his weight down onto the bed and stretched out. The grieving wails of Stapleton's thin wife continued to fill his soul, and he wondered how he'd be able to block them out so he could sleep. Wishing Maggie were awake so they could at least talk and maybe set his mind on something else besides death, he glanced her way. He wanted to hold her; pull her back against his body and let the balm that flowed from her earlier ease the rawness inside.

"Told you I'd be here," she said quietly with her back to him.

Humor twitched his lips. Yet another surprise, and such a welcome one that he asked without thought, "Can I hold you?"

The big brass bed creaked as she scooted to his side. He drew her to him and wrapped her in his arms. Her warmth, softness, and sweet scent brought such peace he never wanted to let her go. "This is all I want."

Her reply was hushed. "And if I want more?"

He stilled. She turned in his arms and he could see her looking up at him through the silvery moonlight. "Just one night. No claims or ties afterwards. That okay?"

Bewitched, he studied her with wonder. He wanted what she was offering more than anything he'd wanted in a long time, so he soundlessly lowered his mouth to hers.

Once again, the sweetness made him ache. Her

mouth fit his perfectly but she kissed him back with an inexperience he found surprising yet stirring. He drew away and traced the sassy mouth he'd been longing to taste. "Still new at this, aren't you?"

"Why do you ask?"

"The way you kiss."

"What's the matter with it?"

He chuckled at her defensive retort. "Nothing, you just don't do it like someone with a lot of experience at it. That's all." He moved a finger over her lips and down her throat.

"I'm not a virgin, if that's what's worrying you," she said, reacting to his caresses by closing her eyes.

"I know, and it isn't." He couldn't believe how soft her skin felt.

She slowly traced his mouth in much the same fashion he'd traced hers. Her touch made his senses flare like July 4 fireworks. "Are you changing your mind?"

He kissed her again. "Only unless you want me to."

"I don't."

So he spent the next few moments learning the taste and textures of her mouth, sampling the soft skin of her jaw, brushing his lips against the smooth copper column of her throat, and thrilling to the feel of her curves and hollows veiled by a thin, silky fabric beneath his mapping hands. "What are you wearing?"

"A peignoir. Lola says it's a French nightgown."

"Lola?" he echoed while he continued to explore.

"She thought I should wear it tonight," she breathed.

He couldn't suppress his chuckling and teased his tongue against a berry-hard nipple. "You two teaming up on me?"

"Sort of," she said, and her breath caught as he took the veiled berry into his mouth. He circled it with his tongue and pulled at it gently with his teeth.

"It's very pretty," she choked out while he continued to play and tug. "Do you wish to see it?"

He raised up to capture her mouth again, "Maybe later. Bit busy as the moment . . ."

Kissing his way back down the thin expanse of her throat while his hands continued a slow exploration of her form, he planted a line of lazy kisses over the swells above the gown and then filled his hands with the pliant flesh. The weight burned his palms and he rubbed his thumbs over the nipples until they turned as hard as gemstones. He bit each one gently. When she moaned and tipped her head back against the pillow, he used the tip of his tongue to trace the hollow of her arched throat.

She groaned again. He smiled and ran his hands down her ribs and over her thighs. The short peignoir had risen up to bare her thighs and hips. He impatiently tore the bedding away so he could feast his eyes and touch the lean, firm limbs. He teased a finger over the curling hair and bent to kiss the circle of her navel.

Maggie shuddered in response to the languid delight she was being treated to. The few men she'd been to bed with in her past hadn't done any of this, so she was unprepared to be touched like she was made of priceless crystal or to have her breasts fondled so deliciously. She never knew that her nipples could be made to plead, or that a man's tongue against the corners of her lips could leave her breathless. Every place he touched, kissed, or sucked left a torrid flame in its wake and she was on fire. She wanted to ask him why he was going about this so leisurely when the others before had not, but she was too busy trying to keep from crying out in celebration of the gloriousness of it all.

And as he placed his blazing lips against her navel, she crooned and then shimmered to the possessive pass of his large hands traveling boldly up and down her thighs. His journeying hands found her ankles and then her toes. He bent and paid each one searing tribute, and she just knew she was going to die.

He kissed his way back up her inner thigh. In response her swollen core pulsed in tandem with the sinuous rhythm claiming her hips. She assumed he'd push himself into her now, and she steeled herself for the part of coupling she didn't particularly care for, but once again he showed her how little she really knew. Wicked, wicked hands plied the damp gate to her soul and then focused lustily on the tiny temple of flesh that adorned it, making her spread her legs shamelessly. Desire stacked up inside her like a burgeoning summer storm and she found herself twisting and crooning and rising in uninhibited response. When he lowered his head and flicked his tongue against the throbbing kernel, it was too much. She shattered. Crying out hoarsely as her body buckled and trembled, she felt the red-hot pieces of herself swept away like cinders on the wind. The sensations were so powerful she fell back to earth with tears in her eyes.

Ian heard the sob and froze. "Maggie? Did I hurt you?"

"No."

"Then what's wrong?"

She sat up and used the backs of her hands to dash the tears from her cheeks. "I'm not sure." She looked at him in the moonlight. "The way you touched me. Is that how it should be?"

Ian wasn't sure he understood her question. "You mean that last part that gave you release?"

"Is that what all that shuddering is called?"

"There's a few other names for it, but *release* is one of them." He paused a moment and tried to see the expression on her face. "You never had a release before?"

"No," she replied in a subdued tone. "Never had a man touch me like I was fine crystal, or kiss me so sweetly, either."

Ian was floored. He ran his eyes over her shadowy form. *What kind of men had she been with in the past?*

"Carson Epps. And—the man. The one he brayed about on the train. Those were the only ones, and it was never like what you and I just did together."

He reached over and lifted her onto his lap. She

wrapped her arms around his waist and leaned into his chest. Filled with all that she was, he placed his lips against the crown of her mussed hair and murmured, "You deserve to be touched like fine crystal, every woman does."

"If that's your philosophy, you must have made a great deal of women happy in your life, Marshal."

He supposed she was right but he didn't keep tally.

"So, why didn't we do the joining?"

"Wanted to pleasure you first—make sure you were ready."

"I don't particularly care for that part, but with you, it might be different. The rest of it certainly has been."

"Shall we see?"

She leaned up and whispered through the kiss, "Yes."

So they began again. She boldly undid the buttons on his shirt. "I want to touch you . . ." she whispered hotly. Once the buttons were freed, he removed the shirt and tossed it on the floor.

Maggie had never run her hands up and down a man's muscular arm before; never felt the warmth of his chest pressed against her bare flesh, or been so inspired to touch more. He was very well made, but all her thoughts took flight under his renewed sensual claiming. He treated her breasts to another prolonged round of teasing that left her breathless and groaning.

Scintillating touches made her part her legs to allow him to rekindle the heat still simmering from her release. She never knew being with a man could leave her crazed and straining, and not caring how she looked or where or how he touched her, as long as he didn't stop.

Ian undid the placket on his trousers and shucked them down his legs. She was lying on the bed with the peignoir twisted erotically around her waist, and the moonlit tableau made him harder than he'd ever been in his life. He touched a finger to the ripe, slick center and reveled in the moans his loving evoked. He never imagined she would be so uninhibited or that the prospect of not having her by his side like this every night for the rest of his days would leave him bereft, so he didn't think about it. Instead he concentrated on the hard tips of her nipples, her sweet, sassy mouth, and making the rose petals between her thighs bloom like springtime. Only after she was running wet with his magic did he ease himself inside. She was virgin tight. Her muscles closed around his shaft, and heaven couldn't have been more satisfying. She'd voiced an aversion to this part of the act, so it became his charge to make sure she felt nothing but pleasure. So rather than stroke her hard and fast as his manhood was demanding, he held back so she could acclimate herself to his size and the feel of him inside. It was difficult. "You all right?" he whispered through the soaring passion rising within.

"Oh my."

Humor touched him. Emboldened by her breathless response he stroked her gently; teasing her with his hardness, drawing the tip of his shaft almost free before reentering the channel once more. He repeated the move again and again until she was gasping, and her inner muscles clung to him in greedy, lusty reply. She was now rising to meet his strokes. Her hot hands were moving up and down his arms and circling over the taut muscles in his back. He moved his hips faster and she answered with a welcoming pace. He did his best to keep her pleasure in the front of his mind, but she was so responsive and so supple his hold on his control began to fray. Stroking her as if there would be no tomorrow, he felt white-hot release rising and demanding to be given its head. Instead he bent low and bit her nipples, slid his hands down her trembling torso to grasp her hips and raised her high. Her answering cry signaled her release. Her rippling flesh made him grip her tighter, stroke her harder, and when she cried out again, he broke; shuddering, yelling her name, and not caring if he woke up everyone for miles around. He rode the orgasm until he thought the top of his head would explode, and then he slowly collapsed onto her softness.

When he withdrew and rolled away, Maggie was left breathless, twisting and throbbing. She looked over and found him watching her. All she could do was smile and reach for his hand. He locked his fingers with hers. "I stand corrected," she whispered.

"Enjoyed yourself, did you?"

"Very much."

She moved closer and laid her head on his

outstretched shoulder and his arm enfolded her. "Thank you."

"No, thank you."

In the silence she trailed a finger slowly down the hair on his bare chest and leaned up to give him a sweet kiss. "Are my kisses better?"

"Give me another sample or two and I'll render a decision."

So she did, filling them with everything she'd learned and all she felt. His decision was to turn her on her back, deepen the kiss, and make love to her all over again.

Chapter 11

Ian awakened the next morning with the still sleeping Maggie sprawled across him in the same intimate manner as yesterday, but this time he didn't have to imagine how it might feel to spend the night with her, he knew. Knew that she tasted of roses and that she was as uninhibited as she was sassy in life. He also got his first true look at the peignoir. It was black, transparent, and tipped with silver piping. The filmy fabric allowed him a veiled view of the breasts and nipples that had enthralled him so, and of the arousing length of her lean legs and hips. His manhood rose in instant response and he closed his eyes to keep from touching her. Lord knew he wanted to, but he couldn't. Now that dawn had broken, last night would have to be put away. He'd have to don his role once again and forget about the pleasures they'd found in each other's arms. In order to do so, he'd have to let the ice encase his heart and feelings once again because that was the only way.

For the moment, however, he savored the sight and feel of her against him one last time and then quietly left the bed to wash and prepare to meet the day.

Maggie awakened alone. That he wasn't there made her sad, but she'd promised him no ties, so she put the sadness away. They'd shared a night she would remember for the rest of her life. She would have to be content with that. She sat up and thought back on the bleakness she'd seen in his eyes after Stapleton's death last night. It confirmed her suspicion that there were places inside him that no one knew, places that were bruised and hurt. That realization was what made her want to offer him solace with the only thing she had to give, herself. She hadn't planned to seduce him, but after he left to accompany the Stapleton sons home, she asked Lola for a nightgown to wear to bed. When she was given the peignoir, the die was apparently cast. She had no regrets. In his arms she'd learned the true meaning of making love and would be forever grateful. If she never experienced such sweetness again, so be it. She had her memories.

She assumed he'd left without waking her to spare them both the awkwardness of having to resume their roles, and a part of her appreciated his thoughtfulness. She'd been around him enough to know that if her assumption was true, he'd show very little emotion when they met face-to-face again, so she planned to do the same.

She took the time to wash and dress herself in her freshly laundered shirt and trousers. She also packed the clothing and toiletries Lola had given her into her weathered saddlebag and carried it with her so that she wouldn't have a reason to return to the room with its memories.

She found him downstairs having breakfast at one of the tables. She dropped her pack on the floor by one of the unoccupied chairs and greeted him nonchalantly. "Good morning, Marshal. Did you sleep well?"

He eyed her over his mug of coffee and searched her face silently as if trying to determine what she was about. She kept her features bland.

"I did," he finally replied. "And you?"

"I did as well. Is there more food?"

"Kitchen."

"Thank you." Walking away she thought she'd handled that as well as could be expected. *That was that.*

In the kitchen, Maggie found Lola pouring herself a cup of coffee. Apparently it was too early for the girls to be up and about because the house's owner was alone. "Morning, Miss Lola."

"Morning, Maggie. How'd the night go?"

Maggie shrugged noncommittally.

Lola raised a tweezered eyebrow. "That good, huh?"

Maggie got herself a cup of coffee but didn't respond.

"There's eggs and bacon and bread on the counter behind you. Get yourself a plate and let's talk."

Maggie wasn't keen on sharing her evening with the marshal, but she got a plate of food and sat down at the small table anyway.

"So did you ask him to let you go?"

"No."

"For heaven's sake, why not?"

"Getting him to let me go wasn't the reason," Maggie said as politely as she could manage around the forkful of eggs in her mouth. "I'm not a whore."

Lola tossed back with a laugh, "You say that as if being a whore is a bad thing. Plenty of women whore and many of them are married. How else are they going to get that new hat or that fancy stove? You'd be surprised how weak-minded a man can be after a good tumble in the hay. A smart woman should take advantage of that."

Maggie shook her head. "Guess I'm not that smart."

"Oh, you're smart enough."

But not enough to keep from wanting a man she'd never have. She wondered if Lola had a magic salve that could somehow uproot the seeds of feelings that had taken root in her heart for him. Changing the subject, she asked, "What's Abilene like?"

"Much tamer than it used to be. Back in the late sixties, early seventies, folks called it the Queen of the Cow Towns. Hundreds of thousands of cows went through the stockyards. Almost as many cowboys, too. Me and my girls did good business there back then, so did all the brothels and saloons. Lots of shooting, drinking, and carousing."

"But it's calmer now?"

"Yes. There are still saloons and madams, just not every five steps like it used to be. Wild Bill Hickok was the sheriff there for a while. Spent most of his time playing cards and drinking at the Alamo Saloon though. After he shot his deputy during a misunderstanding, the town council decided the place needed cleaning up, so that's when I packed up my business and moved here."

Maggie wondered what she'd find in Abilene. She hoped the reply to the wire would be there and have a positive response written on it so that she and the marshal could part ways and her feelings for him could wither.

Lola's voice interrupted her thoughts. "Things will work out, you'll see."

Maggie nodded and focused on finishing her breakfast.

They reboarded the crowded train without incident. Ian found them two seats together in the second car. Maggie sat by the window while he took the aisle. He hadn't spoken much, so neither had she. According to the conductor the train would arrive in Abilene by early evening. Out of her window she watched the plains roll by. She wished the train could go faster so this would all be over, but it was moving as quickly as the engines would allow. She'd just have to be patient.

Ian was impatient to get to the end of the journey, too. After making love to her last night, his hold on his commitment to keep his heart in check now had cracks in it large enough to send a herd of buffalo through. His feelings didn't care about his resolve, they wanted Maggie and to hell with everything else.

* * *

The train arrived in Abilene early that evening and they rode Smoke to the sheriff's office. The man who greeted them introduced himself as Pete Granger. He didn't appear to be very old; mid-thirties at the most. Ian knew that many sheriffs were corrupt individuals bought and paid for by the local power brokers and therefore controlled like puppets on a string. Granger, however, shook Ian's hand firmly and looked him in the eye. His decent manner reminded Ian of Sheriff Wells.

Granger assured them that he'd gotten the wire. "Sorry about the pickle you're in, Miss Freeman," he told her kindly. "Wells wants you to be jailed here until he gets the paperwork finished showing he dropped the charges. Once he sends them you'll be free to go."

She nodded.

"We'll try and make your short stay with us as comfortable as we can. I'll wire him back and let him know you got here safe and sound."

"Thank you."

Granger asked Ian, "So where you headed now, Bigelow?"

"Home."

"Where's that?"

"Wyoming." Ian forced himself to stay focused on Granger and not look Maggie's way for fear of what it might do to his resolve.

"Well, have a safe journey. We'll take good care of her. I promise."

Only then did Ian turn her way. She faced him with unflinching eyes and her chin held high.

"Thank you for your kindness, Marshal. Safe travels."

"Where will you head, once you're done here?"

She shrugged. "Try and make it to Ohio, I suppose. I'll see." Her business with him seemingly done, she asked Granger, "So where do I go, Sheriff?"

"How about you just take a seat over there for now, and we'll get you something to eat first."

She complied.

It was apparent to Ian that she had nothing else to say to him and that she wasn't going to meet his eyes again. He tightened his jaw. "Thank you, Sheriff."

"You're welcome."

Maggie watched him walk out of the door, and the pain closed her eyes for a moment. Hoping to appear nonchalant, she angled her head towards the window and watched him mount up and ride away. She was glad the ordeal was over. She didn't mind staying in Abilene until the papers were wired, but the idea of going on with her life without him was difficult.

"So," Granger said.

Maggie turned to him.

He had his hip propped on the edge of his desk and was viewing her speculatively. "How'd you get the black eye?"

"A fight."

"A little face paint should cover it fine."

Maggie stilled. "Face paint?"

The smile on his face gave her both pause and a chill that ran down her spine.

"You sing?" he asked.

She tried to determine where this conversation might be heading, so she responded warily, "A bit, yes."

"Good. Open your shirt. Let's see what you got?"

She stared, outraged. "No!"

He pulled his gun and pointed it her way. "Open it now, or I'll shoot you and swear on a stack of Bibles you were trying to escape."

Eyes wide, she searched his face and realized he was serious. She hid her fear behind her fury and after getting to her feet, undid the buttons on her shirt and spread the halves wide to reveal the worn white shift beneath. He studied her for a long moment, then looked up again with pleased icy eyes. "You'll do. Grab your pack and let's go." Still holding the gun on her, he gestured her towards the door.

They walked a few streets away to a place called the Red Garter Saloon. On the way, she'd prayed the marshal would appear, but of course he hadn't. She was in this new nightmare alone.

Holding her by the arm, Granger guided her in through a back door and up a flight of stairs that led to a hallway on the second floor. A number of painted women in various stages of undress were rushing back and forth, apparently in preparation for the night's activities. They viewed the sheriff malevolently and her with various degrees of curiosity, suspicion, and in one case, pity.

"Where's Bunny?" he asked.

"In her room." The woman who'd replied had been the one eyeing Maggie so suspiciously. She was tall, and her long blonde wig cascaded past shoulders bared above her tight black corset. Her legs were covered by patched knee-length drawers. Years ago she'd probably been quite beautiful, but now the twin demons of age and a hard life had taken the bloom off the rose. "Who's she?"

"Your new sister."

The mocking reply drew a sneer and the sight of her back as she walked away.

"Bunny!" he yelled angrily.

A loud female voice hollered back, "What the hell are you bellowing about now!"

The voice belonged to an older woman who came charging out of one of the rooms dressed in a pink satin robe. Her sparse graying hair was in pipe-cleaner rollers, her feet were bare, and she had a lit cheroot in her hand.

"Got a new one for you," Granger explained.

Maggie watched the woman size her up.

"Says she can sing."

"That's what they all say," Bunny replied, inhaling her cheroot. She blew out a thin column of smoke. "Okay. Leave her to me."

He turned his icy gray eyes on Maggie. "Nice meeting you, Miss Freeman."

The angry Maggie didn't reply.

While he departed, Bunny said in a far kinder voice, "Come on with me. Place opens in an hour. We need to get you ready."

Maggie followed her down the hallway.

Once the two of them were sequestered in a room behind closed doors, Bunny tapped ash into a small saucer on the old desk dominating the interior and asked, "So, how'd you wind up in Granger's net?"

Maggie hesitated for a moment, not sure she wanted to share the story.

Bunny must have read her mind. "It's okay. I hate him like everybody else up here does."

That surprised her.

"We're all wanted for something, but rather than letting us plead our cases before a judge, we're working for him and the bastard owner of this place, McQuade."

"Who's he?"

"Town's crime boss, and a fine upstanding member of the Kansas legislature. Wants to be governor eventually. With any luck, someone will stick a shiv in his ribs before that happens and save the good citizens a lot of grief."

"All of you are here against your will?"

Bunny nodded.

"But what if you decide to just leave?"

"You wind up in the cemetery on the edge of town."

Maggie's eyes widened.

"Saw Granger shoot a girl in the back a couple months ago. Said she was trying to escape."

"But how can he hide you away like this?"

"If no one knows you're here . . ."

Maggie found this appalling. Had Granger lied about the reply he'd gotten from Sheriff Wells? "How long have you been here?"

"Be three years in July. Most of the others a year or less. Some are here because they answered flyers McQuade posted back East for singers and dancers."

Maggie thought about Carson Epps. This was more of a nightmare than she'd originally imagined. "So what do we do in the saloon?"

"Dance, sing, make sure the rubes buy lots of drinks."

"No back work?"

Bunny shrugged. "If you want to. He has a whole 'nother operation for that. Most of those girls are willing. They stay in the cribs in the building next door."

Maggie dragged her hands down her face. At least she wouldn't be forced into prostitution, but it made her captivity only mildly more acceptable. *What am I going to do?*

"You really sing?"

"Yes."

"Ever been on a saloon stage before?"

"Yes. Even have my own dress and a pair of shoes."

"Well, good." Bunny reached into a desk drawer and handed her a pair of new fishnet stockings. "You get the first pair free. After that it comes out of your tips."

"Tips?"

"Yeah, you get a small cut for every drink you sell, and any that the customers buy you, too." Granger takes most of it back for rent and food. If you're frugal you can save a little bit for things like underwear and feminine supplies."

Maggie found this unbelievable.

"Get dressed and I'll take you downstairs before the place opens up so you can meet Vincent the piano player. He'll want to know what you're planning on singing."

Maggie was grateful the woman seemed to have a kind heart, but for the life of her couldn't figure out how she was going to get out of this.

Bunny showed her into one of the bedrooms and left her alone to get dressed.

Maggie took the bright red dress out of her pack, along with the matching glittery shoes, and felt the sharp sting of tears. Crying wouldn't help, so she dashed them away and laid the wrinkled taffeta dress on the bed. It needed an iron but she assumed Bunny could supply one. In the meantime, she tried not to think about being held there against her will for maybe the rest of her life, otherwise she'd go screaming out into the streets like a madwoman.

Chapter 12

Ian pushed the food around on his plate with the fork in his hand. He missed her already. Even though she'd been with him less than a week he'd grown accustomed to having her near. *Now she wasn't.*

It was his plan to take the train in the morning to Denver. From there he and Smoke would make the long journey home to his ranch. All he had to do was survive the night without her. He was in one of the local boardinghouses. It was small but clean. The woman who ran the place, a widow named Winthrop, had thrown in dinner with the price of the room, along with breakfast in the morning. She'd said there were three other boarders in the house, but Ian hadn't seen anyone else, not that it mattered. The only person he wanted to see was Maggie.

He forked up some of the beef and potatoes. They weren't the best he'd eaten nor the worst. A man entered and walked over to the table. Ian realized it was the gambler from the train.

"Evening, Marshal. Didn't think I'd be seeing you again."

"Evening."

"Mind if I join you?"

Ian gestured to one of the empty chairs.

"Let me get a plate first."

Once that was accomplished, the gambler sat down and introduced himself. "Name's Franklin Denton."

"Didn't expect to see you again, either. Where're you from?"

"Born right here in the Queen of the Cow Towns. Live in Denver now though. Was back East a few weeks ago, and thought I'd stop in Abilene and see family before going home."

His suit was well made and gave the impression that his career as a gambler was a successful one. "What brings you to Abilene?" he asked Ian.

"Business with Sheriff Granger."

"Hope he's not a friend."

"Why not?"

"Man's a snake."

Ian went still. "Explain that."

Denton cut into the slices of ham on his plate. "He's been sheriff here going on four years, and he's owned lock, stock, and balls by Benjamin McQuade."

"Who's McQuade?"

"Controls the sin trade. Gambling, whiskey, whores. Grew up in a soddie in Nebraska but has made himself over into one of the town fathers. Wants to be governor I'm told. He's the reason I moved away. Gambler can't make a living competing against marked cards, crooked tables, and cheating dealers, all of which is business as usual at his place."

Ian knew that the crooked gambling establishments were common everywhere.

Denton continued. "My sister, who still lives here in town, said one of McQuade's girls was shot by Granger over the winter, trying to escape."

"Escape what, jail?"

"No. The Red Garter, one of the saloons."

Ian was confused. "Why escape from the saloon? Was she being held against her will?"

"Something like that. From what my sister said, Granger reels women in by hook or crook and puts them to work at the Garter or in the whore cribs."

Ice ran through Ian's veins. "I left Maggie with him a few hours ago."

"The little lady with the black eye who was with you on the train?"

Ian pushed back from the table and got to his feet. "Yes." He reached into his pocket and pulled out a box of cartridges and began feeding them into his guns.

"Why?"

"She was under arrest."

Denton cursed. "You'd better go after her. There's no telling what Granger's done with her."

"For his sake, it'd better be nothing. Where's this Red Garter?"

Denton told him, and a cold-eyed Ian set out.

Decked out in her low-cut taffeta dress, fishnet stockings and her worn, red satin shoes, Maggie was doing what Bunny called working the room, which entailed flitting from table to table and flirting with the customers. It was the job of the floor girls to make the farmers, businessmen, and cowhands happy with their attention, and entice them into buying the house's watered-down spirits. If they purchased drinks for the girls all the better, but the ones the girls consumed were tea, so as to keep them from becoming as drunk as the customers. The saloon was loud. Bunny had explained that on a good night, the aging place with its stage and faded red-and-gold drapings could hold as many as fifty people. Maggie guessed there were that many inside presently, if not more. The noise of all the conversations, Vincent banging on the piano, and the high-pitched laughs of the girls, coupled with the clink of glasses and the clouds of cigar and cheroot smoke, were conspiring to make her head ache, but she had to keep smiling, and flirting, and sitting on laps until the time came for her to take the stage and sing.

Presently, the blonde, suspicious-eyed Sylvia was doing the entertaining. While Vincent pounded out "Camp Town Ladies," she sang along, prancing back and forth. Maggie had heard cats stuck in a fence carry a better tune, but no one in the audience seemed to mind. They were more interested in the way she kept flipping up the hem of her dress to flash them looks at her thighs in the fishnet stockings. She'd then stop and lean over so that the raucously yelling men seated near the stage could peek down the front of her dress. Maggie wasn't looking forward to being next. All evening she'd forced herself not to think about the marshal, how far along on his journey home he might be, or if he was thinking about her or not, because the questions wouldn't get her out of Granger's clutches. She could see him on the far side of the room leaning against the bar. He seemed to be keeping a close eye on her, probably to make sure she didn't run.

To her further displeasure he was now walking in her direction, weaving his way through the tables of drunk men still cheering Sylvia's bad singing performance.

"So Miss Freeman," he asked against her ear so he could be heard above the din. "You seem to be having a good time."

Maggie wasn't, but she didn't respond.

"Do you see that man over there in the gray suit?"

She saw a portly but prosperous-looking man sporting muttonchops seated at a table with three other men who looked to be in the business trade.

"His name's Benjamin McQuade and he owns this place. Think of him as your master and me as your overseer."

Maggie balled her fists to keep from showing a reaction.

"You're a pretty girl. If you're nice to me, I can make life here real smooth for you. Think about that."

Sylvia was leaving the stage.

"Excuse me. It's my turn to sing." Walking away, the only thing she wanted to think about was running him over with a train.

* * *

During the height of Abilene's reign as the country's premier cattle town, the drunken antics of the thousands of cowboys who accompanied the herds from Texas were legendary. If they weren't drunk and disorderly or having shoot-outs in the streets, they were riding their horses into saloons, guns blazing, and scaring the hell out of folks. As the son of an actress, Ian had a flair for the dramatic, which was why he rode Smoke slowly into the Red Garter Saloon. The look on his face was as deadly as the drawn, sawed-off shotgun in his hand.

Maggie was onstage in the middle of a song. It was hard not to miss a man on a smoke gray stallion entering the center of the room. She stopped singing, Vincent stopped playing, and the room went silent enough to hear a ghost walking as everyone in the place stared with wide eyes. She wanted to jump up and down and cheer.

His voice was low, clear, and sinister. "Name's Preacher. I'm a bounty hunter and a United States deputy marshal. If your name isn't Granger or McQuade, I suggest you leave in the next thirty seconds."

Men got up and fell over one another trying to reach the exit.

The absolute surprise on Granger's face made her want to cheer again but fear quickly grabbed her upon seeing the bartender raising a gun hidden behind the bar. Before she could call out a warning, the marshal turned and fired. The loud blast from his weapon sent the barkeep running and ducking. The next shot blew apart the big fancy mirror behind the bar, shattering stacks of glasses and bottles of whiskey.

Just as quickly, he leveled the gun on Granger, whose hand was frozen in position on the gun in his holster. Apparently he'd been thinking about drawing, but being caught dead to rights, she was pretty sure he'd changed his mind.

The two armed thugs Granger employed to keep the peace in the place had stayed behind when the other customers fled, but in the face of the marshal's opening act, quickly laid down their guns, stuck their hands high up in the air so that he could see they posed no threat, then slowly backed across the room to the front door and disappeared outside.

Granger and the marshal continued to stare each other down. The sheriff must have decided he didn't want to be in a casket come morning, so he slowly undid the gun belt and dropped it to the floor. Beside him, McQuade was wiping a handkerchief over the sweat pouring down his face.

A concerned Bunny stepped out from the stage's wings in response to all the commotion. "What the hell is happening?" Seeing the marshal, she stopped and asked Maggie, "Who is that?"

Maggie had tears of joy in her eyes. "Deputy Marshal Bigelow."

"Friend of yours?"

Maggie nodded. Bunny smiled.

He then yelled, "Maggie Freeman! Where are you?"

"Here, Marshal!" She was amused that he hadn't recognized her when he rode in.

He moved his attention to the stage. If he was surprised by her attire he didn't show it. She wanted to jump off the stage and kiss him until she turned one hundred years old.

Ian had trouble reconciling the Maggie he'd left with Granger and the dolled-up woman on the stage wearing a low-cut red dress and fishnet hose, but he'd deal with that later. Now that he knew she was safe, he could direct his anger towards Granger and his keeper. "Why's my prisoner on that stage?"

"It—it was her idea," Granger said quickly. "She wanted—"

The blast from the shotgun ended the lie, and both he and McQuade screamed like sheep and tried to find cover. They ran into each other, knocking themselves down. Another blast blew up the floor, which caused more screaming.

Having gotten their undivided attention, he quoted Proverbs: "'A false witness shall not be unpunished, and he that speaketh lies shall not escape.' Now, tell me, what did Wells's wire really say?"

Granger didn't look like he wanted to perish. "He—said she was free to go."

"No restrictions?"

"Just that she should stay out of the state of Kansas for a while in case the Langley charges don't stick."

Ian wanted to blow him to hell. "Rumor says you're keeping a bunch of women here against their will."

Both men, now sweating and shaking, looked

at each other with fright in their eyes. McQuade, apparently deciding he wanted no further part of this, turned to Granger and asked, "Is this true?"

Up onstage, Bunny shook her head. "Cowardly bastard." She then called out, "It's true, Marshal! McQuade's lying if he says he didn't know."

Ian looked to her. "Tell the ladies to get their things. They're leaving."

Bunny didn't have to be told twice. Waving her hands joyously in the air, she hurried backstage.

Ian speared his prey with hard eyes once again and announced quietly, "This is what's going to happen. Granger, you're going to give the town your resignation."

"The hell I will."

"Then I'll arrest you for false imprisonment, abduction, and anything else I can think of, haul you down to Fort Smith, and let you tell Judge Parker what a fine and upstanding lawman you are."

Granger's lip curled in reaction, but he kept his mouth shut.

"As for you Mr. McQuade, same thing."

"You can't talk to me this way. Why, I'm a duly elected member of the town council."

"I hear you're thinking about running for governor."

"I am, and once elected, I will make sure that crooked sheriffs like Granger never get the chance to terrorize—"

An answering blast from the shotgun sent both men scrambling again. In the tense silence that followed both were trembling. "You either resign or I wire every newspaper from San Francisco to Boston and see what they think about a duly elected official of the state of Kansas keeping a bunch of women locked away like slaves. Reporters will come from miles around to hear you tell your side, but that'll be after Judge Parker sends you to jail. Knowing him, he'll probably see to it that you and Granger share the same cell."

McQuade puffed up. "How dare you threaten me."

"And how dare you not remember that the slaves were freed in '65."

Silence.

By then Bunny had returned with the eight girls. She handed Maggie her saddlebag.

He asked Bunny, "Is that everyone?"

"Yes, sir."

"Maggie, you ready?"

"Sure am."

He walked Smoke over and she climbed aboard, wrapping her arms tightly around his waist. Tears filled her eyes again as she pressed her cheek against his strong back in silent gratitude.

He directed his attention at Bunny and the girls. "Ladies, after you."

The women scrambled off the stage and together walked past the stony-faced Granger and McQuade to the exit. Ian and Maggie followed on Smoke, and left behind another chapter in the still-growing tale of the legendary bounty hunter, the Preacher.

Outside, the male customers lining the walk looked on silently. Paying them no mind, but keeping his eyes on the upper windows and doorways of the buildings just in case someone was dumb enough to try and take a shot at him, Ian escorted his party of painted women away from the Red Garter Saloon.

They set up camp at the depot. It was closed for the night, but when it reopened in the morning, they all planned to buy tickets and board the first train to come through. None of the women had enough money to go far but didn't care as long as they put distance between themselves and Granger and McQuade.

Upon hearing of the women's limited funds while he and Maggie stood talking with Bunny, Ian offered a solution by pulling out his grandfather's leather pouch and handing the old madam enough gold to buy tickets to take her and the girls wherever they wanted to go.

Bunny stared dumbstruck. "I can't take this."

Ian didn't respond to that but said instead, "Give the ladies what they need, then settle down for the night. I'll keep watch in case Granger or McQuade decided to make trouble."

Bunny was still staring at the small pile of gold coins in her palm but finally looked up to meet his eyes. "I doubt that. You scared the hair off them." She glanced down at her hand once again. "You sure about this?"

Once again, no response.

She shook her head. "Never knew being a marshal paid so well."

He responded to the humor in her voice with a hint of humor in his eyes.

Maggie was surprised by his generosity, too. Granted he'd been paying for everything since they'd been thrown together, but she'd had no idea he held so much coin. She had to agree with Bunny; being a marshal was way more lucrative than she'd imagined.

When Bunny walked over to where the girls were gathered and told them the news, their whoops and hollers of joy filled the night. They all came over to offer their thanks, even Sylvia, who seemed to be viewing Maggie in a different light. "Is he your man?"

"No. Just an acquaintance." She didn't look his way.

"Wish I had an acquaintance like him. You married, Marshal?"

Bunny clamped a hand on her arm. "Go back over there and find a seat. Rest of you go with her."

Maggie hadn't known any of them long enough to call them friends; she didn't even know most of their names, but she was glad that they were no longer under Granger's boot.

Bunny's voice cut into her thoughts. "Maggie, you and your marshal will always have a soft spot in my heart."

"Thanks, Bunny."

Bunny walked over to join the girls, leaving Maggie and her marshal alone.

Chapter 13

The night songs of the crickets played around them like music and all Maggie wanted to do was look at him, even if it was too dark to see her hand in front of her face. The idea that he was there, and that she was now free, made her soul rejoice. "Quite an entrance you made back there."

For Ian it was good to have her near again, too. "Wanted to get their attention."

"You certainly did. Thank you for the rescue."

"You're welcome. My apologies for putting you in harm's way." Although they'd only been apart for a few hours, it felt like ten times that.

"You had no way of knowing Granger wasn't being truthful about the wire."

"He didn't hurt you?"

"No." She paused for a moment as if thinking back. "Do you think he and McQuade will really do what you told them to?"

"Probably not, which is why I'll be wiring Fort Smith as soon as I get to Denver."

"Is that where you're going next?"

"Yes."

They studied each other in the darkness. "What are you going to do now that you're free?"

"Don't rightly know. If the sheriff wants me to stay out of Kansas, I suppose I'll have to, but all the trains connect here."

"True."

"Maybe I can find work in Denver, wait six months or so and head back East to Ohio. I don't know." She sighed. "Add to the fact that I don't have a penny to my name."

"I can buy your ticket, that isn't a problem."

"Thank you. I'll pay you back soon as I can, I promise."

Ian wanted to tell her she was going to Wyoming with him but he doubted that would go over well. "Once you get to Denver I'm sure you'll come up with something."

"Probably. I also need to change clothes so you'll recognize me from now on."

"I saw a woman on the stage when I rode in, but didn't know it was you. You look different."

She bent over and took stock of herself. "I do, don't I?"

"Did Bunny give you the dress and shoes?"

She hesitated for a moment before responding quietly, "No, I had them in my saddlebag."

Ian tried to see her expression but it was hidden by the darkness.

"Which means of course that I've sung and danced in places like the Red Garter before." She added. "Carson Epps."

"So when you joined his troupe this is how

he made his money." It was more statement than question.

"Yes."

Ian found himself amazed by her once again. How many facets of her were there? Just when he thought he had her figured out, something else about her rocked him back on his heels. "My mother was an actress."

"Really?"

"Sang, dance, recited. Audiences loved her. She'd've liked you."

"Because I sing on a stage?"

"There's that, but she'd've been more taken by your spirit."

"Are you complimenting me, Marshal?"

"I think I am."

"Then I think I say thank you."

Ian wanted to sneak her off into the darkness and reacquaint her to the feel of being in his arms, but that would only further complicate matters, and the situation was complicated enough. Standing near her and thinking back on their night together while the wind whispered around them and the moon above played in and out of the clouds, was going to lead to trouble if he didn't back away, so he did. "You go ahead and change clothes. I'll set up here and keep watch."

She glanced up as if surprised by his abrupt end of their conversation, but instead of speaking to it, she said simply, "Sure." And walked off.

Ian sighed and removed Smoke's saddle. He patted the stallion affectionately. "Doesn't look like we'll ever make it home, does it, boy? You as tired of getting on and off trains as I am? Promise I'll never take you on a trip like this ever again. Making myself the same promise. In the meantime, what are we going to do about Maggie?"

Smoke had no answer and neither did his rider, so Ian untied his bedroll and prepared to settle in for his watch. Lying back against the saddle, he made himself comfortable and lit a cheroot. As the smoke curled up and drifted off into the night, all he could think about was Maggie.

Dressed in her shirt, trousers, and battered boots once again, Maggie folded the red dress and carefully wedged it back into her pack along with the stockings and shoes. Using the saddlebag as a pillow and her father's coat as a blanket, she made herself as comfortable as she could on the depot's plank floor and thanked the gods of both her parents for the marshal. Without his intervention there was no way of knowing how long Granger might have held her prisoner. Now she was free from everything, and still giddy because of it, but the marshal remained on her mind. He'd broken off their conversation back there rather sharply and she wasn't sure why. It might have helped had she been able to see his face, but even in full light she had a tough time discerning his thoughts, and in the darkness it was impossible. While they'd stood talking his presence brought back the memories of the night they'd spent together. Her senses bloomed recalling the thrill of his kisses and the heat in his touch. She wondered if he'd been remembering, too, and if that might have been the reason for the quick retreat. Did he not want to be reminded, or were the memories as potent as her own? The woman in her wanted it to be the latter. That woman also wanted to be loved by him again, even though keeping her distance made more sense because he'd soon be gone from her life.

The rest of the women from the Red Garter were spread out nearby. A few, like Bunny, were already asleep. Others seemed to be lying silently and minding their own thoughts. It was a warm May night, so there was no danger of frost, and if it rained, the long flat roof above their heads would keep them dry. She raised up to see if she could see him out in the grass. The moon slipped free of the clouds just long enough to illuminate him before it disappeared and plunged him back into the darkness. All that remained was the faint glow of his cigar. The woman inside hoped he was thinking of her.

The depot agent arrived for work early the next morning and the sight of the women made him stop and stare.

Ian intercepted him and after introducing himself explained, "The ladies are under my escort."

"You're the marshal everyone's talking about this morning. The good people in Abilene have been trying to get that place closed down for years. Been trying to get rid of Granger, too, but he was handpicked by McQuade and there was nothing any of us could do."

"I asked them both to resign. Figure they won't so I'll send a few wires when I get to Denver and have the courts look into those two."

"Thanks, Marshal. Let's get these tickets issued so you and the ladies will be ready to board when the train arrives."

The agent's name was Lerner and with his help the process went smoothly. By the time the train pulled in, everyone in Ian's party was lined up and ready to board the westbound train for Denver.

The conductor stepped off and Ian was surprised to see it was the same redhead who'd been on the train when Ian's journey with Maggie first began.

The man peered around at all the women. "This harem yours, Marshal?"

The glare he received made him swallow visibly. "Um, well, you all will have to ride in the smokers' car. Don't think I have enough seats up front."

"That's fine, just get us on board."

They got on moments later. None of the colorfully dressed women paid any attention to the shock and disapproval on the faces of the other passengers as they made their way to the smoking car. It wasn't the first time they'd been sneered at.

Inside the car was already crowded with card players and other men smoking and drinking. As the women filed in, the faces of the men widened with delight and then someone began to applaud. The rest joined in and the ladies from the Red Garter smiled in reply.

Ian searched the men's faces for any that he might know were wanted by the law or he'd had run-ins with in the past. He felt responsible for the women now and wanted to make certain none of them came to harm. None of the men he saw fit either category so he relaxed. They were all still eyeing Bunny and her girls though, and he knew it would be just a matter of time before one of them got up the courage to make an approach. In the meantime, he found a seat in the back, took out the Sherlock Holmes novel he had in his saddlebag, and settled in to read and keep a discreet eye on the woman he wanted to protect the most. The trip to Denver would take the better part of three days, what with stopping to take on more passengers, fuel, water, and mail. He hoped to give her the space she needed to figure out her future and for him to figure out how to contend with his future without her.

Just as the train began pulling away from the depot, the gambler Frank Denton entered the car. Denton gave Ian a nod and walked over to join a card game.

One of the men produced a banjo and soon the car was awash in singing, laughter, and gaiety. Over the course of the next few hours word must have gotten around because the presence of the girls began drawing men to the car from other areas of the train, probably much to the displeasure of their wives traveling with them, Ian supposed.

Over his book, he watched Maggie sitting with Bunny and enjoying the singing. To his surprise she stood and added to the entertainment with a song of her own. In a pure soprano voice that had everyone in the car enthralled, she offered up the haunting tale of a woman waiting for her love to come home from the war. She sang of the woman's anguish, and her broken heart when the news came that her love had been killed. Ian saw Bunny dab at her eyes and a few of the men did the same. When the final beautiful note faded into the silence, thunderous applause broke out. Eyes sparkling, she curtsied in her trousers and retook her seat. When she glanced over his way, he gave her a nod of approval and was once again rocked on his heels by another fascinating facet of Miss Maggie Freeman.

Ian noticed the eyes of a young Black man watching her as well. He'd been seated at one of the tables when Ian and the women walked in. His nice brown suit and clean-cut manner made Ian assume him to be well employed or of good family, or both. During her song, he'd stared at Maggie unabashedly.

And now he was approaching the table where she was seated. Ian watched Bunny give him a smile and gestured an invitation for him to sit and join them. He accepted, and as they spoke Maggie gifted him with her beautiful smile.

"Who are you glaring at?"

Ian looked up to see Frank Denton standing by his chair.

"Nobody."

Denton turned his eyes in the direction Ian had been looking and upon seeing Maggie in conversation with the young man at the table, shook his head knowingly and sat down, saying "I see."

"I don't remember inviting you over."

Denton grinned as he took a pull from the drink in his glass. "I don't either. Just came to relay my family's thanks for what we heard happened at the saloon last night."

Ian was only half listening because he was watching Maggie. Bunny had moved on to another table, leaving her and her well-dressed companion alone.

Denton said amusedly, "There's no cure for that, you know."

"For what?"

"Longing after a woman who's all you can see."

"Don't you have a card game somewhere?"

Amusement flashed across his thin face. "Thanks again."

"You're welcome."

Maggie was enjoying the pleasant conversation she was having with the young man who introduced himself as Justin Taylor. He was from Boston and studying to be a doctor at Meharry, the Black medical college established in Tennessee in 1876. He was journeying to Denver to apprentice with an established doctor. Taylor was well spoken, his manner polite and his smile engaging. As he talked about his studies, she found herself wondering what it might be like to have such a man for a husband. He was presently unmarried, but after his apprenticeship, if he was successful in establishing his own practice, taking a wife would be his next step, he'd revealed.

She thought the wife of a doctor would be very respected by members of the community and would undoubtedly have a fine house to oversee, and a servant or two to help with things. She'd probably wear nice clothing and be able to pause now and again to read a book. More than likely she'd be able to plant flowers and vegetables; all of which Maggie dreamed of having, but in real life a potential doctor wouldn't seek out a former prisoner and saloon singer for such an honor. Not that he moved her. He was polite and very good-looking, but she didn't sense any heat beneath his polished exterior. In her pretend world, marrying him might be rewarding for her pocketbook, but she wasn't sure about her bed. Having spent a night in the marshal's strong arms, she knew now how moving it could be, and the heat and fire was something she wanted from a husband no matter his station. Life with a man like Justin would be safe and secure. There'd be no shoot-outs with bitter old men or the need to mount rescues.

He interrupted her thoughts by saying, "I'm not accustomed to so much smoke. Would you like to step outside for some air?"

Around them the saloonlike atmosphere in the car continued. Some of the girls had found partners and were up dancing to the banjo. She spotted Sylvia seated on a gentleman's lap while he played cards. They both looked tipsy.

"Um." She cast a quick glance at the marshal. He was seated in the shadows by the door but she knew that he was watching, had been watching.

"I'm not trying to be forward, I just thought it would be nice to breathe some clean air."

She looked at the marshal again. "Sure, thanks."

As they stood and headed to the door that led to the outside platform, she saw the marshal put down his book. As they approached, he stood. Maggie hoped he wouldn't interfere.

"Where you headed?" he asked. She could see him gauging Justin and he didn't appear pleased.

"Just out for some fresh air. We'll be right back."

Justin was viewing Bigelow warily, so to forestall any kind of confrontation, she said, "Come on, Justin."

He followed but he shot another quick look back at the marshal.

Outside, Maggie pulled in deep breaths of the fresh air. She had to admit stepping out had been an excellent idea.

Justin asked, "Who was that man?"

"His name is Bigelow. He's a bounty hunter and a deputy marshal."

"He looks dangerous. Is he your father?"

It took all Maggie had not to burst into laughter. She imagined Bigelow would shoot him a hundred times had he heard that. "No. I was in his custody for a short time."

Justin froze and then asked, "Why?" But as if suddenly realizing the rudeness of his request, he apologized. "I'm sorry. That wasn't very polite."

"No. It's a natural question."

Like the handsome farmer she'd met at Lola's, Justin studied her as if her crime could somehow be discerned by the features of her face. So she explained to him how she'd come to be in custody.

"That's quite a story, but now you've been released?"

"Yes."

"So, what are you going to do?"

Before she could respond, the door opened and out stepped the marshal.

Justin's eyes widened. Maggie's mouth thinned.

Bigelow didn't say a word, but apparently Justin heard something because he offered Maggie a hasty "I'll see you back inside."

Once Justin was gone, she stood silently at the rail with her back to him, her attention focused on the passing landscape. Ian sensed he was about to be verbally flayed and he didn't know whether to smile or start running.

"He's been making cow eyes at you since the minute you walked in the car. Just came out to make sure you were okay."

She didn't respond at first. "He's studying to be a doctor."

"The race needs good physicians." *But not one intent upon Maggie,* grumbled a testy voice inside.

"And what if he has been making cow eyes at me?" she asked, glancing over her shoulder.

"Is that what you want?"

She turned away. After a few moments of silence, she said, "His mama would probably keel over dead if he brought me home."

"Probably."

"You don't have to be so agreeable, you know."

"Trying to be helpful."

She looked back. "What am I going to do with you?"

He shrugged. "Wondering the same thing about you."

"And have you come to a conclusion?"

"Not yet."

"Neither have I."

"At least we're in agreement."

Ian ran his eyes over her beautiful copper face, the lush petals of her lips, and wanted to pause time so he could make love to her there and then. He wanted to slide his hands over her breasts and hips and kiss his way up her thighs. He wanted to hear her soft moans when he entered her and take her screams into his mouth when she came. He closed his eyes to get a hold on himself. When he opened them, her eyes were waiting and sparkling with a quiet smile, as if she'd been party to his thoughts.

"Shall we go back in?" she asked softly.

"Might be a good idea."

"Or we can stay out a bit longer."

"You trying to tempt me?"

"Maybe. Maybe not?" she said playfully. "Which would you prefer?"

Ian had yet to meet a bolder, more confident woman. He wanted to eat her up. "The former."

"Then shall we meet later to explore why?"

He folded his arms and studied her. She had every inch of him alive and aroused. "I can make time for that."

"Good. I'm ready to go back in."

It took all Ian had not to drag her into his arms. "After you."

For the rest of the afternoon her saucy invitation filled his mind. He doubted a woman like her would ever blaze across his life again and he'd be a fool to just sit back and watch it go by. He refused to deny himself any longer. It was his plan to enjoy these last few days with her and let her sunshine brighten his darkness.

However he was presently glowering in the gloom over the attention Taylor was paying her. He doubted she was encouraging him in a way that would lead the young man on, but even so, Ian was jealous. He couldn't remember ever being jealous before, not even with his wife, Tilda, but he was honest enough to admit that with Maggie everything seemed to be different. He didn't want her near another man, let alone a pup like Justin Taylor.

Chapter 14

Dusk had fallen when the conductor entered the car to announce that the train would be making a stop to take on fuel and water. They'd be able to get off and stretch their legs, if they had a mind to, and take advantage of the food stands manned by some of the local families waiting beside the tracks.

After his departure, the train slowed and Ian saw Maggie rise to her feet and look his way. He set down his book and threaded his way through the small throng of people moving to the exit.

"Do you want to get something to eat?" he asked.

"I'd love to. Is it okay if Justin joins us?"

Ian eyed the doctor. Of course he wanted to deny the request, but he also wanted to keep her happy. "Sure."

The three of them stepped down onto the tracks and followed the others over to the food stands. There were offerings of everything from paper bags holding roast chicken and vegetables to sandwiches and slices of pie. Maggie settled on some sliced beef between large wedges of bread and a piece of apple pie.

Justin dug into his suit coat. "I'd be honored if you'd let me pay for that."

But Ian had already handed the coins to the woman behind the stand.

Justin's face registered his annoyance but he didn't argue. Instead he asked Maggie, "Do you want to sit in the grass or go back inside and eat?"

"Let's sit out here until the train's ready to leave. The evening air is nice."

Most of the other passengers had chosen to sit in the grass as well.

"How about here?" Maggie asked. They were close enough to keep the train in view but far enough away to have a bit of privacy. However, before she could sit, Justin removed his coat and laid it on the ground.

"A gentleman never lets a lady dirty her clothes in the grass."

Maggie thought the gesture unnecessary seeing as how she was wearing trousers but she appreciated his chivalry. She glanced at the marshal, but his face was as emotionless as always, so she sat. "Thank you, Mr. Taylor."

"You're welcome, but please, call me, Justin."

He took up a seat at a respectful distance.

Maggie looked up at the marshal, who was still standing. "Are you going to join us, Marshal, or just stand there and loom?"

She thought a smile crossed his lips as he sat.

They ate in silence until Justin asked, "How long have you been a marshal, sir?"

"A few years."

"Must be exciting."

"It has its moments."

"Who's the most interesting character you ever encountered?"

"You're sitting next to her."

Justin choked on the water he'd taken from his canteen.

Maggie shot Bigelow a look that was part disbelief and part amusement. He held her eyes for a moment and went back to his sandwich.

Justin was still looking bemused, so Maggie said reassuringly, "I'm sure the marshal is just pulling your leg."

"No, I'm not."

She shot him another look. She could see Justin eyeing them both before he asked, "Does being a marshal require any formal schooling?"

His tone, though neutral, was a bit more superior-sounding than Maggie cared for.

"No."

"I didn't think so, but wanted to be sure."

Again he'd kept the tone neutral, but again it rubbed her the wrong way. "The marshal is from Scotland, Mr. Taylor."

"Now I know he's pulling our legs. Say something in Scottish."

So the marshal obliged.

"And that means?" the still skeptical doctor asked.

"Arse hole."

Maggie choked on her sandwich.

Taylor's jaw dropped to the grass.

The marshal took a sip from his canteen.

Taylor had no more questions.

The train's whistle blew, alerting the passengers that it was time to return, so they disposed of their trash in a bin by the vendors and boarded. She was still reeling from the marshal's translation. The doctor had earned the set-down with his condescending behavior, but all she'd wanted was food and a little fresh air, not be in the middle of whatever they were intent upon.

Back inside the smoking car, a fiddler had joined them and was sawing away. Men and women were up dancing festively. Watching from the edge of the room, Maggie was unconsciously tapping her foot to the lively music.

"Would you like to dance?" Justin asked.

"No," she replied kindly, "but thank you." Any more snide remarks out of him and the marshal was liable to draw his gun, so she thought it best if Justin made himself scarce for a while. "I'm sure there's a lady here wanting a partner."

When he hesitated she said encouragingly, "Go on, I'll be here when you return."

Only after his departure did she allow herself to acknowledge the heated presence of Bigelow standing behind her.

He said quietly, "You did him a good turn by sending him off."

"I didn't want you filling him full of holes."

"Might be a good way for him to get in some doctor practicing."

She chuckled softly and turned to look up into

his eyes. Even in the shadows they held power, but then again, she already knew that.

"Turn back around before I kiss you."

Her knees went weak but she tossed back, "Oh really?"

"Right here in front of everybody."

"And what brings this on?"

He traced her lips and she trembled as he whispered, "You."

Maggie didn't hear the musicians end the song or the opening notes of the fiddle introducing a slow melodic waltz. All she was aware of was his blazing eyes.

"Come dance with me, first."

She studied him as if she'd never seen him before. "You dance?"

"One of my mother's lovers was a dancing master. I used to be fairly competent."

He offered his hand. Stunned, she laid her hand across his palm. He placed his free hand against the back of her shirt with a touch so light she could have been wearing silk. Next she knew, he was waltzing her expertly out into the room. Maggie was speechless, and if the shocked faces of the passengers looking on were any indication, so was everyone else in the room. Bunny had her hands over her mouth and sparkling delight in her eyes. Young Dr. Taylor didn't appear delighted at all.

Maggie however saw none of this; she was too busy being overwhelmed by the marshal's mastery and skill. Having been a dance hall girl, she knew most of the current dances including the waltz, and whoever his teacher had been had taught him excellently. He was a marvelous dancer and even though she was wearing old boots, trousers, and a too large shirt, he guided her as if she were a queen. The intensity in his gaze holding hers made memories rise of kisses that parted her lips and hardened her nipples like wild cherries. That night was one she'd readily repeat because this surprising enigma of a man had her enthralled. They stepped and moved in rhythm with the music as if they'd been dancing together their entire lives, and his hand on her back burned like a brand.

And then the music slowed and faded away. As they drank each other in, and her heart started beating faster in response to his mesmerizing presence, applause rang out, along with a bunch of whooping, hollering, and whistling. He slowly traced her mouth and then swept her up into his arms. Neither of them heard the deafening roar that followed them as he carried her through the door and out into the night.

The kissing began immediately; hot, seeking, melding of their mouths punctuated by roving hands and breathless sighs. Heat from his lips trailed down the side of her throat while his hand relearned the feel and weight of her breast, and it berried in welcome. As he boldly undid the buttons on her shirt and bared the camisole beneath, winds of passion blew across her skin. When his mouth closed over the thin cotton to artfully pleasure the nipple beneath, lightning flashed, setting off booms of sensual thunder that made her moan. He moved his attention to the twin and the bliss was so brilliant, she thought she might dissolve. His hands tugged the camisole free of her trousers and pushed it high so he could enjoy her without hindrance. The licks, sucks and gentle bites were buffeting; glorious. As he continued to feast, her hips moved sinuously in the age-old rhythm of the lovers' dance. Rising up again, he captured her mouth, filled his hands with her hips, and pulled her flush against the hard promise of his need. It matched her own, so she pressed back shamelessly while her palms moved blindly up and down the tensed muscles of his arms.

"This is not the place for this . . . ," he husked out.

"I don't care . . ."

He opened her trousers and slid them down her legs. She quickly undid the buttons of his shirt and moved her hands possessively over the soft hair on his chest. His hot hands explored her drawers-shrouded hips and then the soft, damp place in between. She could feel the storm of completion building, and although she wanted to be swept away by it she didn't want the pleasure to end, so she widened her stance so he could ply her as decadently as he pleased.

He found her wet and slick, and he was so hard and ready he was on the urge of exploding. He turned her around. Tracing a finger down the satin skin of her back, he savored the softness at the base of her spine and the heart-shaped rise of her hips. His touch left her a moment so he could undo the placket of his leathers. He then eased his shaft into the place he most wanted to be.

She gasped as her muscles tightened and held.

He clenched his jaw and fought against his male need to stroke himself to completion.

The positioning was as new to her as it was scandalous. While he moved within, his hands kept her nipples pleading with plucks and tugs before they toured roughly down her ribs to toy with the trembling nodule at the apex of her thighs. All the while he brushed his lips across the edges of her arched throat.

He stroked her with long, drawn-out teases that closed her eyes. Her trousers were pooled down by her ankles, effectively hobbling her movements so all she could do was take what he was giving her and gorge herself on the intoxicating rhythm of his thrusts.

When the rhythm increased her body answered; moving, twisting, bending as pleasure replaced all else. Completion was rising, she couldn't delay it any longer and when it exploded it flung her up into the stars.

Her orgasm triggered his, making him pump his hips and hold her tight and yell out his release until all that remained was the clattering of the train against the tracks.

Maggie felt ripe and lush, as if she were an exotic fruit ready to be plucked, and what a plucking it had been. Even now, his hands were running slowly over her spine in a calming and soothing manner that was accented by slow, gentle strokes. She melted back against him in weary surrender, and he kissed her lovingly. His final withdrawal made her groan with longing and dismay.

"Wait here," he whispered against her ear. "I'll be right back."

Maggie had no idea where he was going, nor did she care. All that mattered was his pledge to return.

Alone in the darkness, she continued to be dazzled by the memories of his thrusts, caresses, and kisses. The night air brushed against the places he'd left bare and damp. She knew she should pull up her trousers and right the rest of her clothing but the wantonness he'd placed in her blood lingered like a fever, making her want to bask in her night-shrouded, half-naked state. Who knew people made love that way? Being with him was quite an education, and her throbbing, pulsating body was eager for the tutoring to resume.

He announced his return with the warmth of his jaw against her cheek and languid, teasing passes of his hands over her breasts. "Brought you some water so you can clean up."

But she didn't want to move, and what he was doing only reinforced that stance. His hand now circling hotly inside her drawers over the surface of her hips added more fuel. "I can't do anything until you stop . . ."

"No?" he questioned quietly.

The touring hand made her spread her legs in response to the searing plucks and circling of already blooming flesh.

Ian knew this interlude should end, but he couldn't stop touching her. Her skin was like silk and her lithe body fit against him perfectly. He couldn't refrain from brushing his lips against her neck any more than he could stop stroking his hands over the velvet curves of her behind. Forcing himself to step back, he took in a deep, calming breath. Once he felt capable of controlling himself he used the water from the canteen he'd fetched inside, along with a clean handkerchief from his saddlebag to slowly banish the remnants of their loving from her thighs.

She righted her clothes. When she was done, she stepped back into the circle of his arms and he placed his lips against her brow. The tight, answering pressure of her arms around him filled his soul with a surge of emotion he couldn't name but didn't ever want to lose. "Do you want to go back inside?"

She shook her head negatively against his chest. "Can we sit out here for a while?"

During his outlaw years, Ian had made love in a variety of places but never on the small connecting platform between two railroad cars. She continued to astound him.

He used a hand to get his bearings on the short iron fencing and made himself comfortable on the wooden floor. She cuddled up in his lap, and he whispered, "Perfect."

Chapter 15

Maggie thought the moment together perfect as well. Cuddled against his chest and heartbeat, she felt sheltered and precious, rare concepts in her life, and she wanted to bask in his nearness for as long as the fates allowed. "What's the first thing you want to do when you get home?"

"Sleep."

That amused her. "And after?"

"Ride my land to see how it's been faring without me."

"How long have you been away?"

"Almost a year."

"That's a long time."

"It is. Left a friend behind in charge of things."

"How big is your place?"

"About fourteen hundred acres."

She pulled back. "So much?"

"It's smaller than some, larger than others. Wyoming's a big place."

She made herself comfortable again. "That's still a lot of land. The farm I grew up on was half an acre."

"What happened to it after your parents died?"

"Sold for back taxes. It hurt knowing I'd never be able to go back." And it had, but she had the memories of it and her parents to let her know that once upon a time she'd had family and love.

"Were you still living there?"

"No, by then I was at the convent."

It was his turn to pull back and stare down.

"It was the only place I could find work. I'm pretty sure the sisters took me in out of pity, but they worked me from sunup to sundown for a good six years. Been drifting since." Maggie quieted and listened to the rhythmic sound of the train on the tracks. She craved permanence in her life, but it remained elusive and she got the sense that her future would hold more of the same. "May I ask you something?"

"Sure."

"Why'd you become an outlaw?"

When he didn't offer a ready reply, she said apologetically, "I'm sorry. I didn't mean to be nosy."

"No. I'm thinking about the answer." Finally he said, "I don't know. Seemed like a grand idea at the time. I had no money, no way to make any. I met Neil July and when he asked if I wanted to join him and his friends, I said, Why not? I'd always liked adventure, and it was a way to get even with America for not letting me practice law."

Maggie went still. "Law?"

"I've a degree in the law from the University of Edinburgh."

Once again, this surprising man left her all but speechless. "Truly?"

"Yes. Changed my name to Bigelow though. Didn't want to jeopardize my certificate by being arrested under my real name."

"Bigelow isn't your name?"

"No. I was christened Ian James Vance."

"How many people know this?"

"Only a few, and now you."

"Why tell me?"

"Felt you should know I suppose."

"Because of what we just did?"

"No, because of who you are."

She wasn't sure she understood. That he would trust her with such a secret filled her heart, though.

Ian wasn't sure why he'd revealed the truth about his identity to her, either. It wasn't anything he'd planned, but it seemed right, and he supposed that when they parted and went their separate ways, he wanted her to remember him as the man whose feelings for her were growing by leaps and bounds, and not the marshal who'd had her in custody.

And his feelings for her were rising like floodwaters. For a man who'd sworn to never risk his heart again, the last few days had been humbling. She'd managed to breach the walls he'd built around himself without exerting much effort, leaving him to wonder how to prevent the burrowing from spreading further, or even if he wanted to. In truth he might as well try and stop time for all the success he was having keeping the walls in place. He was powerless to resist her smile, the effects of her spirit, or the desire to make love to her. "Do you have your heart set on Ohio?" He wanted to know if he had a chance of changing her mind.

"I do. That's where I was heading when I gave you the slip at the Tanners'. I was going to find work there and save up enough to take the classes I'll need to be able to teach children someday."

"As starving as folks are for someone to open a school, you wouldn't even need the certificate in a lot of places."

"I know, but the certificate would give me the standing I need to inspire my students to aim even higher."

Ian understood. In spite of the disenfranchisement taking place across the country, men and women of the race continued to battle for education in hopes it would offer their children and grandchildren better lives.

"My father grew up free in Philadelphia, and after receiving his Oberlin certificate he returned home and taught school until Mr. Lincoln's war."

"I'd heard Philadelphia was very important during abolition."

"It was. He'd often talk to me about the rallies at Mother Bethel AME, and the people he met during those times, like Douglass and the Forten family, and the great William Still and his daughter Caroline, who grew up to be one of the race's first female doctors. Mostly, though, he talked about education, and how important it was to me. My mother emphasized the same. She'd been forced to attend the missionary schools when she was young, and although she hated being away from her family and told on a daily basis how godless her people were, she hoped her education would help her tribe better understand the forces lined up against it. She read voraciously."

Ian listened as she told him about the Black colleges established in Pennsylvania before the war, like Cheyney State Training School, which opened in 1837; Avery College, which began taking students in 1849; and Lincoln University, founded in 1854. Having not resided in the States during those years, he found the information helpful in filling in some of the blank spots he had about the journey America's African descendants had taken on their way to the present day.

"My father always said that he was inspired to aim high by his father and other men like Edward Jones, who graduated from Amherst College in '26, and John Russworm, who graduated from Bowdoin College that same year. Had he not lost his life in that fire, I believe he would have accomplished much."

"Where'd the fire happen?"

"In our barn. He'd gone in to make sure the livestock were bedded down for the night. No one's sure what happened next—whether he fell or tripped—or if one of the cows kicked over the lantern he was using to see by, but a fire started. My mother was in the house with me and by the time we smelled the smoke the barn was fully engulfed. She ran inside to try and find him but a second later, the roof collapsed and they were gone."

Ian felt her pain.

"I still miss them," she whispered.

He tightened his hold and pressed his lips to the top of her head. He couldn't imagine having lost his mother at such a tender age. Beneath the tremendous grief and sorrow she had to have been terribly afraid. Were it within his power to build her a school wherever she wanted, he would, and make certain her pupils had access to everything they needed to be successful, to make her and their parents proud. His mother had been keen on education as well. She once told him that although he'd never be able to stop the bigots from calling him a half-Black bastard, she'd make sure they'd never be able to call him an ignorant one.

"You must've had an awful lot of schooling to be able to study the law."

"I did. Some of Mother's lovers were kind enough to not only give me dancing lessons but a few arranged for the occasional tutor. Once I was able to read well enough on my own, my natural curiosity drew me to books of all types, and I read whenever I had the opportunity." It was a pastime he enjoyed. His mother had been well read for a woman of her times, and he felt a special connection to her whenever he picked up a book. Ian felt her give a shiver. "Cold?"

"A bit."

"Do you want to go back inside?"

"Truthfully, no. I'm enjoying being cuddled up with you."

The darkness hid his smile. "We can't sleep out here, though."

"I know. I'll miss you when we part in Denver."

His heart twisted at the thought of her leaving him. "I'll miss you, too. Why don't you come to Wyoming with me?"

She looked up. "As what?"

He shrugged. "We could use a schoolteacher."

"Really?"

"Yes."

"But where would I stay?"

"With me."

She was still studying his face. "That wouldn't look right. People would think I was your whore."

Marry me, then, he almost said, but stopped short. "I've a neighbor you could board with. Her name's Georgina but everyone calls her Georgie. She's in her seventies and sharp as a bear trap. You two would do well together."

For a moment she didn't reply but then asked, "How many children are there?"

Ian had no idea, so he lied. "A dozen or so."

"Is there a school building?"

He lied again. "Yes." He couldn't believe himself, but chalked it up to a desperation he'd never experienced before.

"May I think about it and give you an answer when we reach Denver?"

"Of course." His lying notwithstanding, he'd wanted her to agree now but knew she'd have to come to a decision on her own.

"That's a very sweet offer, Marshal."

"Just want you to have an alternative to having to scrape by."

"I appreciate that." Her voice softened. "May I call you Ian now?"

"I'd like that."

She reached out and stroked his cheek. "You're such an outstanding man." Her hand brushed his scar. "How'd you get this?" she asked softly.

"A fight in a Mexican cantina during the first year I rode with the Julys. Man accused me of coveting his wife. I'd thought I was a pretty competent fighter up until then, but he was better, and had a knife."

"Was she beautiful?"

"No, but he thought she was."

She chuckled softly.

A flash of lightning filled the dark sky, followed by a loud clap of thunder. "Looks like we'll be getting a storm," she said. "Which means we should probably go inside."

Ian didn't want to move. Spending the rest of his life with her curled up in his lap suited him just fine, but they had to go inside. "In a minute." He raised her chin and brushed his lips across hers until they parted to receive his kiss. As they caught fire, the sweetness of her poured into him like spring rain, and he drank until he had his fill. "All right. We can go now."

It took a while, however, because neither wanted to leave the other, or the desire they'd rekindled. Finally, reluctantly, they pulled away, rose to their feet, and stepped over to the door.

They entered just in time to hear the last sour

notes of Sylvia's off-key rendition of "Jeanie with the Light Brown Hair." In response to the rousing applause that followed, Maggie shook her head. "Drinking must make men deaf," she said as the dancing and fiddling resumed.

He seemed amused by that and gave her a soft, playful swat on the butt. "Where's your charity?"

"Wherever she got that voice." The echoes of their lovemaking were still coursing through Maggie's blood and she wondered if anyone could tell. She was certain her lips were kiss-swollen and her eyes still slightly lidded from the haze passion always produced. Before coming back in, she hadn't thought to check her hair to make certain it wasn't all over her head, so she smoothed her hand over the crown just in case.

"You look fine," he said at her side. "Just fine."

Although the lit lamps and sconces bathed the central area of the car in light, it barely penetrated the darkness near the back wall where she and Ian stood. She met his eyes in the shadows. "Thank you. For everything." If he hadn't been on the train the day it pulled into the Dowd, Kansas, depot, where she might have ended up was anyone's guess. In many ways, she owed him more than she could ever repay.

"You're welcome." He touched her cheek. "I'm going to lie down and try and catch up on my sleep. You think you can stay out of trouble?"

"Maybe. Maybe not. Pleasant dreams." Giving his hand a parting squeeze, she walked into the light to rejoin Bunny and the other passengers.

Justin was seated at the table with Bunny when

Maggie sat down. He studied her face silently for a moment before asking, "So are you and the marshal lovers?"

Before Maggie could respond to the rude question, Bunny replied, "You're awfully nosy for someone we met just today. Mind your own business."

He pushed his chair away from the table and went to find another seat.

She and Bunny shared a smile. Content, Maggie turned her attention to Sylvia, who was standing to grace the assemblage with yet another selection from her off-key repertoire.

After what seemed like a dozen or more stops to take on fuel, mail, more passengers, and a small herd of sheep, the train arrived in Denver two days later. While the men and women in the smoking car said their good-byes, Bunny gave Maggie a parting hug. "Take care of yourself, you hear?"

"I will. You do the same."

Ian walked over with his saddle and gear.

Bunny gave him a kiss on his scarred cheek. "Thanks again for the tickets."

"You're welcome."

"And take care of Maggie."

"Will do."

Bunny hurried away to catch up with her girls.

"Have you come to a decision?" he asked Maggie as the passengers flowed around them to leave the train.

"I have. I've decided to go with you."

He looked pleased.

She was, too. Not only would she get an opportunity to live out her dream as a teacher, she would continue to have him in her life. "So what happens next?"

"We buy tickets for the trip to Cheyenne."

"Another train?"

"Afraid so, but it will be the last one."

They began the walk to the door. "I'm holding you to that." Maggie was so weary of all the travel. "And how far is your ranch from Cheyenne?"

"Two days by horseback."

She sighed. "Goodness, but I've come this far, so what's another few days?"

"It will be worth it. I promise."

"I'll be holding you to that as well."

They deboarded, and while Ian talked with the conductor about where to buy tickets for the trip to Cheyenne, she watched knots of travelers being greeted by those who'd come to meet their arrival. Some of the men from the smoking car passed by and tipped their hats her way before disappearing into the crowd. Justin Taylor stood a few feet away talking to a well-dressed man and woman who she supposed were his sponsors. He must've felt her presence because he glanced her way, then deliberately turned his back. She rolled her eyes. She hadn't seen him since Bunny's set-down. He'd left the car right after and never returned. She assumed he'd taken a seat elsewhere.

Ian finally had the information they needed and Maggie was about to turn to him when the sight of Carson Epps hobbling on a cane in the thick of the crowd stopped her in mid-motion.

She had no way of knowing whether he was departing or arriving. Their gazes met and his widened like the moon. In the same motion he turned around swiftly and scuttled away in the opposite direction like a bug seeking a place to hide.

"What's so amusing?"

"Nothing. Just happy."

She watched him scour the crowd as if he were still curious about whatever it was she'd seen, but she didn't say anything, so he led them away.

Back in Kansas City Maggie had been impressed by the size of the depot, but the one in Denver put it to shame. It was as crowded as a big city.

According to the information pamphlet she picked up on their way to retrieve his stallion, Smoke, the depot consolidated the traffic of thirteen other stations. The cavernous building boasted a one-hundred-and-eighty-foot central tower, a clock on the front of the beautiful Romanesque structure so large it looked to be the size of her barn back home, and electric lights! She found the glowing fixtures fascinating.

"Everything of value in the West runs through here," Ian told her as they waited to be given access to the cattle car. "Timber, silver, gold, beef. If the West needs it or produces it, it comes through Union Depot."

They finally retrieved Smoke and went to buy tickets for the trip to Cheyenne.

After Ian paid for them, the agent handed them over. "Train leaves tomorrow around three in the afternoon, folks."

Outside, he said to her, "By this time tomorrow we'll be on our way."

She mounted up behind him and he slowly guided the stallion into an area of the city built near the depot. It was early evening. The hotels and businesses they passed were a bit run-down, some were constructed of beams worn gray by the weather. She knew from the pamphlet that the city had a grand opera house and many luxurious hotels, but so far, she'd seen nothing but a few rouged-up girls standing in doorways, and lots and lots of saloons, boasting names like the Gold Nugget and Miner's Paradise in signs of red neon. "What part of the city are we in?"

"Poor side. Have a friend who owns a boardinghouse a few block ups, or at least she did the last time I was in town. Name's Jade. We'll spend the night there."

"That's a different-sounding name. Is she Chinese?"

"Yes. I met her during the Hop Alley race riot back in '80."

"Where was this?"

"Right here in Denver."

"A race riot in Denver? How'd it start?"

"As a fight between some Chinese and White pool players A White man wound up dead. No one's sure how, or even if he did die, but once word spread, all hell broke loose."

While she listened, appalled, he told her about the mob of over three thousand men that tore through Denver's Chinatown, or Hop Alley as it was called because of the opium dens, like one of the plagues of Egypt. They burned and sacked businesses, and assaulted the residents while shouting, "Stamp out the yellow plague!"

"And you were here during all that?"

He nodded. "I met Jade when I took her youngest brother up on my horse two steps ahead of the mob."

"Was anyone killed?"

"One Chinese man. Authorities said he died from being kicked to death. The Chinese say he was lynched."

"Where were the police?"

"Doing their best, but there were only eight men on duty that night. Firemen came and turned hoses on the rioters but that didn't stop them, either."

She was pleased to hear that not all of the locals were in the mob, though. Some citizens did their best to shelter their Chinese neighbors, like saloon owner James Veatch and Madam Lizzie Preston.

"She and her girls kept the mob from storming her place by arming themselves with champagne bottles and high-heeled shoes."

Maggie offered a bittersweet smile in response to the image in her mind. "How long did the rioting last?"

"All night. Might have been longer if the town council hadn't appointed Dave Cook acting police chief."

According to Ian, the city had no chief of police, so Cook, a former marshal was given the post. "After he took the oath, he enlisted fifteen of his men and a bunch of gunfighters, including myself, and we waded in. By morning it was over."

Maggie shook her head. "I had no idea."

"The worst part is that Jade and her family moved to Denver after fleeing a similar riot in Los Angeles back in '71. Eighteen Chinese were killed in that one. She said lynched bodies were hung all over the city."

Maggie was very familiar with the atrocities perpetrated on her own family, but to learn that the Chinese were being subjected to the same violence and fear was surprising and sad.

Jade's boardinghouse was located next to a laundry that bore her family's name. There were two menacing-looking Chinese men holding rifles out front, so when Ian and Maggie dismounted, he said to her, "Stay here for a moment and let me find out if she still lives here."

The men watched him as he approached and he noticed them tighten their hold on the weapons. "I'm a friend of Jade's. Is she here?"

"What's your name?"

"Preacher."

"Wait here."

One man went inside while the other remained at his post. Ian wondered again about the armed guards. Had there been another riot? His last visit to Denver had been nearly three years ago, so he had no idea what might have transpired during that time.

The man who'd gone inside returned promptly with Jade. She greeted Ian with a smile and extended hands, which he took in his.

"So good to see you again, Mr. Bounty Hunter. How are you?"

"I'm well, Jade. And you?"

"They haven't killed me yet, so I suppose that means I'm doing okay. Who's that by your horse?"

"A friend. Maggie Freeman."

"Not a wife?"

He shook his head.

"Well, she is still welcome."

He ignored her teasing for the moment. "Why the armed guards?"

She sighed. "We've had a bit of trouble lately. Come on in and I'll tell you about it."

He beckoned to Maggie. They left Smoke to be looked after by the armed guards and followed Jade inside.

Maggie thought Jade quite beautiful. She was small in stature and dressed in a long-sleeved waist-length black garment with a high collar. Beneath it were loose-fitting trousers that brushed the worn slippers on her feet. Her black hair, drawn back from her face, matched her eyes.

The room she ushered them past first appeared to be a parlor. It was well furnished with a settee and colorful lacquered vases and lamps sitting atop small carved wood tables.

She then led them around a tall wooden screen, carved with birds and flowers, and into a small room centered by a long table covered by an embroidered gold cloth. Against the walls were side chairs carved out of similar gleaming wood that had lovely embroidered cushions embellished with flowers and birds on the seats. Maggie got the sense that the furnishings had come from

China because she'd never seen anything like them in an American home.

Jade gestured them to take seats. "Would you like something to eat?"

Maggie was famished and was pleased when Ian said yes.

She left them alone and Maggie asked, "She seemed disappointed that I'm not your wife."

"She thinks I need to marry."

"Why?"

"Says I need sons."

"Ah." Maggie thought back on the passionate moments they'd shared and realized she could very well be carrying his child. Deciding not to think about that, she turned her mind away.

"You okay?" he asked, as if having seen the clouds crossing her thoughts.

"Little tired," she said, which was not really a lie.

"I'll go over to the telegraph office once we've eaten and send word to my friend Charlie to meet us in Cheyenne."

"I can't wait to see your place and to meet Georgie. Thanks for offering me the position."

"Every community needs a good teacher."

Jade returned with a tray holding bowls of rice that were topped with vegetables and succulent pieces of chopped fish. The tea was bracing and smooth.

"So," Ian began, "why the guards?"

"The new crime boss. Name's Soapy Smith. Wants the Chinese to pay him protection."

"From whom?" Maggie asked.

"Him. And because I've been refusing, he's been taking his anger out on some of the other business owners. There have been threats and a few fires, but once we took a couple of shots at his thugs, they've left us alone, at least lately."

Ian asked, "What about the police?"

"Oh, they come and say all the right things, but they aren't going to do anything. Many of them are on his payroll." She paused and looked at Ian. "I'm thinking of pulling up stakes and going back to California. The Exclusion Act is making living very difficult."

Maggie had read about the 1882 Chinese Exclusion Act, but just in passing, so she knew little about the details. "The act forbids Chinese immigration, am I correct?"

"Yes, for ten years, and denies us the right to return here should we go to China for any reason."

"So if someone who lived here had to go back to China to, say, bury their father, they can't come back to the States?" Maggie asked with surprise.

"No. The bigotry practiced against us is in many ways just like the bigotry your race endures. We are lynched, arrested without reason, beaten and jailed, and accused of everything from being the cause of White men not being able to find jobs, to the spread of disease. We are also denied citizenship. Forbidden to marry outside of the race, too."

Maggie shook her head at the wrongness of that.

"So back to California?" he asked.

"Yes. Since the forties, the Chinese there have been forming these associations to help one another, but only recently have they been able to exercise real power. There's a group in San Francisco that seems very promising and I believe that's where I'll go. They call themselves the Chinese Consolidated Benevolent Association and have been somewhat successful in counteracting some of the violence. They are also mounting legal challenges to this disgusting Exclusion Act and what we call the Chinese tax."

She must have seen the confusion on Maggie's face.

"The first immigrants were men who came to America to work in the mines and gold fields and to lay track for the railroads. The California government needed to fill their coffers so they issued a tax on foreign born, non–United States citizens. Since the Chinese are legally barred from citizenship, we were the only ones made to pay it. Back then, my father and uncles made six dollars a month in the mines. The tax took half."

"What happened if they didn't pay?"

"The tax collectors would take their homes and property. Some Whites masqueraded as tax collectors and took property illegally. California law prohibits us from testifying against Whites in court, so we couldn't take the complaints to the courts."

Ian said, "The Exclusion Act is nothing more than legalized bigotry."

Maggie thought about men like Frederick

Douglass and Chief Joseph of the Nez Perce and their efforts on behalf of their people. "Do your people have any champions?"

"Not in the government. President Hayes vetoed the first version of the act back in '78, but the forces lined up for its passage were like dogs with a bone, and in '82 they prevailed. Now I hear there's a move afoot in Congress to add even more restrictions."

Maggie could see the fire and anger in Jade's eyes and so offered, "My father said that one day, America is going to have to live up to the promises of the Constitution."

Jade replied, "He may be correct, but it doesn't appear as if it will happen anytime soon."

Maggie had to agree.

Ian asked about her brothers.

"They still can't return to America." She explained to Maggie that her twin brothers had left for China in '81, a few months after the riot, to fetch their two younger sisters and bring them to the States, but the act was keeping them out. "I'm hoping that if and when the act is struck down, I can see them all again. In San Francisco I have a few family members, so that's one of the reasons I wish to relocate there. I miss my brothers very much."

Maggie remembered her mother's sadness when recounting how her family and other tribal members of the Kaw had been forced to leave for the Indian Territory. There was a similar note in Jade's voice. The United States government and the people in power apparently didn't care that their unfair policies were separating families and making day-to-day life difficult. She wondered if they ever would.

After they were done with their food, Ian stood. "I need to send a telegraph. Is the office in the same location?" he asked Jade.

"Yes, and be very careful. The people in the office are on Soapy Smith's payroll. They may give you trouble, and they may not."

"Thanks for the warning."

"Maggie, are you going with him?"

"No. I'd like to lie down for a while if I may."

"Most certainly."

Ian said to her, "I'll see you when I return."

"Be careful."

"I will."

As he departed, Jade said to her, "Come. I'll take you up to one of the rooms and you can rest."

The room was small and furnished with more beautiful furniture. "How long have you and the Preacher been together?"

"Almost two weeks."

"So you've just met?"

"Yes."

"He needs a wife."

Maggie smiled. "It won't be me."

"Why not?"

"I don't believe he's looking for one."

"I see the way he watches you, though."

"And?" Maggie thought back on a similar observation made by Cleo at Lola's place.

"You will be his wife. If not soon, sometime." Jade had a glimmer of satisfaction in her gaze. "Trust me. I know of what I speak."

"You're not married?"

"No. It's difficult to find a husband here. One more reason for me to move to San Francisco. I'm hoping my family knows someone there who is looking for a woman without parents or a dowry."

"Your parents are deceased?"

"Yes. Both died a few weeks after the riot. They died without seeing my brothers again."

More heartache, Maggie thought.

"You go ahead and lie down. I'll let the Preacher know where you are when he returns."

"Thank you."

Chapter 16

If a grown man could be giddy, Ian was that as he rode Smoke through thick traffic on Market Street. Having Maggie in his life had brought him more joy and satisfaction than he ever would have imagined on the day he first saw her sitting so defiantly on that horse. Never in his wildest dreams had he thought she'd help restore his soul. After Wells put her in his custody, had someone told Ian that he'd become attached to her, make love to her, and become her champion in less than two weeks' time, he would have asked what they were drinking, but all that had come to pass and more. And now, thanks to a few small lies, he'd ensured her presence in his life hopefully for a long time to come. When they reached his ranch, he'd eventually have to own up to the truth about the number of students she'd be teaching and the nonexistent school. At the moment, that wasn't a worry. All that mattered was that she'd agreed.

He still wanted her to live with him even though she'd been right to turn down his offer. Although Wyoming with its women voters was an unconventional place, some things were still considered sacrosanct, and a lady's reputation was one. Her staying with Georgie would allay any potential slurs on her reputation, and allow her to be embraced by the community in a way he knew they would. Georgie didn't live very far away so he'd be able to see Maggie whenever he wanted and she would get to fulfill her dream of teaching children.

Were he not so eager to return home, they'd spend a few more days here so he could take her shopping and buy her a trunkful of new dresses and whatever else she wanted. Then he'd get them a room at one of the fancy hotels so he could show her the town. He rode by the hotel once owned by Barney Ford. He wondered if Ford's famous restaurant and chop house was still open over in Breckenridge. At one time Ford, a former slave, had owned top-notch hotels in Central America and Cheyenne, as well as the one Ian just passed. Ford's hotels had played host to presidents and royalty, but Ian was too anxious to get home. He made a promise to himself to bring Maggie back to Denver before the snow fell. He couldn't wait to show her the beauty of the Colorado and Wyoming autumn with its riot of fiery colors.

He spotted the telegraph office up ahead and reined Smoke over to the post. After securing the stallion and giving him a parting pat, Ian strode into the office.

"Can I help you?" The voice belonged to an older woman with graying hair and suspicious blue eyes.

"I'd like to send a telegram."

"To who?"

The tone of her voice held the same suspicion as her gaze.

"Friend of mine in Cheyenne."

She looked him up and down and quoted him a price for the service that was outrageous even for a crime-ridden Denver. Her eyes held a hint of triumph. "If that's too steep, write a letter."

It was hard for him to tell whether she'd been born this nasty or if the dismissiveness had to do with his race. Some places wouldn't give water to a dying man of color let alone allow access to the telegraph, but Ian decided he didn't care about the reason behind her attitude. Instead he reached into his pocket, placed his star on the counter where she could see it, and asked, "What's the charge for a United States deputy marshal?"

Her eyes bugged and she turned red as a beet. "Um, no charge, sir."

He gave her a tight smile.

Her hand shook as she pushed a pen and a piece of paper his way. "Just write down what you want me to send."

"Thank you." When he was done he handed it over.

"There might not be an answer until mornin'," she told him nervously. "It's getting kinda late in the evening."

"I understand. Can you have it sent around to me when it arrives?"

"Where are you staying?"

He told her.

Her eyes widened again.

"Problem?"

She swallowed visibly. "I, um, we don't usually send our runners to that part of town."

Ian waited.

"But there's a little colored boy whose mother works across the street at the hotel. I'll send him, if that's okay with you, Marshal. He runs errands for me sometimes."

"That's fine. What's his name?"

She went red again and replied softly, "I don't know. Never asked."

Ian held her eyes for a moment. He could only imagine how she addressed the child then. "I'll expect him in the morning."

And he strode out.

Remounting Smoke, Ian shook his head and rode back towards Jade's place.

Upon his return, he was informed that Maggie was asleep. Needing to see her anyway, he walked up the stairs to the second floor. The door to the room was closed, so he opened it quietly and just wide enough to see inside. And there she lay. Her soft snores gently filled the silence. What he felt for her filled him with a joy that touched his soul. Although they hadn't broached the subject, it was quite possible that they'd made a child at some point on their journey together, and if intensity played even a small role in conception, it was all over but the shouting. That possibility was something they'd need to talk about. Growing up in Scotland, he'd had the slur *bastard* hurled at him seemingly every day of his life, and no child of his would be forced to suffer the same fate. The thought of having children with her pleased him as well. Tilda hadn't wanted any, so out of respect he hadn't pressured her, but he wanted babies with Maggie. For that to happen they'd have to marry. Drinking in her sleeping form for a short while longer, he closed the door and left her to her dreams.

He found Jade in the parlor and before he could tell her about his interaction with the surly lady telegraph operator, she said, "You love her, don't you?"

The question caught him off guard.

"The reason I ask is this. I have known you for eight years. Granted, I have only seen you on four or five occasions since you saved my brother's life, but there's a light in your eyes I've never seen before."

"And you attribute that to Maggie?"

"Do you have another explanation?"

He didn't of course. "I do care about her. Whether it can be called love, I don't know." Even if he was pretty certain it was.

"You watch her with eyes of love."

"You just want me to get married," he responded with amusement.

"I do, and do you know why?"

"No."

"Because the world needs sons and daughters with the courage of their fathers, and you are a courageous man."

He had no idea how to respond to such a compliment, except to say, "Maggie's very courageous, too." Any young woman who'd been on her own since age twelve, and whose spirit hadn't been broken by the hardships she'd faced, was one of great courage, strength, and resilience. A child of hers would be one to reckon with. He wondered what she'd say if he proposed marriage. He came back to the present to find Jade's eyes on him.

"Life always works out, even if it's not the way we intended it to."

"So, are you going to look for a husband when you get to San Francisco."

She laughed. "Turning the tables on me?" In answer to his question, she shrugged. "I may. I have always wished for children."

"Then may life grant you your wish."

"That's my wish for you as well."

Jade rose to her feet. "I have to see about some sheets that need to be delivered to one of the hotels. Once I do, I will return. If you're hungry there's more food in the kitchen."

"Okay. Do you need my help?"

"No, but thank you."

She exited and left him alone with his thoughts. The more he contemplated marrying Maggie, the more certain he felt it to be the right thing to do. She'd unfrozen his heart and his world, and yes, the specter of losing her the way he'd lost Tilda was foremost in his mind, but wanting her in his life made him bury that fear as much as he was able in order to take a chance at the brass ring. He'd made many enemies over the years and there was no guarantee one of them wouldn't show up intent upon revenge, but she'd become as necessary to his existence as breathing. Now he just had to convince her that marrying him was right for her as well.

Maggie awakened to a dark room. She startled at the sounds of gunfire and high-pitched squeals of glee.

Ian's voice came out of the dark. "It's okay." He was seated in a chair beside the open window. "It's just Denver having a good time."

"What time is it?"

"A little past ten."

She sat up and wiped at the sleep in her eyes. "Why'd you let me sleep so long?"

"You needed the rest."

"Have you slept?"

"No."

"Then come to bed, Ian," she said softly.

He removed his boots and slid in beside her. She scooted back until their bodies were flush. His embracing arm held her close and she smiled contentedly. "Did you send the telegram?"

"I did. If I get a reply it won't be until tomorrow."

She turned over to face him. "I've had a wonderful time with you."

"So have I."

He traced her cheek, and the touch resonated so deeply her eyes closed.

"Will you marry me?"

Maggie went still. She searched his face in the dark. "Are you joking with me?"

"No."

His serious tone gave her pause and she searched his face again and wished she could see him better. "Why?"

"Why what?" he asked as he placed his lips against hers.

His kisses were making it difficult to think. "Why do you want to marry me?"

"Because I want this adventure we're on to continue. Because you fill my heart. Because I want you to have that garden." He'd opened her shirt and was moving his hands over her breasts, which were responding with joy. "Pick one."

His tongue dallied with her nipples, and desire began to unfurl inside like the smoke from a sensual fire. "You're making it hard for me to be logical."

"Good . . ."

"You don't want to marry me."

"Why not?"

His hands were sliding up and down her thighs and up over her torso and ribs. His mouth was making her nipples plead for more. "Because . . ."

He bit her gently and she moaned softly.

"Because why?" he asked.

"But . . ."

"Let's take these off." He was referring to the trousers she'd been too exhausted to remove before falling asleep.

"Ian?" she protested weakly, but he was dragging her trousers down her legs. "We need to talk," she countered in a voice that was even less firm. His caresses were making her body come alive.

"I'm listening."

It certainly didn't feel as if he was because he was planting lazy kisses on the soft undersides of her breasts while his hands continued their possessive roaming. She wanted to discuss this outrageous proposal, but the haze clouding her mind from his touch made forming a counter nearly as impossible as he was.

"Just say yes," he whispered.

But his hands had drifted below her waist and the slit in her drawers conspired against her and she couldn't say anything but "Oh my."

While he boldly coaxed and teased her legs to widen, he husked out against her ear, "I'm going to give you silk dresses, and books . . ."

"Ian . . ."

"And more of this . . ." His fingers entered the throbbing vent he'd prepared so lustfully and her hips rose up off the bed. ". . . until death do us part."

The orgasm slammed into her, and she screamed soundlessly in response to his wicked voice and erotic manipulation. Before she could retrieve the far-flung pieces of herself he entered her with something harder and more substantial, and she groaned with greedy delight.

"Say yes, darlin'."

His initial thrusts pushed her past mindlessness and into a realm of sensation so enticing she answered his rhythm blindly and wantonly. "Let me give you babies, Maggie."

That hot invitation almost sent her over the edge again, but she held on because she didn't want to surrender to the rising tide just yet. She wanted more of the strokes that made her lock her legs around his waist; the impaling that left her breathless when he changed their positioning and she found herself on top. She was speechless, ripe, and so filled with bliss she thought she might go mad from the brilliance burning inside.

"Say, yes, Maggie."

Maggie couldn't say anything, she was too busy riding the horn of paradise, too inflamed by his hands and mouth on her breasts, and when his hot hands cupped her hips and rocked her faster, and then faster still, she broke and cried out; he did, too, and they both exploded in the dark.

Later, after their breathing quieted and his hand was moving lightly up and down the damp skin of her spine, she asked, "Do you really want to marry me?"

"I do."

She rose up slightly and looked down into his shadowy face. "But why?"

"Weren't you listening?" he asked, and gave her a playful thrust.

She grinned and brought her body back down to his chest and savored the feel of their intimately entwined bodies and the arms holding her close. "I was a trifle distracted."

His answering chuckle rumbled beneath her ear. "Do you need a repeat performance so I can explain it again?"

"Maybe, but in a minute." She felt so happy lying atop him, happier than she'd ever imagined she could be, considering the rough-and-tumble world she'd been living in. "You fill my heart, too."

He hugged her tight. "So you were listening."

"Yes, I was." And what he'd confessed still amazed her. She'd never been in love before so she wasn't sure if this was it, but whatever her feelings for him were called, it was good enough for her if it was good enough for him. "Ian?"

Snoring answered her. He'd fallen asleep. She couldn't fault him. Neither of them had gotten any real rest for days, and him in particular. He'd kept watch the night they spent sleeping on the floor of the Abilene train depot, and since then had slept only in fits and starts. She gently untangled herself and then sidled close enough to feel him against her back. It was a positioning she looked forward to enjoying for many years to come, but at the moment, she was too bowled over to join him in sleep. He wanted to marry her. The declaration continued to amaze her. Sometime soon, she would be Mrs. Ian Vance, or whatever name he'd want her to go by, she thought with a smile. He'd already offered her a teaching position and now he wanted to gift her with the security and companionship she'd craved. She'd be a nitwit to tell him no. Happy all the way down to her toes, Maggie closed her eyes and joined her soon-to-be husband in sleep.

Chapter 17

A groggy Maggie awakened the following morning to a gentle fondness flowing from green eyes.

"Morning," he said quietly, and brushed a stray lock of hair away from her face. "Did you sleep well?"

"I did, but there was a man in my bed last night who made me do all sorts of naughty things. Luckily for me he fell asleep so I could get some sleep, too."

Amusement crossed his lips. "I don't remember that part."

She tenderly stroked his scarred cheek. "Because you were too busy snoring."

"My apologies, madam."

"None needed. Neither of us have gotten much rest these past few days. You'd earned it."

Ian brought her fingertips to his lips. Kissing them affectionately, he thought back on last night. She'd agreed to be his bride, but was she still willing? She hadn't exactly been in control of her faculties while he was proposing. Had he asked her if her name was President Benjamin Harrison, more than likely she would have agreed. It hadn't been a fair way to get the yes that he'd wanted to hear, and now, under the full light of day, his method didn't sit well.

"Something wrong?" she asked.

"Do you still want to marry me?"

For just a moment, Maggie saw something in his eyes she'd never seen before and it gave her pause. She realized he was unsure of her response. Considering how deadly and fearsome he could be, she found that surprising. "Yes. Have you changed your mind?"

"No, but wanted to make sure you didn't feel pressured to say yes."

For a moment she studied his face. Amused and touched, she shook her head at her magnificent, caring man before saying frankly, "Ian Vance, you are the first and only man to propose marriage to me. Smoke must have kicked you in the head while you were asleep if you think I've changed my mind. You're stuck with me whether you care to be or not."

His laughter rang out and he pulled her on top of him. They rolled around the bed in mutual joy, and she was so happy she thought she might burst. She looked down into his smiling face and echoed, "Stuck, Mr. Marshal. Forever."

"Good, because I want to get married today."

She stilled. "Today?"

"That a problem?"

"A girl wants to be dolled up for her wedding. I don't mean to be fussy, but no woman should have to say I do wearing the same wrinkled clothes she's been traveling in for over a week."

He slid a warm palm down the bare spine and hips, asking playfully, "What clothes?"

She punched him in the shoulder. "You know what I mean."

"Then how about I take you shopping?"

She stared down in wonder.

"No?" he asked, tracing a fingertip over her lip.

"Yes!"

He gave her a playful smack on the butt. "Then up with you. We've a ton to do before catching the train to Cheyenne."

Her voice quieted. "You are so wonderful to me."

"You make it easy."

He hugged her tight, she dashed away tears of emotion, and they left the bed to begin the day.

The little boy who ran errands for the lady telegraph operator arrived at Jade's while they were eating breakfast. He looked to be seven or eight years old. His clothes were worn but clean.

"What's your name?" Ian asked, taking the folded note from his small hand.

"Anthony, sir."

"How old are you?"

"Eight, sir."

"Thank you for delivering this to me, Anthony." Ian reached into his pocket and took out a five-dollar gold piece. "Give this to your mother and tell her I said thank you for raising such a prompt and polite young man."

Anthony looked at the coin in his hand and then back up at Ian. "This is too much, sir."

"I know, but it's still yours."

At first it appeared as if Anthony didn't know what to say. Finally a smile widened his features and he beamed. "Thank you, sir."

"You're welcome."

After Anthony departed, Ian looked over at Maggie, who said, "That was very nice of you."

He nodded and read Charlie's response. "My friend will meet us in Cheyenne."

"What's his name?"

"Charlie, and he's a cantankerous old coot I hope you'll like. We've been friends for years."

"Then I hope he likes me."

"I don't think you've anything to worry over."

Jade entered the room, having returned from her morning errands. She'd been up and gone before sunrise. "I see you found my note about the food?"

"We did," Ian replied. "Thank you for the breakfast."

"You're welcome. Any plans for the day before getting on the train to Cheyenne?"

He glanced Maggie's way and she smiled. "We're getting married."

Her mouth dropped. "Oh my goodness! Congratulations. That's wonderful."

"I want to take her shopping. What's the best place?"

"A good friend of mine has a place. Her name is Bethany and she's a woman of your race." Jade gave them the location. "I'm so happy for you two. When will the wedding take place?"

"Hopefully before we board the train."

"Ah," she voiced dreamily, "that's so romantic. I wish you much happiness." She embraced them both with a strong hug. "I have to get back to work. I will see you before you leave Denver?"

Ian nodded.

"Good."

She hurried off, and Ian pulled Maggie into his side. He kissed her gently. "Ready?"

"For what?" she asked, with a sassy light in her eyes.

"Shopping, you incorrigible woman."

She gave him a mock pout. "I suppose."

He laughed and they walked to the door.

To be truthful, when Jade said the shop was owned by a woman of color, Maggie had been expecting a small, cramped place with few choices, not the large, airy place she and Ian walked into. There was a slew of readymade dresses, colorful hats, shoes, and other fashionable items beautifully displayed on headless dress forms and smooth glass-topped counters and gleaming wooden tabletops. One of the tables held fancy ruffled bloomers; another, frothy feathered hats that ladies of leisure might wear, and at a price that widened her eyes. While fashionably dressed White women browsed and tried not to stare at her wrinkled and travel-stained shirt and trousers, Maggie told Ian quietly, "The things here are very expensive."

"And?"

Before she could recommend they find a dress shop with better pricing, a tall, black-skinned woman approached and asked, "May I help you with something? I'm the owner, Bethany Adams."

Ian said, "Jade recommended we come and see you; my lady needs a new wardrobe."

Maggie was taken aback by being termed his lady, as if she were a countess or a duchess, but it pleased her immensely.

Bethany asked, "When you say new wardrobe, what do you mean?"

"I mean everything. The train misplaced our luggage and she has nothing to wear."

Maggie fought to keep surprise from exploding over her face.

Bethany eyed Maggie sympathetically. "I understand. Would you like to take advantage of our bathhouse before we begin trying on things?"

"Bathhouse?" Maggie echoed, trying not to sound excited.

"Yes. I offer many services here. I even have someone who can do your hair if you like."

"I don't mean to be crass, but how much will this cost?"

Ian said in a reassuring tone, "Don't worry about that. Get yourself gussied up and buy whatever you think you need."

"But Ian—"

The soft kiss he gave her closed her eyes and ended the discussion. The other ladies in the shop smiled openly.

While Maggie fought through the sensations left by the kiss, he asked the shop owner, "When should I return for her?"

She assessed Maggie critically. "Two hours."

Maggie wanted to take issue with that, but she knew how ragtag she looked, so she said nothing.

"Then two hours it is. Enjoy yourself, Maggie."

As he made his exit, both women stared after him, and Bethany asked, "Does he have a brother, honey?"

Maggie laughed. The shop owner laughed, too, and led Maggie to the back of the shop.

Ian's first stop was to buy himself a new set of clothes. Even though he'd kidded with Maggie about their clothes, he'd rather be married in something other than his worn leathers and dirty shirt, too. Not that his present attire would cause any commotion. He was in Denver, after all. The miners who came in and out of town often looked and smelled worse.

He walked into a reputable men's clothing shop where he'd purchased garments before and looked around at what they had to offer. He picked out a gray Western-cut suit and a pair of hand-tooled black boots that would undoubtedly be hell on his feet until he got them broken in, but Maggie was worth the discomfort. He also tried on a few hats, one of which was made in Mexico, according to the smiling salesman, who added that the shiny metal ovals interspersed along the braided black band were high-grade silver.

Ian met the man's eyes coolly. It was a common ploy used by salesmen to separate greenhorns from back East, the local farmhands, and cowboys from their gold. Ian didn't believe the silver claim for a minute, but he added the hat to the rest because he liked the look of it. He handed over the payment and walked out.

Next he went in search of a bathhouse. Because of the city's sprawling size there were plenty to choose from. Some were cleaner than others and more than a few offered feminine companionship for a price. He walked to an establishment he'd used on previous visits and found the interior as clean as he remembered. He paid extra for a private space.

"You want someone to wash your back?" the woman behind the desk asked coyly.

He shook his head.

"I'm real good," she promised.

By Ian's eye she was more child than woman. She had the thin, emaciated look of someone trying to scratch out a living but was harvesting dust instead. He gave her a nod in parting and walked to the back.

For the price of the bath you also received a bar of soap. For a few cents more you could add a shaving kit, which he had.

While he soaked, he held up the small mirror and shaved. He wondered how Maggie was doing. Her excitement at becoming his wife made him smile. He planned on being the best man and husband to her that he could be. The two years he'd been married to Tilda, he had done his best then as well, but she hadn't cared for being touched and stroked, and he couldn't joke and play with her as he could with Maggie. He knew now that as much as he'd loved Tilda, she'd had no fire. Her beauty and poise had been so captivating that it never occurred to him before they married that there might not be any passion underneath. Once it became clear that there wasn't, he hadn't let that alter his commitment to her, nor the place she held in his heart. On their wedding day, he'd vowed, "Until death do us part." And death had taken her.

And now he'd been blessed with Maggie. He still found her presence in his life unbelievable. With her Ian would get to put into practice what he'd learned from watching the men around his mother. They knew how to be kind, and what it took to make a woman smile. The earl his mother was mistress to for more than a decade had delighted her with small gifts of chocolate, flowers, and the occasional piece of jewelry. The affair ended when he married a young duchess who supplanted his mother, Colleen, in the earl's bed and heart. His mother's devastation notwithstanding, the earl's tender devotion to her in the early years of their relationship left a lasting impression.

Once he was done with his bath, he dried off, dressed himself in his new clothes, stuffed the old ones in his saddlebag, and left to search out a barber to get a haircut.

Maggie viewed herself in the full-length mirror and thought she could easily pass for a duchess with her brand-new gown, sleekly styled hair, and fashionable hat. She'd bathed, then soaked in scented water and had her hair done. Every garment she was wearing from her drawers to the gloves on her hands was brand spanking new. She felt like a lady.

Bethany stuck her head in the door of the room Maggie had been using. "That gorgeous man of yours is here."

Maggie walked out to meet him and was instantly taken aback by how cleaned up he was as well. More important, he looked dumbstruck by her own transformation and the reaction added to what was turning out to be a spectacular day.

"Do you like it?" she asked, turning slowly to give him the full effect of the new green dress and jacket, silky white underblouse, and jaunty green hat with its matching green feather.

He cleared his throat. "You look dazzling."

She curtsied elegantly. "Thank you."

"Very beautiful."

Bethany appeared pleased as well by the results. "What else did you buy?"

She gestured to the four boxes on the counter.

"That's all?"

"I didn't want to spend you into the poorhouse, Ian. This dress and a few other items were more than enough for me."

"Maggie."

Bethany waded in, "I tried to convince her that you'd want her to purchase more, but she stuck to her guns."

Eyes sparkling with humor, Maggie put her hand on her hip and told the shop owner, "Stay out of this."

She saw Ian shake his head as if he didn't know what to do with her.

"Okay, madam, you win this round, but next time, remember that I can afford whatever it is you may need. I promise."

"And I spent quite enough of your hard-earned money, thank you very much."

Their eyes held, and a smile crossed his golden features. "Sassy woman."

Her attraction to him rose and blossomed. "Would you want me any other way?"

"No darlin', you're perfect. Sass and all."

Heat slid between them.

Bethany chuckled and started fanning herself with the bill of sale. "You all need to pay what's owed and get out of my place before it catches fire. Maggie, are you sure he doesn't have a brother? What about a cousin?"

Maggie laughed.

After he paid Bethany what was owed, Maggie's purchases were retrieved and they left the shop after a chorus of thank-yous and waves of good-bye.

As they walked down the street, Maggie was impressed by all the people, the fancy buildings, and the wealth of traffic going back and forth, but even more impressive was the man walking by her side. He was already eyeball-aching handsome, but cleaned up he was something to see. Tall and gorgeous, he still appeared dangerous even in the gray suit. The fancy black hat only added to his allure. And if all the veiled but appreciative eyes of the females they passed were any indication, the verdict was unanimous. "Where are we going now?"

"Courthouse."

Excitement filled her face.

"Unless you've changed your mind?"

She punched him. "Stop that."

The gleam in his gaze made her grin show. "Loony man, let's go and get married so I can say I do."

At the base of the courthouse steps, Maggie held back for a moment.

"What's wrong?"

"Do you have a knife of some kind on you?"

He stared. "Why do you need a knife?"

"A bride needs flowers and I'd like a sprig or two of those lilacs over there."

Ian saw the bush she was intent upon, so he walked over to it. And taking a few seconds to find a branch with the most sweet-smelling purple flowers, he cut it off and brought it back to her.

Putting the blooms to her nose, she sighed. "You're such a wonderful marshal. Do you know that?"

He presented his elbow, she hooked her arm in his, and he led her up the steps and inside.

They stepped back out into the bright sunshine as man and wife. Maggie still couldn't believe her fortune. She wanted to pinch herself to make sure she wasn't walking in a dream, but the words they'd shared and the love in his eyes were as real as the love in her own.

"We're married, Maggie," Ian told her as they turned back onto Market Street.

"Now you're really stuck with me."

"And I couldn't be happier."

They had a celebratory lunch at one of the fancy hotels. Maggie was overwhelmed by the beauty of the large room, and all the well-dressed diners of all races. Although she had difficulty pretending she wasn't a rube, Ian seemed right at home with all the cutlery and courses.

While they were eating the main dish, squab for her, and steak for him, he said, "We'll have just enough time to go back to Jade's and grab our things and Smoke and get to the train."

She'd already expressed her disappointment at the prospect of more travel, so she kept the wanting to whine about it to herself. She didn't want him to think he'd married a complainer.

He seemed to have read her thoughts. "Not looking forward to another train ride, either, but I am to getting to the ranch so we can have our wedding night."

She thought about the saucy little black peignoir she'd purchased at Bethany's shop especially for the occasion and smiled. "As long as we have it and it isn't on a train, I'll be fine."

"It'll be worth the wait, I promise."

"It better be," she replied with her usual sassiness.

After lunch, they strolled back to Jade's. Maggie wondered if all brides felt as happy as she. For a woman who only two weeks ago was certain she'd never marry, she'd somehow landed herself a pretty good fish.

Jade looked at them in their new finery and said to Maggie, "You actually got him out of that old duster, congratulations."

"I had nothing to do with it," she responded with a laugh and turned an adoring gaze on her husband. "But he does look fine, doesn't he?"

"You both do."

Ian squeezed Maggie into his side affectionately. "We came back to pick up our bags and then we'll be off. Thanks for the food and the room."

"Anytime. I've enjoyed seeing you again, and meeting you, Maggie."

"Thank you for your hospitality. You'll write to us when you are settled in San Francisco?"

"I will."

Ian added, "Send it in care of the Cheyenne post office. Hope you get to see your brothers soon."

His sincerity seemed to touch her. "I do, too. Safe travels."

Upstairs in their room, Ian closed the door and pulled Maggie into his arms for a kiss. After letting her come up for air, he traced her cheek. "Thank you for marrying me."

"Thanks for asking. Am I supposed to be this happy?"

He shrugged. "I think so."

"I want to be a good wife to you, Ian."

"And I want to be a good husband."

"We'll probably argue over some things down the line."

"Probably, most married couples do."

"You aren't a hitter, are you?"

He stared down, confused. "You mean will I hit you?"

"Yes. I know that some men are."

"No. Never." He gathered her back in and held her tight. "Never."

"Good. I didn't think you were."

He pulled back and scanned her face. "If I do you have my permission to shoot me."

"I'll shoot you permission or not."

He laughed. "We're going to do well together."

They shared another lingering kiss and began gathering their belongings.

At five that afternoon and after fetching Smoke from the livery, Mr. and Mrs. Ian Vance boarded the northbound train to Cheyenne, Wyoming.

Chapter 18

On the train ride, Maggie sat by the window and marveled at the changing landscape. Gone were the flat, golden brown grassy plains of Kansas. Replacing them were mountains and forests and more green landscape than she'd ever seen before. She was also still marveling at the change in her circumstances. A week ago she'd been a prisoner contemplating the possibility of being hanged, and now she was seated next to her husband. Thanks to her new clothing, there'd been no disapproving, sideways glances from the other passengers when they boarded. The conductor greeted them respectfully and directed them to seats in the main car. Granted the train was all but empty so there was plenty of seating available, but he didn't summarily relegate them to the cattle car or smoking car simply because of the color of their skin.

But the land continued to draw her attention. The vastness of it was most striking. They were traveling through acres and acres of unpopulated land for as far as the eye could see. Rivers of crystal water and towering peaks still holding snow dominated the skies. The beauty of it took her breath away. "This is pretty country."

"Prettiest around."

"Whose tribal lands are these?"

"Arapaho. Crow. Lakota. Land to the west and south belonged to the Cheyenne, Blackfoot, Bannock, and Apache. Many of the mountains were sacred."

"And no doubt still are. Are their people all on reservations?"

"Mostly yes."

She thought that a shame. How wonderful it must have been for them to walk, hunt, and live in such beauty. It saddened her that here, too, a way of life had been destroyed just as it had been for the Kaw. The once proud and self-sustaining tribes that stretched from the Atlantic to the Pacific were now mere shadows of themselves.

They spent the night at Fort Collins. At the small rest stop that housed passengers overnight, the food was bad, the accommodations poor, and Maggie's heart broke at the sight of the teepees set up outside the fort.

"Arapaho, maybe," Ian told her.

She thought about the despair and poverty the people were being forced to endure and how powerless and frustrated they must feel knowing they no longer had a land to call home and were not free to seek out another. As she and Ian cuddled together on the narrow cot that served as a bed, it took her a long time to find sleep.

They boarded the train the following morning

for the last leg of their journey. As they took their seats Maggie gently moved her neck and shoulders around to free up the kinks in her back.

He eyed her fondly. "There's a nice big feather bed waiting for you at the house, so hold on."

That was music to her ears, but she hoped she wouldn't be sleeping in it alone. Even though they'd been sharing a bed, all the upstanding women she'd worked for in the past had maintained separate bedrooms. Personally she enjoyed having his presence in bed with her and she wanted that to continue. She supposed that if desiring her husband made her less ladylike in the eyes of polite society, it wouldn't be the first time.

The depot in Cheyenne was substantial in size but in no way equaled the bustling magnificence of Denver. There wasn't a crush of people and vehicles rushing everywhere, either. As he politely handed her down the steps she could actually hear nature around her.

"Almost home," he said, viewing her intently.

"How far?"

"Day and a half, depending on the shape of the terrain."

"And tonight we sleep where?" she asked skeptically.

Amusement sparkled in his green eyes. "Under the stars next to a fire."

She sighed at the prospect of another uncomfortable night. She'd hoped the journey would be a short one. "I suppose it could be worse. We could be spending it on that cot we slept on last night."

"Once we get home, you can sleep for a week if

you want. Let's go and get Smoke. Undoubtedly he's as tired of all these trains as we are."

The air was chilly for May, so she pulled her jacket closer. "What's weather like here?"

"Rainy during early spring and early summer, but it can get pretty hot come July. Snow as early as September sometimes though, and lots of wind because of all the mountains."

After he guided Smoke down the car's ramp, a short, elderly man approached them with a wide smile. "Well, well, well. Look who's home."

Ian turned, and from the affectionate embrace the men shared she assumed him to be Charlie, the friend Ian had spoken so highly of. "Good to be back. How are you?"

"Considering all the aches and pain old age is giving me, I'm holding together. Who's this pretty lady?"

Ian made the introductions. "Charlie Young, my wife, Maggie."

His dark eyes lit up with excitement. "Well, I'll be. Nice to meet you, Mrs. Vance."

"Same here, Mr. Young."

"Welcome to Dakota Territory."

Maggie was confused. "I thought we were in Wyoming."

Ian eyed Charlie with amusement. "We are. Charlie prefers to live in the past."

Charlie groused, "And who wouldn't? Worst thing ever happened around here was joining the United States of America. Things were perfectly fine before. Now you got the government telling you what you can and can't do. Railroads scarring the land. Indians getting the boot. Game being run off by homesteaders. The past was better."

Maggie had no idea how old Charlie was but his hair was snow white and his nut brown skin was lined with age. His eyes were bright and mischievous, however, and he was looking at her as if he was genuinely pleased by her presence.

"What tribe are your people, Miss Maggie?"

"Kaw."

"Ah. Legendary warriors. Enemies of the Arapaho. I hear there are only a handful left."

"You heard correctly."

"Country ought to be ashamed treating the tribes this way." He eyed Ian while asking her, "He tell you about all the women who are going to be mad at you for being his new missus?"

She turned on Ian. "No."

"Well, he should've. They've been trailing behind him like a remuda for years."

"Oh, really?"

Ian countered, "Don't listen to him. He's just trying to stir the pot. Gives his life purpose."

Charlie's answering smile showed that in spite of his age he still had all his real teeth.

"What are you even doing here?" Ian asked. "Where's Harper? You said you'd send him to meet me."

"Got a lot on his plate right now. Draper's brought in some hired guns, but we can talk about that when we get to the ranch. And by the way, Harp's been bedding down at the house."

"Whose house?"

"Yours."

"Why?"

"Vivian kicked him out for keeping company with one of the girls down here."

Maggie watched surprise spread over Ian's features. "And she let him live?"

Charlie grinned. "Amazing, isn't it? Only reason she didn't shoot him was because no one would give her a gun. She settled for divorcing him."

"When was this?"

"Almost a year now. A few weeks after you left for Scotland."

"And they haven't reconciled?"

"Nope. Told him he could sleep with the bears for the rest of his life as far as she's concerned. He really stepped in it this time."

"Why would he cheat? He's got one of the prettiest women in the state."

"Also one of the most stubborn and testiest. He said she was spending more time being mayor than his wife, and he was lonesome. Add to that the fact that he's a July, and there you have it."

A fascinated Maggie asked, "Are these people I'll be meeting?"

Ian nodded. "Vivian Palmer July was the schoolteacher for a while, but she's now the mayor. Little town called Osprey. Harper July's the Osprey sheriff."

Maggie mulled over the name. "Is he kin to the outlaw Julys?"

"One of the younger brothers."

"And he's a sheriff?"

Charlie replied, "Miss Maggie, you're going to

find that up here, folks can shake off whomever they might have been in the past and resurrect themselves as somebody new, and folks don't care. Harp's a good sheriff. She's a good mayor. They love each other like the mountains love the snow but she's stubborn and he's bullheaded. They clash a lot."

Charlie turned his attention to Ian, who appeared to be deep in thought. Maggie wondered if he was thinking about the Draper business.

"You ready to go home?" Charlie asked.

"Yes. Does the ranch need anything?"

Charlie shook his head. "But your Maggie might. She got boots, things like that?"

Maggie answered, "No." She liked Charlie. "Do you live nearby?"

"Yep. Live right behind you. Do most of his cooking and cleaning."

"Really?" Another surprise. She wondered what role he'd play now that she'd come into the picture. "Then I'm looking forward to you helping me get settled in."

"I'd like that."

Ian cracked, "Trouble, meet trouble."

Maggie punched him playfully in the arm. "Stop that."

Charlie chuckled. "I like her."

Ian met her eyes. "Me too."

Maggie hooked her arm in theirs, and they walked into town to see about buying her boots and things like that.

They spent most of the morning getting Maggie

outfitted with the boots she needed and the denims she insisted on having. "I'm not going to be able to help with the cows or the horses or whatever it is you do in what I'm wearing," she told him.

"You won't be doing anything with the cows or horses, Maggie," Ian tried to explain.

"Why not?"

He glanced over at Charlie, who didn't bother hiding his grin. "Don't look at me."

She asked in a serious tone, "Is this not something women do in Wyoming?"

"Well, yes. Some do."

"Then I'd like to learn as well."

The storekeeper glanced between the two of them and cracked, "This comes from giving them the vote."

A raised eyebrow framed her glare.

He reddened and coughed. "I'll just go and see if I have some denims to fit you, ma'am."

"Thank you."

While he went off to do that, Ian asked her, "I thought you wanted to wear nice dresses and read?"

"I do, but not all day every day."

The storekeeper returned. Maggie took the trousers and shirts he'd added into a small stockroom to try them on. Both pairs fit, so she put one on, added a shirt, folded up her new green dress along with the rest of her feminine attire, and walked out to rejoin the men.

"They're a bit snug," she said, showing Ian a back view.

He looked over at Charlie, who appeared to be having the time of his life.

"What's the matter?" she asked.

"Nothing," Ian said. "Are you ready?"

"Yes."

He paid the store owner and they made their exit. Behind her she heard Charlie ask Ian in a humorous voice, "You sure you brought the right woman home?"

Ian replied, "Shut up."

As they crossed the street, Ian paused in mid-step.

"What's wrong?" Maggie asked.

A man on the opposite walk had stopped, too.

Charlie said, "That's one of Draper's new hired guns. You know him?"

The man in question stepped off the walk. He slowly strode their way and Charlie got his answer when the man drawled, "Well, if it ain't the Preacher man."

Ian answered in a winter-cold voice, "When'd you get out of jail?"

He replied smoothly, "About a year ago." He was clad in black leather studded with silver. The long black hair beneath the thin-brimmed hat was tied behind his back. The left side of his face was horribly disfigured as if it had been melted and hardened again. He glanced Maggie's way and the ice in his eyes sent a chill through her blood.

"What are you doing here?" Ian asked, bringing his attention back around.

"Was about to ask you the same thing."

"You go first."

The responding smile had a reptilian quality. "Working for a man named Draper. Know him?"

"Yes."

"Friend?"

"No."

"Good. Hate to break up a friendship."

"And I'd hate to shoot a trespasser, so have Draper show you where my land begins and ends."

"So you live around here, huh?"

"I do."

"Good to know."

The men were of equal height, but the stranger was heavier, thicker. The air between the men was charged. People on the walks seemed to sense it and paused to watch.

As if the man knew the confrontation to come wouldn't be that day, he gave Ian a nod. "You all have a good day." He tipped his hat politely to Maggie and went on his way.

Beneath his anger, Ian sighed. His past had already come calling, and he hadn't even gotten Maggie home.

"Who is that?" she asked.

"Pratt Ketchum."

"How do you know him?"

"He's the half brother of the man who killed Tilda."

Ian saw her eyes widen. "Ketchum was wanted for a murder a few months later. I hunted him down and brought him in. Jury gave him twenty years. He's out early."

"Then he's going to be trouble," Charlie offered knowingly.

"More than likely." His eyes were emotionless when they met Maggie's. "Let's get you home."

Chapter 19

Charlie had ridden down in a wagon. "Didn't know how many trunks and things you might be coming back with," he explained as they walked to where he'd left it parked at the livery.

Ian put Ketchum out of his mind for the moment. "Wagon's fine. I'll have to get Maggie a horse once we get her home."

"A horse of my own?"

"Unless you'd prefer a carriage."

"No. A horse would be more than enough."

Ian decided he'd make arrangements for both. There might be days she'd prefer the carriage when she wasn't busting broncs or herding cows. Once again her unconventional approach to life made him shake his head at the wonder of her.

They placed Maggie's Denver purchases and her saddlebag in the bed along with Ian's bag and gear. Ian mounted Smoke. Maggie climbed up on the wagon seat beside Charlie. Once they were all settled they headed west.

Ian tried to concentrate on how good it felt to be home. He and Smoke were once again riding, the air was clear and sweet, and the spirit of the wide open land resonated with familiarity, but Ketchum's presence loomed like a dark cloud over the sunny day. First thing he planned to do after getting Maggie settled in was sit down with Charlie and hear what Draper had been doing and why he felt it necessary to hire a murderer like Ketchum. Ian's mind quoted a verse from Lamentations: *He is a bear lying in wait for me, a lion in waiting . . .*

As Ian rode in pace with the wagon, watching Maggie and Charlie chatting away lifted his mood. He was pleased the two seemed to have taken to each other because Charlie was well known for his curmudgeonly ways and would have been silent as a totem had he disapproved of her. He and Charlie had been friends more than a decade and Charlie was the closest thing Ian'd ever had to a father in America, maybe ever. Charlie'd taught Ian everything he knew about ranching, cattle, and horses. If Ketchum harmed him, Ian would send him to hell. The same thing went for Maggie. If Ketchum targeted her as a way to get back at him, his death would make what happened to his half brother Bivens seem like a day at the fair.

Maggie was enjoying riding next to Charlie and the beauty of the land around them. Everything was so big; from the trees, to the large expanses of green plains that they journeyed through, to the blue sky and snow-topped mountains rising majestically against it. She now understood why the native tribes thought them sacred. Even from a distance she sensed their power.

She glanced over at Ian riding so relaxed on Smoke. She and her husband were finally on their way home. If Ketchum hadn't slunk into their day like the serpent in Eden, she'd be over the moon with happiness. Instead she worried that like that serpent he would somehow spoil their paradise. In the back of her mind was Charlie's reference to Ian's remuda of women, but the knowledge that Ian had proposed to her, and not one of them, made her more curious about them than anything else.

The sun was high overhead when they stopped for a lunch. The fare consisted of beef sandwiches between slices of a sweet meal bread. They washed them down with ice-cold water from a small meandering stream. According to Charlie, rivers and lakes were few and far between in their part of the country and owning land with water increased the value of the land. She noted that Ian no longer seemed distant and apart. In fact, the eyes she looked into were openly teasing, making her remember the feel of his lips and touch of his hand. She couldn't wait to be with him in the big feather bed he promised would be at his home when they arrived.

Before she could enjoy that feather bed however, she had to spend the night next to a fire beneath the stars. As night fell, Maggie would have agreed to sleep in a tree if it got her off the thinly padded wagon seat. They'd covered a fair amount of miles since leaving Cheyenne and her aching bottom was groaning from all the sitting. By the time they stopped to make camp for the night, she could barely make it back down to the ground.

"Are you okay?" Ian asked with concern.

The slow-moving Maggie lied, "Just a bit stiff from so much sitting. I'll be better once I move around for a bit."

Ian wasn't so sure. Her posture was akin to a bent-over old woman and she was moving way too gingerly for his liking. "Let me get the bedroll, and you can lie down."

"Thank you."

While Charlie worked on the fire, he hurried to the back of the wagon. Returning, he laid the bedding on the ground and stood by while she lowered herself inch by inch to meet it.

"Whoever thought a bedroll on the ground would be such a relief," she said, lying on her back with her arms spread wide in surrender.

Charlie cracked, "That part of you will toughen up, don't worry."

Ian almost asked, *Who wanted a woman with a tough bottom?* but kept the question to himself, mainly because of the answer he might receive in reply. Personally, he preferred that portion of her anatomy to remain as soft and yielding as he knew it to be. He watched her snuggle in and wished he was beside her so he could savor her warm skin.

Charlie's humor-laden voice broke the spell, "Hey, you with the glassy eyes. You want to take the first watch or shall I?"

He saw a sleepy smile cross Maggie's face just as she closed her eyes. "I'll go first."

Covered by a blanket and lying with his back resting against his saddle, Ian kept watch while

Maggie and Charlie slept. A fire sometimes drew curious predators, both the four-legged kind and the kind who walked upright on two, so having someone awake to keep watch was a necessity at a night camp. By early afternoon, they'd be home and his journey that began on the rocky, windy coast of Scotland would finally end. His grandfather's parting words slid past his mind for a second like a star blinking in the sky. The old man would get his wish; Ian would never return. He'd be lying to himself if he said it didn't matter, but the memory of his mother and her love for him would always be in his heart, which was more than his grandfather could say.

Also in his heart was the little lady bundled up in his bedroll beside him. Had he not made the trip to Scotland, would he have met her? He watched her sleep while the flickering flames played across the portion of her features visible above the dark cocoon. No matter how many times he looked at her, it was never enough. Never. And something told him that would be forever. Life with her was going to be exhilarating. Knowing her, she'd learn to bust broncs and herd cows, or break a leg trying. He was also certain he'd only viewed the top of the mountain of who she really was beneath all that toughness, and yet she could be incredibly tender. He would remember the night at Lola's until the day he died. When he returned from helping the Stapleton sons take their father's corpse home, how had she known that he'd been so deeply in need of salving? She'd offered herself to him as if she were the living embodiment of the water his parched soul craved, and he'd been drawing from that wellspring ever since.

As if sensing his thought, she stirred and opened her eyes. The soft smile made his heart open even wider. "You're supposed to be sleeping."

She struggled up to a sitting position and kept the bedroll around her to stave off the cool night air. "How are you?"

"Other than wishing I was in the bedroll with you, I'm fine."

"You're welcome to join me."

He liked the idea of that, but with Charlie sleeping on the other side of the fire, he couldn't take her up on the offer. "I'll wait until we get home."

She gave him a mock pout.

"Outrageous woman."

"Speaking of women, how large is this remuda Charlie talked about?"

"Not very?"

"So, there is one?"

Ian wondered why he felt like he'd just stepped into a bear trap. "I never led anyone to believe I was going to marry them." He could see her studying him by the dancing light of the fire. "That's the truth. Are you angry about this?"

"No," she said easily. "You proposed to me. Not to one of them." He leaned over and gave her a soft kiss. "You are an amazing woman, Maggie Vance."

"More amazing than your remuda?"

"By ten thousand miles."

Charlie lifted up and groused, "Would you lovebirds pipe down. Old men need their sleep."

They chuckled softly. Maggie gave him a parting kiss before snuggling down again and closing her eyes.

Ian resumed his watch.

Early afternoon of the next day they arrived at his ranch and Maggie marveled as they passed through two large wrought-iron gates. On the gate on her left was an iron plaque that had on it a large letter N with a bar running through it. Below were the words: "Night Hawk Ranch."

Charlie grinned. "Welcome to your home, Miss Maggie. You'll be able to see the house in just a minute."

A pleased Maggie glanced Ian's way and found him watching her with sparkling yes. Even Smoke seemed happy to be home. Had Ian not had a firm hold on the reins, the prancing stallion would have taken off.

He reached down and patted the stallion affectionately, "Just a few more minutes, boy. Hold on."

Up ahead, Maggie saw acres and acres of open green grass bordered by distant trees, then outbuildings, which by their size and positioning had to be barns. As the wagon rattled down a gravel and stone paved road, the house came into view. Built partly of stone and timbers, it was two stories and was much larger than she'd expected. It looked like the residence of someone of importance and it made her wonder what kind of standing Ian had in the community. She was just about to ask Charlie about it when she heard him mutter, "Aw hell."

Confused, she looked first at him and then over at Ian. His face had gone from open to closed and he was staring ahead. Turning in that direction, Maggie went still at the sight of a brown-skinned woman riding fast to meet them. She had on a lacy white blouse and a skirt that was divided like a pair of trouser legs that showed off expensive black boots. Her hair was in a fashionable chignon and a happy smile dominated her face.

Nearing, she called out in a mock scolding voice, "I should take a whip to you for being gone so long. Welcome home, Ian. How could you stay away for a year and not write or send a telegram knowing how worried I'd be."

On the wagon, Maggie quietly asked Charlie, "One of the remuda?"

"Yep. Head mule."

Assessing the woman as any wife would, she took in the very beautiful face and the costly clothing while waiting to see how this would play out.

"Henny, meet my wife, Maggie," Ian said.

The woman froze. Her mouth dropped in astonishment. She swung widened eyes Maggie's way.

"Pleased to meet you," Maggie said.

"Your wife!" she screeched.

He glanced at Maggie and she winked. As she'd told him last night, he'd proposed to her and to her alone.

Maggie then announced, "Ian, Charlie and I are going on to the house. I'll see you when you and Henny are done." She gave Henny a smile. "Nice meeting you."

As Charlie drove them off he chuckled and remarked, "Little lady's got balls."

"You ain't seen nothing yet."

He howled.

Ian watched them roll away before turning his attention back to the furious Henrietta Benton. Her father, Tom, was one of the biggest and wealthiest landowners around and had investments in everything from cattle to mining. Ian liked him a lot. He liked Henny, too, but not enough to make her his wife. This homecoming was an awkward situation but it would have been more so had he led her along. He hadn't. She'd been after him for years to marry. Even though he'd made it clear on numerous occasions that they'd never be more than friends and neighbors, she refused to take him seriously. Her father's money and influence had gotten her everything else in life, so why not him.

"How could you do this to me?"

"How many times have I told you I wasn't going to marry you."

"But I thought it was because you were still grieving for your wife."

"No."

"I'll be a laughingstock! And to marry someone like—that? Can she even read? Can she—"

The blaze in his eyes stopped her in mid-rant. "I'm sorry. I'm just so stunned."

"You shouldn't be."

Her chin went up. "Where'd you meet her?"

"Kansas."

"Does she know how cold it gets in the winter?

Does she know a yearling from a barbed-wire fence!"

Ian wheeled Smoke around. He'd had enough. "Tell Tom I'll be by to see him in a couple days. You be careful riding home."

He spurred Smoke forward, leaving her to glare and fume alone. He was unhappy enough about having to deal with Henny, but now the thought that Charlie was showing Maggie the house only added to his mood. Introducing her to their home was to have been his job and it was something he'd been looking forward to. Now, knowing Charlie, all he'd left for Ian to do was introduce her to the corrals. He urged Smoke faster and the stallion responded to his urgent rider.

He ran inside and there she sat seated on his sofa by the cold fireplace. She was frowning.

"What's wrong?"

"I made Charlie mad, I think."

Ian looked around but didn't see him nearby. "Where is he?"

"Said he was going home."

He'd thought the two of them had been getting along well, so this development was surprising. He walked over and hunkered down in front of her. She appeared sad. "What happened?"

She sighed. "He wanted to show me around, but I told him I preferred to wait for you."

Ian forced himself not to smile.

"I think I hurt his feelings. I know he's a good friend and I don't want to start off on the wrong foot or have him think I don't want him around."

"I'll talk to him."

"Should I apologize?"

He shook his head. Standing up, he took her hands and gently urged her to her feet. In the snug-fitting denims and blue flannel shirt, she couldn't be more beautiful than if she were gowned in silk. He traced her cheek and the wonder unfurled again. He kissed her softly. Kissing him back, her arms slowly crept around him and tightened. He did the same and soon they were lost in a tender reunion that was filled with the passionate joy of finally having no barriers between them; no trains, warrants, or rented rooms. Now they were together and able to explore all they could be.

Ian reluctantly pulled away from her beguiling lips. "Welcome home."

She hugged him tight. "Glad to be here."

After a few more moments of silent savoring, he asked, "Ready to see your domain, your majesty?"

"Very much."

Holding her hand, he introduced her to the room they were standing in. There were colorful tribal-designed rugs on the floor, and blankets of matching motifs on the sofa and two sitting chairs. "I buy them at a trading post in Osprey," he explained. "The Native women make them and the trader sells them, for a profit of course."

"They're very nice, especially the colors." There were scarlets and grays on fields of black and ivory.

The mantel over the fireplace was bare, but mounted on the wall above it hung the head of a bear in mid-growl.

"Does the bear have a story?" she asked.

"One of Charlie's trophies. The bear wanted Charlie's horse."

"And Charlie took issue with that, I assume."

"Yes, he did."

He led her into the kitchen next. It was large and very spacious. The modern stove with its four top plates and large oven surprised her.

"Charlie's pride and joy."

"And with good reason. One of the women I worked for had a stove similar to this."

He watched her look around at the white-washed cabinets and the counters above the lower cabinets and drawers. "Let me show you the pump."

He led her through the back door and outside to the curved-handled pump a few steps away.

"There's another out by the barns, but we use this one for the house."

She looked out at Charlie's log cabin. "Is that where he lives?"

"Yes. Everything will be okay. Promise."

She nodded and for the first time seemed to notice the large garden staked out next to the house. Whatever was planted there had begun to push up from the soil with leaves and curling, sun-seeking vines. He met her grin.

"The garden," she voiced quietly.

"Yep. Charlie takes care of it, but it's yours, too."

She looked very pleased. "Where to next?"

"Come. I'll show you."

Their next stop was a small bedroom. The clutter and clothing everywhere took Ian by surprise for a moment until he remembered Charlie saying

Harper was staying here. He sighed. "This was a spare room, but apparently it's where Harp's been sleeping." Ian was going to have to have a heart-to-heart discussion with his friend. Now that he'd returned home with a wife, the sheriff was going to have to find somewhere else to park his boots. Selfish, maybe, but Ian didn't care. "He'll be moving out shortly."

Chapter 20

Ian's mood lightened as he moved them away from the chaos left behind by Harper. He walked Maggie down the hallway and stopped in front of a closed, polished wood door. "Now, for this part of the tour, I want you to close your eyes."

To his surprise, she didn't question the request. "I'm going to pick you up, so no peeking."

Her answering smile earned her a kiss.

He picked her up, dipped her a moment so he could open the door, and then walked her inside.

"Okay. Open them," he invited with her still in his arms.

Maggie stared around at a bedroom. She saw windows covered by closed shutters and nightstands holding glass-globed lamps. She saw a large armoire and a big ornate mirror on one wall, but mostly she saw the huge wooden bed with its tall posts and large carved headboard. "Hallelujah!" She leaned up and kissed him long and hard in gratitude. Laughing, he set her back on her feet.

"This is to be our room?"

"Yes."

"We'll share it?"

He went silent for a moment. "Unless you'd rather sleep in the room Harper's going to be vacating?"

"No. I want us to be in a room together."

To her surprise he eased her into his arms. She felt the soft pressure of his lips against the top of her hair. She sensed something flowing in him that she couldn't name. "May I ask you something?"

"Sure."

She looked up into his eyes. Maggie hesitated for a moment. The last thing she wanted was to offend him in any way. "Is this the room you shared with your first wife?"

"No," he replied quietly. "She slept in the room Harper's using."

"Oh." She didn't have the heart to ask why, but from the mask now veiling his features, she assumed it had been his wife's choice. Maggie placed her cheek back against his heart. "I want to wake up with you beside me, and close my eyes in the same way."

He kissed the top of her hair again and said softly, "Got one more place, no, two more places to show you."

First was the washroom with its big claw-footed tub. Once again, the size of the space was impressive. The second place he took her to was another closed door next to the bedroom. Maggie couldn't imagine what the interior might hold.

"Close your eyes again."

"Ian," she said with mock warning.

"Humor me one last time, please."

Maggie couldn't remember him ever saying *please,* before, so she closed her eyes and let him lead her by the hand.

"Open."

What she saw was a room filled with shelves and shelves of books, so many that she placed her hands over her mouth and stared around in awe. He'd promised her books, but she hadn't expected a lending library's worth. The sight filled her with so much emotion she had no idea she was crying until she noticed the dampness on her cheeks. "Oh, Ian." Filled with amazement, she walked over to the shelves and was mesmerized by the tomes, folios, and small, cloth-bound volumes of poetry by men like Keats and Spenser, and women like the poetess Miss Phillis Wheatley. There were Shakespeare's tragedies and comedies and bound maps of foreign lands. She eyed neatly stacked newspapers beside magazines from England. From almost ceiling to floor there was something to read. She'd married him, and now had died and gone to heaven. She turned to him standing by the doorway. "I'm speechless."

"You?" he teased.

Maggie began walking past the shelved books again. "This is astonishing." For the first time she noticed the large stone fireplace and the comfortable-looking brown wingbacks sitting on either side. Each had a folded Native blanket across one arm. "It must be grand in here when the winter is raging outside and you're cozied up by the fire."

"That it is."

She hurried across the room to him with her arms outstretched. He gathered her in and swung her off her feet. She threw back her head and beamed. "This is the happiest I've been in my life. Thank you for being my husband."

"Thank you for being my wife."

They heard someone clear his throat. In the doorway stood Charlie. "You two want something to eat?"

Maggie left Ian's arms and walked over to him. Looking into his sun-crinkled eyes, she said with sincerity, "Charlie, my apologies if I offended you or hurt your feelings earlier."

He waved her off. "Not needed."

"It's just that I'd been waiting so long to get here so Ian could show me the house. I wanted him to have the honor."

"I understand."

"Do you?"

He nodded.

She opened her arms and gave him a hug, which widened his eyes. He responded with a few quick pats on her shoulders and stepped back as if unsure how to respond to such demonstrative behavior.

"So," she asked, "how may I help with the meal?"

"You can't. All you get to do is sit down and rest. You've been traveling a long time, but you're home now."

Maggie glanced between the two men, and the kindness in their eyes made her feel as if she truly had come home. "Thank you, Charlie."

After his departure, Ian asked in a Scottish brogue, "Would you like to tour the grounds, my lady?"

She curtsied in her denims. "I would, kind sir."

He held out his arm and they were off.

The land near the house held three large corrals for the wild horses he and Charlie brought in.

"They're empty now, but Charlie and I will go up in the spring and see what we can find."

"Is that where my horse will come from?"

"Nope. I have a mare for you. If she'll let you ride her."

Maggie was puzzled. "What do you mean?"

"She won't let anyone ride her. Charlie's theory is that she wants a female rider. Not sure he's right, but wild horses can be very particular about who they take to sometimes."

"May I see her?"

He led her over to a pasture behind the corral. Smoke grazed nearby and Maggie noted how much larger the stallion looked without his saddle and reins. A palomino walked over and nuzzled Ian affectionately. "This is Jack. He's been with us for almost four years now. He's blind in one eye so we didn't want to sell him."

Jack immediately began searching the front of Ian's jacket. Ian reached into a pocket and produced a carrot which Jack made short work of in two crunching bites. "Good boy. Now, where's the queen? Where's Lightning? I haven't seen her yet."

The palomino wandered off.

Ian shook his head. "He doesn't care. He's

gotten his carrot and he's gone." He stuck two fingers in his mouth and whistled shrilly.

Nothing.

He whistled again, louder this time.

A few minutes later a dazzling black horse walked up. If this was the mare, she wasn't quite as many hands high as Smoke, but what she lacked in muscle and height she made up for in her sleek and powerful appearance. A jagged white blaze between her eyes resembled a lightning bolt. She stopped well out of Ian's reach. "Afternoon, your majesty. We are honored to be in your presence. Not that you care, but this is Maggie."

The mare's dark eyes moved slowly from Ian and over to Maggie, who noticed Smoke watching as if he was interested in how this might go, too. "Hello, missy," she called softly.

In response, Lightning cocked her head. After studying Maggie a second longer, the mare tossed her head and galloped away.

"And the royal visit ends," Ian declared.

"I don't think I've ever received a dismissive look from a horse before."

"She's something."

"How long have you had her?"

"Two years."

Smoke had resumed his grazing.

Looking off in the direction the mare had taken, Maggie pointed out, "She's very beautiful."

"And knows it."

They left the pasture and looked in on the five hens in the coop.

"Charlie says they all have names but I couldn't tell you who's who."

"All hens have names. Shame on you."

"As long as they give me eggs for breakfast, I don't care what they're called."

She leaned into the row of nests and told the cackling and fussing birds, "We'll just have to wait for Charlie to introduce us then, won't we?"

Ian rolled his eyes and took her hand. "Come on, you."

Back outside, Maggie stood and looked around at the beauty and magnificence of the land. There were trees and birds, and it was so silent she swore she could hear the earth's heartbeat. Her voice turned serious. "I'm going to love it here."

"This is a very special place."

"What mountains are those?"

"Wind River chain of the Rockies."

They were still snow-topped. "How far away are they?"

"Over a hundred miles and then some."

"They look so much closer."

"Yes, they do."

She turned to him and felt the need to thank him again for marrying her, but because it seemed as if she'd been saying that to him all day, she simply walked over and wrapped her arms around him and squeezed him tight. No words were needed.

"I'm looking forward to what the future brings us."

"So am I."

On the walk back to the house, Maggie was

moved by all she'd seen so far. His pride in his land was readily apparent and she was honored to be asked to share it.

For dinner, Charlie prepared two succulent, pit roasted hens basted with a sweet, spicy tomato sauce, grilled potatoes, and collards. He was an excellent cook, and his blueberry biscuits made Maggie groan with delight.

"Like those?" Charlie asked from his seat at the table.

"I do. They're heavenly."

"Only make them on special occasions."

"Then I count myself lucky. Thank you."

"You're welcome."

"I don't remember you ever making these for me," Ian mockingly complained.

"What's so special about you?"

Maggie's sip of water came through her nose. She hastily wiped her face with her napkin.

Charlie countered Ian's claim. "I've made these before, you just ate them so fast you don't remember."

Maggie knew she'd enjoy living with Ian, but having Charlie thrown in was a bonus. Seeing that Ian appeared more amused than offended by the irascibility, she guessed the two men went back and forth this way often. She'd never had a friend to banter with and she wondered if Ian knew how blessed he was that he did.

Charlie asked her, "What other kind of things do you like to eat, Miss Maggie?"

She shrugged. "I'm not real particular. Never could afford to be."

He studied her silently as if weighing her and her words. "We know you like blueberries. Do you like them baked in a pie?"

"I do. Very much."

"What else?"

While she and Charlie conversed, Ian realized he'd never seen Charlie go so out of his way to be pleasing. Ian still swore he'd never had the blueberry biscuits before, but Charlie'd made them for Maggie and the gesture was very surprising because Ian thought he knew the old mountain man well.

Once they finished discussing her likes and dislikes they went back to their meal, and she asked, "How long have you lived in the Dakotas, Charlie?"

He gave her a smile. "Hear how she said Dakotas?" the pleased-looking Charlie pointed out to Ian.

"I did." He was getting a real kick out of this. She hadn't been at the ranch a full day yet and already had him eating out of her hand. Ian couldn't wait to see what other miracles she'd bring about.

"Been here since the late thirties."

"Where were you born?"

"Missouri. Left there when I was nine and headed west."

"With your parents?"

He shook his head. "Alone."

She studied him as if evaluating the truthfulness of the tale. Ian could've told her not to bother.

"That's pretty young."

"Yep. Got tired of being a slave."

"Ah."

"Worked my way as a gopher for a wagon train master."

"What on earth is a gopher?"

"You go for this, you go for that."

"Oh," she uttered. She glanced Ian's way but he kept his face impassive and picked up his shot glass of whiskey.

"Got to be friends with a man of color named Jim Beckworth. He was the train's blacksmith. When he left the train in Denver I went with him. After months of trapping and fighting Natives—no offense—"

"None taken."

"We met a Crow woman who claimed Jim was her long-lost son and adopted him into the tribe. Pretty soon, he was a Crow chief."

She looked confused. "Why would she think he was her son?"

"Jim didn't know, and to this day, I don't, either, but she did."

She met Ian's eyes again. He toasted her with his glass.

"Charlie. Is this a tall tale?"

"Nope. As true as the story of old Big Nose George becoming a pair of shoes."

"What! Ian?"

Ian smiled. "Now that's true."

Maggie was speechless for a moment. "You can't turn a man into a pair of shoes."

"Here, you can."

So he told her the story of the outlaw and murderer Big Nose George Parrot, who received his comeuppance for his crimes at the hands of a lynch mob of masked Rawlins citizens.

Charlie interjected. "The mob had to hang him three times because they botched the first two attempts."

Maggie stared.

"Will you let me finish?"

"She should know the details."

Ian smiled. "Anyway, after he was finally dead, the body was claimed by two local doctors."

Charlie interjected, "They wanted to compare his brain to a regular man's brain to see if they could find a reason why Big Nose was a criminal."

"In the name of medical science," Ian added.

"That's understandable, I suppose," Maggie said but not sounding sure.

"But things went slightly bizarre after that." Ian then told her how bizarre.

Maggie couldn't believe her ears. "Ian, this can't be true. Who would take the skin off a corpse and send it to a tannery with a note saying, 'Please turn this into a pair of shoes and a medical bag'?"

"Dr. John Osborne," Charlie said.

"When did this happen?"

"Back in '82," Charlie said.

Ian had a further twist in the story to impart. "Osborne's a pretty big politician now. May even run for governor in the next election."

"What happened to the shoes?"

Ian grinned. "He's wearing them."

Maggie stared agape. "You're joshing?"

"Nope."

Wide-eyed she stared between the men.

Ian saluted her with his empty shot glass. "Welcome to the Dakotas, darlin'."

After the meal was done, Maggie stood and began clearing the table. Ian watched to see how this would play out and sure enough an argument ensued. She wanted to help. Charlie wanted her to sit and rest.

"How am I supposed to learn where everything goes?"

"When you get rested up."

"No."

"Yes."

"This is not up for discussion."

He paused and looked her up and down. "Not used to folks telling you no, are you?"

"No I'm not. I've worked other people's homes all my life because I had to. Now I'm in my own home. I want to work for myself for a change."

Charlie looked to Ian, who declined to intervene. "I'm not getting in this. I've learned she's a lot more dangerous than she appears."

Maggie took a break from her stance to shoot him a smile before refocusing her attention on Charlie. "So, what's it to be? Do I help, or do I nag you to death?"

He grinned. "I like her."

"Knew you would," Ian said.

Charlie finally nodded. "Okay. You win."

"Thank you."

Chapter 21

Later, Maggie was seated on the porch under the stars. Ian and Charlie were out in the barn checking on the horses. She was savoring how wonderful it felt to be sitting on her own porch of her very own home when suddenly her stomach fluttered, and a familiar tingling between her thighs stole her joy. Her monthly bleeding had made its appearance. Disappointed at the timing and the knowledge that she wasn't carrying a child, she went to find the men.

They were pitching clean straw into the horses' stalls and looked up when she entered. "Are there any old pillow slips or sheets I may use?"

She could tell by the puzzlement on her husband's face that he had no idea what she was about. She sighed. A woman's monthly wasn't something to be publicly discussed, especially with men, and she was embarrassed by the reality of having to do so, but she had no supplies. Charlie, however, took one look at her and set aside his pitchfork.

"Come on," he said. "I've some slips you can use."

"Thank you."

Ian still appeared confused, but she didn't enlighten him and followed Charlie out of the barn.

Later with everything in place, Maggie crawled into bed. Lying down was a luxury. Usually life forced her to endure the awful cramping and pain that accompanied her time of the month because her employers didn't care if she wasn't feeling up to par. Wood still had to be chopped, floors swept and mopped, along with all the rest of the duties she was being paid to perform. This, however, was heaven.

Charlie looked in on her once she was settled. "How're you doing?"

"I'm doing well, thank you."

"Brought you something that might help."

It was a warm toddy made of unknown ingredients but it tasted good and slightly alcoholic. "What's in this?" she asked, using a spoon to stir the concoction he'd brought on a saucer and tray.

"Little bit of this and that, and a splash or two of spirits. I used to make it for my third wife. Or was it my fourth?"

She gave him a weak smile.

He made her drink it down. "You should have another one in a couple hours."

Because of the way her head was pleasantly floating, she wasn't sure if she should agree. "Is Ian about?"

"He's out in the hallway pacing like a puma. Should I send him in?"

"Please." The toddy was coursing through her

body that now seemed to be floating as well. "I think I'm getting tipsy."

He grinned. "Maybe less whiskey next time?"

"I think so."

"Okay. I'll send him in."

Charlie left and Ian came in. He sat down gingerly on the edge of the bed. "How are you?"

"Charlie and I think I'm tipsy."

He chuckled.

"He's going to use less spirits in my next dose." Her voice turned serious. "I'm sorry there's no baby."

He caressed her brow. "Quite all right, we'll work on fixing that once you're ready."

"And our wedding night."

"That, too."

"I wanted to wear my new peignoir."

His eyebrow raised. "You have a new peignoir?"

"Yep. Bought it at Bethany's shop. It's black and has two little roses instead of frogs. You'll like it."

"I'm sure I will."

"Can I ask you something?"

"Sure?"

"Why didn't you come in earlier?"

"My mother and Tilda used to lock themselves away during their times of the month, so I didn't think you wanted me here."

"Silly man. I always want you here."

She saw amusement in his eyes.

"What's so funny?"

"You, precious one."

"I like hearing you calling me that. You're pretty

precious yourself, and you looked very handsome when you came to get me at Bethany's. I think she wanted to steal you."

"I think you should get some sleep."

"No. I'd rather talk to you."

"Then how about I tell you a bedtime story?"

"I'd like that."

He sat silent for a long moment and began. "Once upon a time there was a beautiful Scottish princess who fell in love with a man of the sea. He couldn't stay long with her, so before he sailed away, he left her a gift—a curly-haired son."

She stilled.

"Her father the king was very angry when he found out what the princess had done and banished the princess and her son from his lands forever."

Maggie searched his eyes. This wasn't what she'd been expecting and because of that the tipsiness fled. "Where'd they go?"

"To the largest city in the realm, but the princess knew nothing about living away from the castle. She didn't know how to cook, or how to find a new place to stay, or even where to start, so she traded on the only things she had, her beauty, her lovely singing voice, and her wit."

He paused for a moment and she could tell he was reflecting on the past. "But she and her son still had to struggle, so she learned how to slip away in the middle of the night when she had no funds to pay the landlords, and how to steal food, pick pockets, and cut purses, and she taught her son the same so they could eat and not have to sleep outside in the gutters in the rain and snow."

"Oh, Ian," she whispered.

"Life got better after a while. The princess found a very powerful protector who took them in. He loved her very much and because he had a kind heart, he sent her son away to school."

"That was nice of him."

"But the son didn't like it there because the other boys laughed at his curly hair and each night after prayers, they beat him and kicked him and dragged him from his bed to tie him to trees and force him to eat mud, and poured coal oil over him so he'd look like the night."

Tears filled her eyes.

"But he got taller and stronger and began to fight back. He became so successful at seeking revenge on his tormentor that he was expelled and told not to return. The princess and the protector were understanding and let him finish his studies with them."

His eyes swung to Maggie and held hers for a long moment. "Then the son went to America, and there he found a princess of his own. She had no parents, and had spent her life on her knees scrubbing and begging and being kicked and called terrible names, and he asked her to be his wife."

He reached out and brushed away the tears on her cheeks. "And she said yes, and made the son happier than he'd ever been in his life."

Maggie covered his hand with hers and said softly, "And they lived happily ever after."

He brought her fingertips to his lips and kissed them. "Yes."

"I'm glad the story has a happy ending."

"So am I." He leaned down and kissed her. "Now, get some sleep, princess. I'll be beside you when you wake up."

"Promise?"

"Always."

So Maggie slid back beneath the bedding, and he doused the lamp on the nightstand and left her alone. Lying in the silence, she thought back on the story. It had given her many of the missing pieces she'd been curious about and now that she had them, one thing was crystal clear: she would love the multifaceted Ian Vance with all her heart for the rest of her life.

When Ian returned to the front room, Harper July was standing by the hearth taking off his gun belt.

"Welcome back, Ian. You were gone so long I thought you'd gotten yourself abducted by one of those Scottish lassies."

"Good to be home. You look bushed."

"I am. Chasing rustlers. What is this I hear about you and a wife? Is she a Scot?"

"No. Black and Kaw."

"Really? Probably beautiful then."

"I think so. Which means you'll have to find somewhere else to hole up until Vivian lets you back in."

"Charlie told you?"

"Yes."

He sighed. "Most hardheaded woman I've ever met."

"You cheated on her?"

"Not in the physical sense."

"Did you tell her that?"

"Tried. I came home after three days of being in the saddle chasing rustlers. I wanted a bath, my dinner, and my wife, not necessarily in that order. She wasn't home. I got my dinner, took a bath, went to town to find her, only to be told she was in Cheyenne at some kind of women's rights meeting. Went back home, got up the next morning, rode to Cheyenne, and after finding her was told, 'I'm busy right now, Harper. I'll be home in a couple days.' "

Ian shook his head.

"I missed my wife. Been missing her since the day she was elected mayor. Call me selfish but I don't like sharing. So I went and had some drinks with Charlene."

"At the cathouse in Laramie?"

"Yeah. How Vivy found out, I don't know, but she did. Next I know, we're arguing, she's crying, I'm swearing. She told me I was no longer welcome, and I left."

Ian felt sorry for his friend. As Charlie'd said, Harp and Vivy loved each other like the mountains loved snow. Ian hoped they'd be able to come together and recognize that before it was too late. "So now you're divorced?"

"Yep."

"I'm sorry."

"Me too."

"Tell me about Draper."

"He's trying to take advantage of all the ranchers caught short by the blizzard last year and loaning them the money they need to start over."

The blizzard of 1888 killed most of the cattle on the plains. From Kansas to Wyoming they froze to death. Many ranchers were now scrambling to rebuild their herds. "How are the big associations responding?"

"For the most part ignoring him. He can't possibly make a move on them, they're bigger, stronger, and better armed, and they know it. So he's putting pressure on the smaller ranches, hoping to convince them to join him because they'll owe him for bailing them out."

"I ran into one of his hired guns today. Man by the name of Pratt Ketchum."

"Met him. How do you know him?"

Ian explained.

Harper sighed. "Wonderful. That's all we need, a madman."

"Who else is on Draper's payroll?"

Harper recited the names, but they weren't men Ian was familiar with.

Harper added, "Draper has this idea that after he consolidates all the small herds, he's going to drive them up to the rail lines in Canada because the big associations have the southern routes into Laramie and Cheyenne in their pockets. He's already got his route in mind, too. And guess whose land his main drive will have to go through?"

Cattle needed water on a drive and Night Hawk

was one of the few ranches with fresh water flowing through it. "Mine."

"Yes, so it's a good thing you're back."

Ian thought so, too. "Whose side is Tom Benton on?"

"His own as usual, but Draper needs Tom's support. He knows Tom hates the big boys and if Draper could get him on board that would be a tall feather in his cap. But we know Tom's not stupid. He's sticking to his guns, and Draper's not happy. Henny thinks her father should throw in with Draper, too. Draper has her convinced the profit will be higher than what she and Tom are getting now down in Laramie." Harper studied Ian for a moment. "Henny know you're married?"

"Yes, she was here to welcome me home."

"That must've been a scene."

"My wife, Maggie, handled it well. Henny didn't. I wound up riding away from her."

"Looks like it's going to be an interesting summer."

"Sure does."

"I'll move my gear out in the morning. Guess I'll have to start sleeping in my office."

"Or work on getting your wife to change her mind."

"The mountains will dance first. I'm going to bed."

"See you in the morning."

Alone, Ian sat and thought back on what he'd learned from Harper. No one knew anything about Draper before he showed up in the county three years ago, except he claimed to be from back East. Wherever his origins, he'd arrived with enough money in his pockets to purchase a good-sized portion of land. Not as much as Ian owned, or Henny's father, Tom Benton, whose land stretched almost to the Wind River mountains, but enough that he figured he should have a say in what went on politically and economically. Many of the neighboring ranchers disagreed, mostly because Draper didn't know beans about cattle or horses. He claimed to know money, however, and had talked a few locals into investing in some enterprises he had a hand in. Ian had no idea how that turned out because he hadn't invested a dime and had no plans to alter his position. Last winter's blizzard had left folks vulnerable to smooth talkers like Draper, especially when that talk had money dangling on the end of it like bait on a line. He decided to put Draper out of his mind. Whatever Draper and Pratt Ketchum were up to would eventually come to light, so he'd face it then.

Ian stepped out onto the porch and looked up at the stars. He was glad to be home. No more trains, or too small beds, or bad food, or hunting down men like prey. For the first time in years he felt at peace, and knew that a lot of that feeling was rooted in the small, feisty jewel sleeping in his bed. He felt so blessed to have found her. Nothing before had ever moved his heart as forcefully as she'd done. It hadn't been his intention to tell her his story in the way that he had. Once he started he couldn't stop and the dregs of bitterness that had been festering inside bubbled up and now seemed drained away. He'd shared details of his school life he'd never shared with anyone else, not even his mother. Now, however, Maggie knew what he'd endured, who he was, and how he'd come to be the man she'd agreed to marry. He felt cleansed and freed of the demons that had perpetually stalked his soul since that part of his life. Maggie had listened and she'd wept just as he had done night after torturous night. So he would reward her for what she'd given him by loving her with every breath he took, and with every beat of his heart for as long as he lived. A verse from Solomon filled him: *Set me as a seal upon thine heart, as a seal upon thine arm: for love is strong as death.*

Ian took one last look at the stars and went inside.

Chapter 22

Ian awakened at dawn to the ringing of an axe. He figured it was Charlie, so he reached out to pull Maggie closer but she wasn't there. Groggy and confused, he sat up. Thinking she might be down the hall taking care of her needs, he waited. No Maggie. He waited longer. No Maggie. The axe continued to punctuate the air and then something occurred to him that made him toss the bedding aside and quickly drag on his denims and boots. With his union suit covering the upper portion of his body he headed to the kitchen.

Charlie was standing at the back door looking out at the yard. He had his blue tin coffee mug in hand.

The axe rang again.

Charlie turned to Ian with an amused look on his face.

"Tell me she's not out there chopping wood."

"Too early in the morning for telling lies, so come look for yourself."

Ian did and sighed at the sight of her swinging the axe with an authority and precision no woman her size should be able to display.

Charlie saluted her efforts with his mug. "Girl's been cutting wood a long time from the looks of her. Good at it, too."

"Why didn't you stop her?"

Charlie gave him a look. "I couldn't even handle her at dinner last night. I'm not arguing with her while she has an axe in her hand."

"I see your point."

"So go on out there and disarm her and I'll get breakfast started. Unless she's hell-bent on doing that this morning, too."

"Where's Harp?"

"Already up and gone."

Ian got coffee to fortify himself for the confrontation to come, then, cup in hand, stepped outside.

"Morning, Maggie."

The smile she shot him could have doubled for summer sunshine. "Morning." The axe came down again. She expertly split the large cord of wood and worked the blade free.

"May I ask what you're doing?"

"Making jam," she tossed back. "What's it look like I'm doing." The axe split the wood again.

He smiled over the rim of his cup. She was dressed in her denims and one of the shirts she'd picked out in Cheyenne. The sleeves were rolled up past her elbows. "Let me rephrase the question. Why are you making jam?"

She stopped and wiped the perspiration from her brow. "Are we about to have another conversation about what I can and cannot do around here?"

"Afraid so."

She sent him a mock snarl.

"You want coffee first?"

"Please."

When he returned, he handed her a cup. "How are you feeling?"

"Fine, as you can see, which is why I'm out here."

"I understand that, however, you have two strong men at your beck and call now. You no longer have to be up before the sun doing chores."

"And suppose I want to be up doing chores before sunup?"

There was a light of humor in her eyes that Ian found irresistible and he knew he was going to lose the argument because he loved her entirely too much to deny her anything, even chopping wood before dawn. "Shall we compromise then?"

"I'm listening."

"Suppose we divide up the duties and you chop wood, say, one day a week."

"Make it two and we have a deal, Marshal."

She hadn't addressed him that way in a while and the sound of it made him remember all the wonder and commotion she'd introduced him to. "Two days it is."

"That was easy," she said, smiling.

Amused by all that she was, he decided he was going to have to find something for his princess to do, like build a school for her to teach in. He brightened inside. That would certainly give her plenty to do besides chopping wood. "Give me a kiss."

She did and once they both saw stars, she said, "We should argue more often."

He laughed out loud.

After breakfast, Ian rode off to talk with Tom Benton about the Draper business and to catch up on what else was going on that he might need to be aware of. Maggie and Charlie were planning to spend the day turning the dirt in the spot where she wanted to put her flower garden, so he left them to their work.

As soon as he departed Maggie and Charlie got to work. The ground had been softened by a bit of rain last night, so getting the soil ready was an easy task. They'd been working a little over an hour when Henny rode up.

Charlie groused as she walked up, "What do you want?"

"I'd like to talk with Maggie if I might."

Maggie stopped what she was doing and wiped at the perspiration on her brow. Henny looked distastefully at her dirty clothing and face but Maggie was too happy about putting in her garden to be intimidated by the opinion of a woman whose opinion didn't matter. "What can I do for you?"

"I've decided to have a dinner party to introduce you to the community."

Maggie pushed the shovel into the dirt and turned the soil over. "I think that's very nice of you." Maggie wondered if Henny had come to terms with Ian's marriage and was offering to host the gathering as an olive branch, or had something else in mind. Maggie thought it might be the latter. "When will this be?"

"On Saturday."

That was only a few days away. "Isn't that short notice?"

"No. People always drop whatever they have planned to attend my parties."

Charlie was digging nearby and Maggie saw him roll his eyes.

"If Ian agrees, we'll come."

"Do you have something appropriate to wear? If not, I may have something you can borrow."

In response to the condescending tone, Maggie bit down on her temper and asked, "How fancied up do I need to be?"

"Very fancy. My father lives in a very elegant home."

"Then I'll be sure to wash my feet."

Charlie laughed out loud.

Maggie turned his way and asked innocently, "What's so funny? Don't people here wash their feet when they get gussied up?"

Charlie was bent over and there were tears of mirth in his eyes. She turned to Henny, who didn't appear to find Maggie's words funny at all. In fact she appeared to be slightly mortified. "What time should we arrive?"

"Six."

"If Ian and I decide to come we'll be there. If we don't show, you'll know we decided to stay at home."

Henny's eyes narrowed. "I'm not hosting this for you not to make an appearance."

"I'll keep that in mind. Anything else? Charlie

and I really need to have this done before the heat of the day arrives."

"No."

"Nice seeing you again."

Henny apparently didn't share the sentiment because without a word, she strode back to her horse, mounted up, and rode away.

Watching her disappear, the pleased Maggie asked Charlie, "How'd I do?"

"Superb, madam. Simply superb."

Later, after stopping for lunch, they were just getting back to work when Maggie saw a wagon rolling towards the house. "Who's that?" she asked Charlie.

He looked out at the nearing vehicle and smiled. "Little Dove and her boy, David."

"Little Dove? Is she Native?"

He nodded. "Arapaho. They live on the far edge of your land."

Maggie was surprised to hear herself referred to as a landowner but she supposed she was. The wagon neared and Maggie got a clearer view of the woman holding the reins. She looked to be about Maggie's age and the boy no more than seven or so. Both had the silky black hair most Natives were blessed with. Little Dove wore hers unfettered down her back and David sported the familiar bowl cut. She was wearing a man's dun-colored shirt and her son one of red plaid flannel. "Please don't tell me she's one of the remuda."

"She isn't. She's a friend."

"Hello, Charlie. How are you?" Little Dove

asked while getting off the wagon. She held her son's hand so he could jump down to the ground. Once there he grinned up at her. The Arapaho woman glanced Maggie's way and stopped with a look of mild surprise.

"Hello, I'm Maggie, Ian's wife."

Her surprise spread into a smile. "So, the Night Hawk has taken a wife. I'm Little Dove and this is David, my son. We're very pleased to make your acquaintance."

"Thank you. Hello, David. Nice to meet you."

"Nice to meet you, too," he replied shyly. He then turned to Charlie. "May I go and see Jack, Charlie?"

"Ask your mother first."

He turned pleading eyes her way and she placed an affectionate hand on his hair. "Go, but just for a minute. We can't stay long, and no pestering Smoke."

"I won't."

Before he could run off, Charlie said, "Hold on, Davey. Let's you and me find some carrots for Jack. We'll let the womenfolk visit."

They headed around to the back of the house.

"Would you like to come in?" Maggie asked. The woman was eyeing her with what appeared to be muted delight.

"That would be nice. Thanks."

"Would like some cold water or lemonade?"

"No, but I appreciate the hospitality."

They took seats in the front room. The bear head on the wall growled silently.

"May I ask why you call him Night Hawk?"

"When my husband and I left the reservation, we hid out in the mountains. Your husband would bring us food and supplies most times in the middle of the night. Like the night hawk of nature we rarely saw him, but he always seemed to know where to leave whatever he'd bring so we would find it."

Maggie marveled at yet another aspect about Ian that she didn't know. She wondered if she'd ever know all that he was.

"He's a good friend. May I ask you a question now?"

"Of course."

"Who are your people?"

"I'm Kaw on my mother's side and Black on my father's."

"Kaw and Arapaho were enemies, but we can't afford to hold on to the old grudges. I hope we can be friends."

Maggie nodded. "I don't know anyone here besides Ian and Charlie, so I'd like that."

Then Little Dove leaned forward and asked with a twinkle in her black eyes, "Now that we're friends, how mad was Henny Benton when Night Hawk brought you home? I'm betting she could've bitten the head off a rattlesnake."

Maggie fell back against the sofa laughing. Little Dove grinned. Maggie knew then and there that she was going to enjoy calling Little Dove friend.

Maggie enjoyed the visit. Because of their shared heritage and tribal experiences Maggie felt a deep connection to her. They talked about the ongoing predicaments faced by the Native tribes, and Little Dove's experiences at Carlisle Institute, the Native boarding school in Pennsylvania.

"I enjoyed the learning," she said, "but not the beatings we received to whip the Native out of us. In many ways the place was horrifying."

Thanks to Maggie's father, she'd been able to avoid the assimilation schools like Carlisle but many Native children and their families weren't given a choice. "So does your son go to the school here?"

"What school?"

"Ian said there's a school here. I'm supposed to lead the classes."

"There's no school, Maggie. Was he courting you at the time?"

Maggie thought back. "I suppose you could say that."

"Then that explains it. Men will say anything when they find themselves in love."

Maggie was no expert on men, but she thought that sounded like a fair reason. Ian had never gone out of his way to lie to her before. She'd talk to him and get it straightened out and then he was going to build her a school. "After Ian builds the school . . ."

Little Dove smiled and nodded knowingly. "It's only fair, I think."

"Will you send David?"

"Yes, I'm teaching him at home presently but a real schoolhouse would be wonderful."

Then Little Dove had to go. Maggie noticed she hadn't mentioned anything else about her husband or even his name. She found that curious but felt it would be rude to ask. Charlie and Ian would know so she saved her questions for them.

She walked her new friend to the door. "It's been my pleasure meeting you."

"I feel the same."

"How far away do you live?"

"About an hour's drive."

"Then we will have to get together again, soon."

"I'd like that."

They walked outside and after finding her son and helping him back up onto the wagon seat, Little Dove waved and drove away.

Charlie said, "Did you like her?"

"I did. Very much. She will be a good friend, I'm thinking. Is she married?"

"Widowed. She lost her husband to tuberculosis, four years back. He caught it on the reservation. She couldn't go see him once he got sick because she didn't want Davey to catch it. He died without her."

That saddened her. "What was his name?"

"Walks Like Smoke. He was a great man to her and to his people."

"Thank you for telling me."

When Ian returned later that afternoon, he was distressed by what he'd learned from Tom Benton and some of the small ranchers. Fences were being cut and there'd even been a series of arson fires of outbuildings. So far, no one had been injured, and no knew who was behind the incidents but Draper had been offering protection for a price to those being targeted. Benton was convinced Draper was involved. Ian thought so as well.

Maggie was seated in the rocker on the porch when he rode up and her welcoming smile touched him inside as it always did. "How'd your day go?" he asked as he stepped up on the porch.

"Very well. Charlie and I worked on the garden. Henny came over to invite us to a party she's throwing for us on Saturday, and Little Dove and her son stopped by for a short visit. She's very nice. We've agreed to be friends."

"She's a good person and you couldn't ask for a better friend."

"Charlie told me about her husband."

"Those were very sad times. We were all affected by his death, but she's held up well."

"She also told me why she and her husband named you Night Hawk. I was wondering how the ranch got the name."

He smiled.

"So, how was your day?" she asked.

He told her what he'd learned from Henny's father, Tom, and his concerns about Draper's possible involvement.

"So he wants folks to pay to have their property protected by that scary-looking Pratt Ketchum?"

"Yes."

"I'd want protection from him."

"True. So far no one has been injured in any of the fires and we won't know until roundup if any of the cattle are being impacted, but in the meantime, Charlie and I will set up night watch to keep an eye on things around here."

"Do you have any plans for this evening?"

"Other than kissing you on and off, no."

"Then in between can we ride out to see the school?"

Ian froze.

She waited and rocked.

"Um." There was a glint in her eye that gave him pause. "You know, don't you?"

"Know what?" she asked innocently. She rocked some more.

Ian hung his head. "How angry are you?"

She shook her head. "Not at all because I know you're going to build a school and have it ready before summer's done."

"You're right."

She chuckled. "I love the way we argue."

"So do I. May I trouble you for a welcome home kiss?"

"No trouble at all."

She came to him, and after a series of searing kisses Ian held her tight. "My apologies for not telling you the truth. Not sure what came over me. I've never done anything like that before."

"It's all right. As long as your feelings for me are true, I have no complaints."

He squeezed. "As true as the spring rains. I'll start building in the morning. How much longer do we have to wait for our wedding night?"

"A couple of days. By the party Saturday night, I should be able to put on my peignoir and watch your eyes pop out."

"That won't be the only thing popping out."

She laughed. "Can't wait."

After dinner, Ian asked, "Want to go riding with me?"

"Of course."

They left Charlie to his own devices and drove away.

"Where are we going?"

"On a hunt."

"For what?"

"Secret."

Maggie took hold of his arm and placed her head against his shoulder. "Gold?"

"Secret, remember?"

They drove a bit farther and stopped along the road in a place that was nearly grown over in shrubbery, tall aspens, and pines. The surroundings were so quiet only birdsong pierced the silence. "Why are we stopping here?"

He hopped down from the wagon and took two shovels from the bed. "You coming?" he asked.

Smiling and slightly confused, she left the wagon seat and joined him. He handed her a shovel. "Follow me."

Maggie did as he asked. They waded into the foliage beside the road and after walking a half mile or so, he stopped. She did, too, and looked around. What she saw made her drop her shovel and bring her hands to her mouth. Lilacs. Everywhere. She was surrounded by what appeared to be acres of the plants growing wild and covered with blooming purple and pink spears.

Maggie had never seen such an enormous array of sizes and colors. The air was thick with the sweet smells.

"Thought you might like to help me dig up a few for us to replant near the house."

She'd held lilacs on their wedding day. "You remembered." Emotion made her throat thicken.

"I'm your husband. I'm supposed to."

Maggie's eyes were filled with love. She embraced him strongly. "Thank you, so much." She was certain she had the most perfect husband in the whole wide world.

They chose two small stands to take back, and when they returned home, she and Ian and Charlie planted them on either side of the front steps. Over time they'd spread in front of the porch, and Maggie couldn't wait for next spring to watch them bloom and enjoy the fragrant scent fill the air.

Chapter 23

The evening of the party, a very pleased Maggie studied her reflection in the large mirror in her bedroom. When Denver dress shop owner Bethany Adams insisted Maggie buy a fancy gown, Maggie had protested, but now she was glad the shopkeeper had been so adamant. She thought she looked real fine in the elegant, ice blue gown. She'd pinned her hair up, added a bit of the face paint she'd purchased from Bethany's hairdresser, and was now ready to go out and meet Ian waiting for her in the front room. Ideally, she'd have some jewelry around her bare throat and in her earlobes, but having none didn't deter from how wonderful being dressed up made her feel. More important, she was finally free of her monthly, and hoped tonight she and Ian would have the chance to have their wedding night and officially consummate their marriage.

"You look beautiful," he said, when she entered. "Where did you get that dress?"

Charlie glanced up from his newspaper and his eyes popped. "Oh my."

She twirled slowly to give them the full effect. "From Bethany's store in Denver. Henny was worried I'd not have an appropriate gown."

Charlie said, "When she sees you she's going to choke."

Maggie hoped so, but it was Ian's response that meant the most and he was viewing her with a subtle delight that put heat in her blood.

On the carriage ride to the Benton home, Maggie wondered how the evening would go. She was looking forward to meeting Ian's friends and neighbors and was hoping to have an enjoyable time. There were butterflies in her stomach, however, mainly because she had little experience rubbing shoulders with people of wealth and she didn't want to say or do anything that might embarrass her husband. He on the other hand appeared to be as confident as always. He was wearing a dark gray suit, a nice shirt, and yet another fine hat. He had a closetful, she'd discovered. Having met him as Vance Bigelow, the duster-wearing marshal and bounty hunter, it was taking her a bit to reconcile that persona with this Ian Vance's impeccable style and taste. This was yet another layer to the man she'd married. "How long have you known the Bentons?"

"Tom bought in here about six years ago."

"I was under the impression that he and his daughter had lived here a long time."

"No. He made his money in the mines and started buying up open range. He used to live down in Laramie but liked the country here so much, he moved here."

"What's he like?"

"He can be bullheaded sometime, but he isn't mean-spirited."

"And Henny?"

"Likes having her way. Tom lost her mother to cholera when Henny was small, and he admits to spoiling her ever since. When they first moved here, she'd just come back from a fancy girls' school out East."

"I appreciate her giving us this party."

"It is nice of her, considering how mad she was when she met you."

They arrived a short while later, and Maggie noted all the wagons, buckboards, and carriages parked on the long gravel drive that led to the house. The imposing mansion with its mixture of stone and timber was three times the height of Ian's and appeared to be ten times larger. Windows with sparkling panes fronted the three levels and the long front porch was anchored by matching stacked stone columns. The Benton home was an unexpected architectural beauty.

"What a beautiful place," she said to Ian as he helped her down. Adjusting her shawl, and holding her little silk clutch bag, she followed him up the walk. Maggie had never worn a pair of evening slippers before and could feel the finely raked gravel against the thin soles. Ian offered her his arm as they climbed the wide front steps. The sight of the well-dressed people spread over the porch made the butterflies take flight in her belly again, so she drew in a calming breath and straightened her shoulders.

Every eye was on them as they topped the stairs, and calls of welcome greeted their arrival.

With Ian making the introductions, she met the Barbers, who owned the trading post. The Hemmings, who lived over the ridge. She didn't know what ridge but she nodded and smiled. Next were the Fields; he was short and balding, she was much taller and stouter. She was named Jolene and had dyed red hair and cool eyes. They introduced their widowed daughter, Sarah Green, and the coolness in the eyes of the gangly young woman matched her mother's. Maggie had the impression that Sarah was a member of Ian's remuda.

"And where did you meet our Ian?" Jolene asked.

"Kansas."

"You're Indian, aren't you?"

"Yes, Kaw."

"Ah."

Before the interrogation could continue, a short, thin woman interrupted, and said, "Welcome to Wyoming, Maggie. Name's Georgina Reed but everyone calls me Georgie." She gave Jolene Fields a quelling look. Georgie's pale blue eyes were set in a sun-lined face that viewed Maggie warmly.

"Pleased to meet you, Georgie." This was the woman Ian had wanted her to board with before he asked Maggie to marry him, and Maggie sensed it would have been a good place for her to be.

"Ian, she is absolutely beautiful."

He looked down at Maggie fondly. "I agree."

"I'll bet Henny wanted to eat her saddle when you brought her home."

Maggie didn't say a word, but some of the people laughed uproariously in response to the elderly woman's outrageous words; Jolene and her daughter weren't among them.

Ian placed a gentle hand on the small of Maggie's back. "Let's go inside before Georgie gets us all tossed out. We'll see you later."

Maggie called back in parting, "Nice meeting you."

Georgie gave her a knowing wink.

Inside, the house was filled with people and the rounds of introductions began anew. Everyone was polite and seemed genuinely pleased to meet her, but there were so many that Maggie knew she'd have difficulty remembering which face went with which name until she got to know them better.

As Ian led her through the vast house in the hunt for their hostess, Maggie marveled at the expensive furnishings and decor, and did her best not to stare like a rube at the first crystal chandelier she'd ever seen hanging from the ceiling in someone's home. From talking to Charlie, she knew that Tom Benton had started life as a slave in Virginia. He'd certainly done well for himself since.

They found Mr. Benton holding court in a large sitting room that had expansive windows, a magnificent fireplace, and a billiards table in the center of the floor. On the wall above the grate hung a large oil painting of Henny dressed in a long-sleeved white blouse and snug brown leathers. She had a riding crop in her hand and such a serious look on her face. She looked like she'd strike anyone who neared. Maggie planned to keep her distance.

Maggie had expected Tom Benton to be as big as life, so she was surprised to be introduced to a fine-boned man of average stature who looked more like a professor than an influential mine owner and rancher. "Pleased to meet you, Mr. Benton."

"Pleasure's all mine," he said, bowing over her hand. "Ian, you did well."

"Thanks."

"Henny's been stomping mad since you returned and now I see why. Welcome to Wyoming, Maggie."

"Thank you, sir."

"No sirs allowed here. Name's Tom."

Maggie inclined her head. "I'll remember that." She found the kindness in his eyes a marked contrast to his daughter's haughty glares.

"I see you two have finally arrived," said a cool female voice behind them.

Maggie didn't have to turn to see whom the voice belonged to, but she faced her anyway. Henny was their hostess after all.

"Thank you for this lovely affair," Maggie said, taking the high road. Only then did she see the well-dressed man at Henny's side. He was White, and the proverbial tall, dark, and handsome. He met Maggie's eyes with an interest that she didn't return.

Henny raised her chin. "Ian, I'm not sure you and John have had an opportunity to see each other since you've been back."

"No, we haven't. How are you, John?"

"I'm doing. Is this your bride? Henny neglected to say how gorgeous you are, Mrs. Vance."

Ian said coolly, "Maggie. John Draper."

"Mr. Draper, nice to meet you."

"My pleasure."

Draper asked, "Vance, any more like her where she came from?"

"I'm afraid not."

"Pity." He was doing nothing to hide the interest in his gaze.

Maggie thought Henny looked so pent-up angry she might burst, but her voice was controlled when she said, "We'll be eating momentarily. John, there's someone in the parlor I'd like you to meet. Excuse us."

He bowed Maggie's way. "Hoping for a chance to chat with you again before the evening ends."

"You're very kind, but I'm sure our hostess wouldn't want me monopolizing your time."

"And neither will I," Ian stated.

Maggie hooked her arm in his and gazed up at him lovingly. "And neither will he."

Draper's face went cold.

Tom Benton smiled.

Henny's lips tightened. "Father, you may as well know that John has asked me to marry him and I've accepted."

Her father choked on his drink. Everyone

within earshot had stopped and was looking Henny's way.

"I'll be making the announcement during dinner. I've asked the help to bring some champagne out of the cellar."

Tom was studying Draper with hard eyes. He tossed back the last of his drink and asked, "She tell you that when I die, all my land goes to the U.S. government and my holdings to Ian here?"

Maggie felt Ian stiffen beside her and she wondered if this was something he hadn't known.

While Henny stared, Tom said to her easily, "Every stock certificate, every bond, title, and deed."

"That's ridiculous!" Henny snapped.

"No more ridiculous than you marrying this joker." Tom looked out at the staring guests and called to one of them. "Hey Sol, how about a game of billiards. Rack 'em up."

The heavyset Sol nodded and walked over to the table.

Before joining him, Tom said to his daughter, "I hope you and John will be very happy."

As he walked away Henny's mouth dropped and she stared up at her fiancé with wide eyes. Draper looked like he'd seen a ghost.

Ian gently covered Maggie's hand with his and said to the frozen couple, "Excuse us. I want to show Maggie the roses."

He led her away, and as they made their exit, the room buzzed with excitement.

Outside, Maggie remarked, "That was very interesting."

"Yes. Henny may want to rethink marrying Draper."

"Did you know about Tom's plan for his holdings?"

"No. I hope he was just trying to get Henny and Draper's goat."

The air in the garden was cool and sweet. They were behind the house and walking on a flagstone path that wandered through a small forest of red and yellow roses in full bloom. Here and there stone-rimmed circles in the ground held flower beds bright with lilies and daisies. The smell was incredibly fragrant. They nodded at some of the other people enjoying the sights, but Ian didn't stop until they reached the end of the path where a bower covered with more fat yellow roses stood. Beneath it was a stone bench.

They took seats and Maggie said, "I thought she wanted to marry you?"

He shrugged. "Guess she changed her mind."

"I guess so. Everyone seemed quite surprised. This is the same Draper causing all the commotion, correct?"

"Correct."

"Handsome, but a bit odious."

"Noticed that?" He glanced her way, smiling.

"Hard not to. The man was attempting to flirt with me with my husband standing by my side. Surely he doesn't believe he's that good-looking."

He chuckled.

"As her father said, I hope they'll be happy."

"I doubt that."

"So do I, and I don't know either of them."

"Are you enjoying yourself so far?" he asked, tracing her cheek.

"I am. Everyone's been very nice. I especially liked Georgie."

"She's a pistol and a true daughter of the territory."

"Is she a rancher, too?"

"Used to be, but now she just owns the land. Spends her days being outrageous and enjoying her position as the area matriarch."

"How long has she been here?"

"All her life."

"Is she a widow?"

"No, divorced a couple of times over the years."

"Ah."

They were interrupted by the sight of a well-dressed woman coming towards them. She was tall and bright-skinned, with chestnut brown hair that was elaborately curled and pinned to the top of her head. Her gown was a beautiful midnight blue and she was wearing round spectacles and a smile.

Ian stood and reached out to take her extended hands. "Hello, Vivy."

"Hello, handsome." She kissed him on the cheek and grinned Maggie's way. "Sorry for being so bold. You must be Maggie. I'm Vivian Palmer July."

Maggie stood and shook her hand. "Pleased to meet you."

"Welcome to our little corner of heaven, or hell depending on the day."

Maggie liked her.

Ian gestured her to take his seat.

She sat down and breathed in as if she'd been rushing. "I was afraid I was going to be late. I had a meeting earlier. Speaking of hell, what's this I hear about Henny getting herself engaged to the devil?"

Maggie really liked her.

Ian shrugged. "I'm as surprised as everyone else."

"I heard she was very upset about you and Maggie, but to marry a snake? Surely she doesn't believe that's going to upset you in any way."

"I don't know what she believes."

"How can she overlook Draper's reputation?"

"And the fact that his hired guns have been intimidating her neighbors."

Vivian shook her head. "She has plenty of education but little common sense." She stood. "Okay. I've caught my breath. I'm supposed to tell you two to come in for dinner but I wanted to meet Maggie first."

"It's been a pleasure," Maggie said, getting to her feet.

Ian gestured for the ladies to lead the way.

Chapter 24

True to her boast, Henny stood up after the main course and announced her engagement to John Draper. Ian took in the terse faces up and down the long table and wondered if anyone considered Henny's choice a good one. Tom sat in his chair at the head of the table and watched the proceeding with a sarcastic smile. As she held up her crystal flute for a toast, Henny appeared to avoid looking directly at her father, but he didn't seem to mind. While she spoke of having the grandest wedding in the state's history, Draper's smile looked forced and remained that way.

As soon as Henny sat, Georgie, seated to the left of Tom, asked, "I thought this was supposed to be a dinner to welcome Maggie Vance?"

Henny had the decency to look embarrassed before saying, "I'm sure Maggie and Ian don't mind me stealing their thunder for just a moment."

Ian said nothing, so Maggie cleared her throat. "Of course not. This is your home, after all."

Vivian stood. "A toast to Maggie and Ian. May their love endure like the mountains."

Thunderous applause punctuated by a male chorus of "Hear, hear," rose in response to her words. Maggie happily touched the edge of her flute to Ian's and they each took a sip.

After dinner, as was tradition, the men went out to the porch to enjoy their cigars and pipes while the women sat in the parlor to talk.

There was one woman with the men, however, and as Georgie lit her pipe, she asked Ian, "How've you been?"

He was standing with her and Tom.

"Well. Went to Scotland to visit my mother's grave which is why I've been away so long."

"Charlie told us," Tom said. "My condolences."

"Thanks."

John Draper walked up. "Mind if I join you all."

No one said anything.

Apparently Draper took that as a yes, and said to Ian easily, "I'd like to talk with you about the cattle association I'm forming."

"Heard about it. No thanks."

"At least hear me out?"

"And if I don't, you going to send your guns over to cut my fences or burn my outbuildings?"

"You got no proof I ordered that."

"No, but I do have proof that one of your hired hands was convicted of murder."

"He was looking for work, I hired him. He said you two had words."

"Words for now." Ian was sure it would be bullets the next time.

Draper asked coldly, "These good folks around here know about your other life?"

Georgie said, "That he's the bounty hunter Preacher Vance Bigelow? Yes we do. We have no problem with it, do you?"

Tom said, "Let me give you some advice, John. Drop this association idea. I'm not joining up, neither is Ian, and without us you have nothing."

Draper gave no indication that he planned to take the advice, saying instead, "I have a question, Mr. Benton."

"Yes?"

"Why would you make him your heir? Henny's your daughter."

Ian sensed everyone on the porch listening in.

Tom tapped ashes into the small ashtray he was holding. "Because I'm not leaving everything I spent my life building to a woman of unsound mind."

"Unsound?"

"No offense, but she has to be to marry you."

Ian saw Georgie smile around her pipe.

Draper looked between them. "Thanks for your candor. Excuse me."

He walked away stiffly.

Georgie cracked softly, "Bastard."

Ian agreed.

Georgie asked Tom, "Anything from the Pinkertons on him yet?"

"Still waiting."

Ian and Tom had discussed this earlier in the week. Tom had hired the Pinkerton Detective Agency to dig up what they could on Draper. If anyone could find the truth they could.

* * *

On the return ride home, Maggie sat close to Ian on the seat of the wagon. "I had a grand time."

"Good to hear it."

"I enjoyed meeting Vivian and Georgie."

"Both are one of kind in their own way."

"How long have she and Harper been married?"

"It would be a little over three years now, but she's divorced him."

"I didn't know that." Maggie had only seen Harper a couple of times before he moved out. So she'd had no idea that the couple were no longer married.

"It's sad that they aren't happy."

"Yes it is."

A crack of gunfire pierced the night. Ian threw himself on top of Maggie to shield her from the attack. Another shot rang out. The horses reared and Ian hissed with pain and slapped his hand over the sting in his shoulder. Another crack. Cursing, he forced Maggie lower while trying to ignore the bullet he'd taken and grab his Winchester from beneath the seat. In the silence that followed sounds of a horse moving away fast could be heard. Still shielding Maggie, he waited and listened. As the sound faded into the distance he slowly rose up. "Are you okay?"

"I think so." She was definitely shaken. She'd never been shot at before.

Seeing him holding his shoulder she asked with concern, "Were you hit?"

"Pretty sure I am. Stings like hell."

"Let me drive."

"No, we're not too far from the house. I can make it."

"If you bleed to death, I will bring you back to life just so I can kill you. Switch places with me, Marshal."

He smiled at that. "Maggie."

"Or if you bleed to death while we sit here arguing."

He sighed and did as he was told.

He had to vocally guide the way of course, but thanks to him and the bright moon, she had little trouble negotiating their passage.

As soon as the wagon cleared the gates, she began calling Charlie's name. Relief filled her to see him on the front porch when she pulled back on the reins to stop the team. "He's been shot!"

Charlie hurried around to Ian's side of the wagon.

Ian groused, "You two act as if this is something new. Do you have any idea how many times I've taken a bullet?"

Maggie replied, "Never on my watch, so hush, and let him help you into the house."

A short while later, Charlie had the bullet removed. Maggie cringed as he cauterized the wound with a hot iron. By the way Ian sucked in his breath when the iron seared his skin, she sensed it hurt as much as she imagined. Once he was bandaged up, she let out her pent-up breath. He on the other hand looked incredibly angry.

"Charlie, keep an eye out here. I'm going to go back and see if I can see any tracks."

"It's dark, may as well wait until morning."

"Maggie could have been hit!"

"I understand that, but if there's something to find, it'll be there when the sun comes up."

His face was mutinous.

"Listen to him, please," Maggie said. "Please. You should rest now."

"I don't need rest. I need to find the person who shot at my wife!" Contrary to the advice, he got up and walked outside.

Maggie shared a worried look with Charlie, who said, "He'll be fine soon as he stops being mad, but whoever did the shooting is living on borrowed time. Hope they know that."

Maggie hoped they did, too. She picked up his bloodstained coat and shirt. Between the blood and the bullet hole, both were ruined. "This was a nice coat."

"He's got more clothes than the king of England, don't worry about that."

Before being married, Maggie had never owned more than a few pieces of clothing at a time and as a result was frugal still. She considered his shot-up coat a waste of money and material. She hadn't thought about her own dress. She tried to look at the back of her gown where Ian had thrown himself on top of her in his attempt to protect her.

Charlie said, "You have a spot or two on your back."

"No!" she cried out and ran to the mirror in the bedroom. Twisting around, she saw a fairly large blotch of her husband's blood staining the gown. "Dammit!" The material was too fine to subject it to bleach or anything else. The idea that her very first fashionable gown was now ruined as well sent her temper up. She walked back out to find Ian. He and Charlie were on the porch.

"There's blood on my new gown and it's ruined, so when you find the person who shot at us, put an extra bullet in them for me, please." She sailed back inside.

Out on the porch Ian looked at Charlie. Her demand drained some of his anger and he chuckled. "That shooter better hope she doesn't find him before I do."

"Amen."

A few minutes later, Ian left Charlie on the porch and went to find Maggie. When he didn't see her he assumed she was in the bedroom, so he went in and closed the door behind him. She was in the process of laying her blue gown across the top of one of the chairs and was bent over with her back to him. Her hips were up and she was wearing a black little something that made every part of his being rise up and take notice. His arm was in a sling but as he continued to feast his eyes, his manhood alerted him that it wasn't injured in the least. "What are you wearing?"

She turned around and his eyes glowed at the black form-hugging, waist-length garment. The tops of her breasts were pushed up above the lace-edged bodice deliciously. "It's a French corset."

"Something else courtesy of Bethany?"

"Yes."

Ian knew she'd only purchased a few boxes' worth of items and he'd complained that she hadn't spent more. Now he realized that each small box apparently held the equivalent of a stick of dynamite. He couldn't wait to see what other surprises the boxes held.

"Do you like it?"

"Very much. Turn for me, please."

She complied, and all he could do was shake his head at the way the corset displayed her luscious behind. "Ever made love to a one-armed man?"

Giggling, she faced him again. "You are so outrageous."

"And I'll be topping that. This is our wedding night, remember?"

"You'll hurt yourself."

"I'll worry about that in the morning. Right now—walk your little self over here."

"Since you are a one-armed man, I'll take pity on you and save you some work." And as she closed the distance between them, she slowly and erotically undid the tiny hooks holding the corset closed. She opened it just as slowly, showing him everything he'd been aching to see and kiss and touch since the day they arrived at the ranch.

When she reached him she stopped. "How's this," she asked sultrily.

He ran his free hand over the soft, yielding flesh and teased the nipples until her eyes slid closed. "How's that?"

She whispered, "Wonderful."

Her hand found him and moved enticingly up and down his hard length. "How's this?" she purred.

He growled and eased her into his chest. Ignoring the fire in his shoulder, he pressed his lips to hers. Desire flared and their long awaited wedding night began.

Maggie couldn't tell where one sensation ended and the next one began. His loving drowned her in a shimmering pool of heat and passion that surpassed anything she'd ever experienced before. Kisses that stung her lips merged with the love-gentled bites on her nipples and flowed into his bold touches between her thighs that made her spread them wide like an eager courtesan. She had no recollection of when they moved to the bed because she was too busy running her hands down his strong back, and up and down his furred chest. He found her rose-tipped toes and after paying tribute there, worked his way up her thighs to make another set of petals bloom. She was on the verge of exploding when he pulled back and whispered hotly, "You'll have to ride me, darlin' . . ."

Maggie didn't have to be invited twice. From above she slid down with a longing and greed that made her clamp down on the rising climax, so she could savor the power of him hard and pulsing inside. He began to move and she responded uninhibitedly. Even with one arm, he was good, so much so that the first orgasm came quickly and with such commanding force she buried her screams in his good shoulder to keep from being heard in Denver. He came right behind her with a roar and a yell that filled the air in the dimly lit room.

They began again, and with that first orgasm

out of the way, they played, enjoyed, and did their best to send the other soaring. The haze parted for a moment and she found herself bending over the edge of the bed with him behind her pumping and driving in the exact same way he'd taken her on the train platform that night. She thought she might die from so much pleasure.

They stopped counting after the third orgasm. Lust, kisses, and thrusts soon became their entire world, and when they'd finally gotten enough, a zombielike Maggie stripped the sodden sheets off the bed, and they slept.

Chapter 25

Maggie awakened the next morning, groggy and disoriented. *Why am I sleeping on the mattress ticking?* As her brain wrestled with that, she realized she was in the bed alone. Last night's passionate activity floated back and she had the answer to the bedding question. She smiled. Not bad for a one-armed man. But where was he? She glanced at the grandfather clock standing stoically across the room and her eyes widened. It was nine A.M.! She should've been up hours ago, but that was the old Maggie complaining. The new Maggie, still preening from last night's lusty interlude, dismissively waved off the old self. All she wanted was to lie there and relive last night. That's when she saw the rifle laid across the chair and the piece of paper on the seat. Curious, she left the bed still wearing her gaping black corset and read: *Gone hunting. Back directly. Stay sharp. I.*

She was no longer groggy. Ian was out looking for the person who'd shot at them last night. The rifle meant Charlie had gone with him and she was in the house alone. She appreciated his faith in her ability to defend herself. Many husbands would have left Charlie behind to do the defending, but Ian must have needed Charlie's eyes and that made sense. She picked up the rifle, fed it some cartridges, and carried it down to the washroom to begin her day.

Clean and dressed, and with the rifle beside her, she sat in the rocker on the porch and ate her breakfast. Charlie had left behind scrambled eggs, bacon, grits, and biscuits, and she enjoyed every bite. She wondered how her men were faring, but thoughts of them fled when Lightning appeared out of seemingly nowhere and walked majestically over to the porch. "Where'd you come from, missy?" she asked with surprise and set her plate aside. "Good morning."

Lightning didn't respond, of course, but Maggie was bowled over by her presence. "If you're looking for Ian or Charlie, they aren't here. Someone took a shot at us last night and the bounty hunter is out prowling." Maggie realized that anyone hearing this would assume she'd lost her mind telling the story to a horse, but the mare seemed content to listen.

"Ian said you won't let anyone ride you, but Charlie said you're just waiting to be claimed by a lady. What do you think?"

To Maggie's wonder and delight the mare walked over to the porch and stuck her big head over the railing close to where Maggie was sitting. "Well, look at you." Maggie raised her hand very slowly and gently touched the sleek head. When Lightning didn't bolt, she stroked her between the ears. "Thank you for coming to see me. Did you know I was here by myself? Is that why you decided to pay me a visit?"

Lightning swung her head towards the road and Maggie saw a rider approaching. He was dressed all in black and had his mount reined to a walk. Pratt Ketchum. He didn't need to be any closer to be recognizable. A frisson of fear coursed through her, but she stared it down and raised the rifle. Lightning threw her head back and screamed out a loud challenge.

Maggie liked that. "Good girl. We don't want this cretin taking us lightly."

When Ketchum was within shooting range, she yelled out, "That's close enough, state your business!"

The ugly disfigured face smiled and he kept coming. Maggie fired a shot that tore past him near enough to widen his eyes.

"I said, close enough! What the hell do you want?"

That got his attention. She could see him studying her in a new light. That pleased her immensely.

"Heard somebody took a shot at your man last night. Mr. Draper sent me over to see if he needs help tracking the person who did it."

"Who told you he'd been shot at!" As far as she knew no one knew about last night outside of her and her men and the cowardly ambusher. She waited for Ketchum to answer.

"Mr. Benton told Mr. Draper."

"Bullshit! Get off my land before you need the undertaker!"

Maggie was two seconds away from blowing him out of the saddle. He might be a killer but he hadn't drawn his gun, and she and her rifle were primed and ready.

He raised both hands in a gesture of surrender. "Okay, little lady. Tell him if he needs help he knows where I am."

Maggie didn't reply, nor did she draw down. He tipped his hat and turned his horse towards the road. She watched grimly until he was out of sight and then a few minutes more to make sure he didn't circle back. When she was finally convinced he'd not be returning, she drew down and dropped back onto the seat of the rocker. Her hands were trembling as she set the rifle down. Lightning nudged her and Maggie stroked her affectionately. "Guess we showed him, didn't we, girl?"

But even as she bragged, she knew he'd be back. He'd tested her mettle and lost. She sensed he'd be better prepared when next they met.

Sound of rifle fire carries a long way across open land so when Ian and Charlie heard the faint report they both stopped. Gunmen also knew the sound and timbre of their personal weapons if they used them with regularity, and because Ian did there was no doubt in his mind that the rifle they heard was the one he'd left with Maggie. "Let's go."

Wheeling their mounts around the men rode hell-bent back to the ranch.

They arrived on the road to the house at a full gallop. From a distance they saw Maggie sitting on the porch. Ian was so happy to see her in one piece he didn't notice Lightning until a moment later. Filled with both joy and consternation he slowed Smoke to a walk and gave Charlie a puzzled look. "Is she reading Lightning the paper?"

Charlie laughed. "Looks like it from here."

Sure enough, when they reached the house, she set the paper aside and stood. "Welcome back. Catch anything?"

Ian shook his head. Before he could ask her about the gunfire they'd heard, she said, "Funniest thing. I was out here eating breakfast and she walked up and joined me. She's kept me company all morning." She stroked the mare's head. "Haven't you, lady?"

Ian and Charlie shared a look. "Did you fire the rifle?"

"Yes. Pratt Ketchum paid a visit and we had to convince him to leave."

Ian's jaw tightened. "Tell me what happened."

She did, and when she was done, Ian viewed her proudly through his anger.

Maggie said, "I think he was here fishing for an answer as to how badly you'd been injured."

"You could be right."

"Or he could've been telling the truth. Either way it was clear he didn't expect me to take a shot at him. Did he, girl?" she asked the mare.

Ian looked over to see Charlie with a bemused look on his face. Ian felt the same way. Her run-in with Ketchum notwithstanding, that Lightning was beside her and acting like a tamed house cat was beyond his ken.

Charlie asked her, "You think she'll let you ride her?"

"No idea."

"Would you like to try it?"

She studied the mare for a moment and shook her head. "Let me wait until tomorrow. I want to see what she does for the rest of the day."

Charlie nodded. "I think we have us a natural-born horsewoman here, Ian."

"Why am I not surprised?" His shoulder was flaring up, but he knew better than to say anything aloud about the pain for fear his rifle-toting wife would banish him to the bed. Alone. "We'll go unsaddle our horses."

She shot him a smile, and he and Charlie walked their mounts around to the back of the house.

The mare followed Maggie around for the rest of the day. Maggie rewarded her with pieces of dried fruit, soft strokes down her pure white blaze, and even softer conversation. Maggie was amazed. Ian and Charlie were even more so.

That evening as she and Ian lay in bed, Maggie asked, "What do you think Ketchum really wanted?"

"Not sure. I wanted to go to Draper's and ask, but Charlie convinced me otherwise. With this busted shoulder, I'd be no good in a fight of any kind."

She snuggled close. "I'm glad you listened. How's it feel?"

"Stiff and sore. I'll be fine in a couple of days."

"Last night probably didn't help."

He grinned. "Helped a lot, just not my shoulder."

"So you all didn't find anything?"

"Found some tracks but lost them eventually in the brush. Whoever it was was riding east."

"Is Draper's place east?"

"No, west and north of here."

"Ketchum rode in from the west. How did his face get that way?"

"Acid. The mother of one of the women he killed threw it in his face during the trial."

"Were you there?"

"Yes and I'm surprised he wasn't blinded. Everyone just knew he would be. It was a pretty ugly sight."

She imagined it must have been. She saw Ian roll his injured shoulder and wince. "What's wrong?"

"Thing's too tight. Charlie's got me bound up like it's broken."

"Do you want me to loosen it a bit?"

"Please."

They sat up and she carefully removed his union suit so she could get at the bandage. Once she had it unwrapped she saw there was no blood on it, so the cauterization had done the job, but the skin around the wound was red and angry.

"There's ointment in that silver tin on the dresser."

She left the bed to get it and opened the lid. The smell wrinkled her nose. "What's in this?"

"Who knows. It's one of Charlie's mountain man concoctions, but it takes the sting out, so it works, whatever it is."

Maggie put a bit of the pale greasy stuff on her fingertip and slid it over the wound. She wiped the excess on the bandage and rewrapped the shoulder. She was kneeling behind him to fasten it with a pin the way Charlie had done and noticed all the marks and scars on Ian's skin. "What are all these puckers?"

"Bullet wounds."

"All of these?"

He looked back at her shocked face. "Told you I'd been shot a lot."

"Ian, there have to be eight or nine of these. There's one here, and here. What's this?" she asked, fingering a long scar.

He peered down. "Knife wound. I've a few of those also but not as many as bullet holes."

Maggie was speechless. "They don't still hurt, do they?"

"Sometimes, but it's the price you pay when you live by the gun."

She thought about all the accumulated pain he must have endured, and then about the little curly-haired boy who'd been dragged from his bed. She placed her lips against each healed scar on his back, and then on the one behind his shoulder.

He whispered, "What are you doing?"

"Turning these into spots of love."

And as he sat, she continued to press kisses to all the places she could see. She flicked her tongue along the scars left by the knife wounds in his side and another that ran horizontally above his heart. With her fingers she tenderly touched the long scar on his cheek, and placed a soft kiss there as well. Looking into his serious eyes, she kissed his lips to let him know that from that moment on she'd always be there to share his burdens and salve his hurts.

The kisses deepened. He pulled her close and

for the second night in a row, Maggie was treated to a long night of love by her one-armed man.

Over the next few days, Ian continued to heal and Lightning showed up each morning to follow Maggie around like a besotted puppy.

The night after that, Charlie came around to the front porch where Ian and Maggie were sitting talking and said, "There's a fire west of us, looks like the Jeffers' place."

"Get the horses," Ian said, rising to his feet. He hurried inside to get his gun belt, rifle, and jacket.

By the time he returned, Charlie was back. Ian set the rifle beside Maggie, gave her a kiss, and they rode out.

It was the Jeffers' place. The barns were fully engaged and flames rose greedily towards the sky. Jeffers was an old man, and having lost his herd to last winter's blizzard he'd had to let his ranch hands go. As a result he and his wife were doing their best to fight the blaze alone. The fire was winning. Ian grabbed the full bucket of water from Mrs. Jeffers's hand. There were tears streaming down her soot-stained face but he had no time to offer consolation. He ran the bucket to the barn and splashed it against the burning door. The horses trapped inside were screaming. He spent a few precious moments trying to find a way in to save the terrified animals but the heat was too intense, so he ran back across the field to where Charlie was working the pump like a madman. It seemed an eternity before the water rose to the top. Once the iron bucket was full again, he sprinted as fast as he could back to the barn. His shoulder was in flames as well, but he ignored it and threw the water against the spot where he knew the horses were. He looked over and saw Harper beside him adding more water. There was no time to question his sudden appearance, there was too much to do.

But in the end, they had to give up. Two lone men didn't stand a chance against flames fed by the barn's wooden frame and the bales of hay and straw within. The cries of the dying horses tore open Ian's heart but neither he nor Harper turned away. Both stood there as if in tribute to the deaths and soon only the crackling roar of the flames remained.

As they walked back to the house Ian spotted old man Jeffers seated on the steps of the porch. He was gasping for breath and his wife was offering water from a cup with a trembling hand. Charlie came out of their front door carrying two blankets and placed one around each.

When the Jefferses were able to talk, Harper asked, "How'd it start?"

Caleb Jeffers shook his balding head. "I couldn't tell you. We were over in Casper visiting our daughter and the barns were blazing when we drove up."

Harper asked, "Any ideas on how it might have started?"

"Course not. You think I'da left my stallions in a barn I knew was gonna burn down? Only way it could've caught fire was if somebody set it on fire."

Ian and Charlie shared a nonspeaking look.

Olive Jeffers was known for speaking her mind.

"If you ask me it was that Draper, or one of his guns. He came to see us the day before we left to see Julia over in Casper."

"Does he do that often?"

"He's stopped by a few times in the last month or so."

"Why?"

She sniffed. "To offer us a loan. Said he wanted to help us get back on our feet. Then asked if we'd been having any trouble with our fences being cut. Caleb told him no."

Caleb took up the telling. "And he says to me that with all that's been happening lately, maybe I should have a couple of his hands ride my perimeter and keep an eye on things. Like maybe I can't shoot my own gun."

Olive added, "And we'd only have to pay him five bucks a month for the privilege of his protection."

Ian heard Harp sigh before saying, "Wish we had some solid proof."

Jeffers grumbled, "So do I. I loved those horses." He wiped his hand hastily over his eyes to keep them from seeing his emotion.

Ian was certain the screams would haunt everyone for some time.

Charlie asked, "You two want me to take you over to Georgie's for the night? You know she won't mind."

"We'll stay put," Jeffers said. "I may be getting old but I've never run from a fight and I ain't starting now."

Olive added, "Thank you boys for your help.

We'll be okay, but find some evidence, Sheriff, and get that skunk Draper out of here. This is God's country, not a place for the devil."

"Yes, ma'am. I'll do my best."

They stayed until the fire was completely out, and then by the light of the moon used axes and pitchforks to turn over what was left of the smoldering rubble to make certain it didn't flare up again. After adding more buckets of water to wet everything down, they waved good-bye to the couple and rode away.

"I was on my way back to town when I saw the smoke," Harper explained. "It's sad that he had to lose those horses."

Ian agreed. "So what next?"

"I'll drop in on Draper. He'll express his concern for the Jefferses, tell me he had nothing to do with it. I'll threaten him and then leave. I know the scene by heart at this point."

"Tom Benton said he's got Pinkertons sniffing out Draper."

"Let's hope they find something, but until they do, how about we meet at my office and talk about putting together some protection of our own? I'm sure most of the men around here would volunteer to take turns night riding to keep an eye on things."

"Good idea."

Charlie said, "Count me in."

"Thanks. I have to go up to the court in Casper in the morning, so let's make it day after tomorrow."

"I don't want to wait that long. I'll be rounding

up riders in the morning, that way when you get back, we'll be ready to ride."

Harper agreed. With a wave good-bye, he rode on to town.

Ian and Charlie rode for home guided by the moonlight.

They returned to find Maggie rocking on the porch in the dark with the rifle across her lap. "Was anyone hurt?" she asked.

Ian dismounted. "Jeffers lost his stallions.

Charlie took Smoke's reins and walked the two mounts around to the stables. Ian sat on the porch and told her the sad story. "Jeffers thinks Draper was behind it and so does Harp. He just can't prove it."

"I hope he'll be able to soon."

"So do I." He then told her of their plan to form a night patrol. "I'll be riding first thing in the morning."

Chapter 26

After breakfast, Ian rode away on Smoke and Maggie stood on the porch until they disappeared. Since the night of the ambush she worried about him riding alone. He was a celebrated bounty hunter, a former gunslinger, and a United States deputy marshal; the man could undoubtedly take care of himself, but he was also her husband and the love of her life. As his wife, she was concerned about his safety.

Charlie stepped out onto the porch and handed her a clean blanket. "Wrap this around yourself and wear it for a little while."

"Why?" It was far heavier than it looked.

"You're going to put it on your mare. If it has your scent, she might take to it better."

"We're going to try and saddle her?"

"May as well see."

Maggie agreed, so she placed the blanket around her like a wrap and sat in the rocker. It had become her favorite place to sit. She could view the endless sky, the snow-capped mountains, her newly planted lilacs; and savor the vast beauty that surrounded the place she now called home. She never wanted to leave Ian's Wyoming. Since the day her parents died, her life had been one hardship after another. Had finding him been her reward for all she'd had to endure? It certainly felt that way. For the first time since being on her own, there was peace in her heart. She was scared to spend too much time dwelling on how wonderful her world had become for fear it might be snatched away, and she'd find herself clawing and scratching all over again, but she had a good life, and she was very thankful.

The blanket had been around her shoulders for only a few minutes, but she felt like she was sitting inside a stove. "Charlie! How long do I have to wear this? I'm starting to melt!"

He came to the door. "Give it a couple minutes more."

She shot him a look.

"Okay, okay."

"Thank you." She dragged it off. "Lordy."

He chuckled. "Come on, let's go find her majesty. Here's some carrots."

They walked out to the pasture. Jack appeared and was rewarded with carrots from Charlie. Lightning was nowhere to be seen, so Maggie stuck her fingers into the corners of her mouth and let a whistle fly into the silence. Seconds later Lightning came galloping to her side and instantly began to nudge Maggie's neck.

Charlie shook his head. "I still can't get over this."

Maggie greeted the horse fondly. "Good morning, sweet pea. How are you?" Talking to her the entire time, she fed the mare a carrot, then unfolded the heavy blanket she was carrying. "Hold still now, honey and let me—"

Lightning neighed and stepped away.

"I just want to put this on you. It smells like me. See? Come give it a sniff."

The horse wanted no part of it, period. Maggie remained patient. She stepped closer. The mare stepped back. She glanced at Charlie. He shrugged.

"Okay, honey. How about we—?"

Lightning galloped away.

Maggie said, "Guess that was a no."

"Guess so."

"I'll try it again later."

But Lightning kept her distance for the rest of the day.

In the days that followed the arson increased. Ian and his night riders did their best with the patrols, but with so many ranches spread out over such a large area, it was impossible to catch the arsonist in the act. Maggie saw very little of him because he slept by day and rode all night. The patrols had about as much success as Maggie had with Lightning, which was no success at all.

One morning while Ian slept inside, Maggie was outside beating rugs when Little Dove drove up. On the seat beside her was Georgie Reed, the area matriarch. Maggie hadn't seen her since the night at the Bentons' and was honored by the unexpected visit.

"Morning, Maggie!" Georgie called out as Little Dove pulled back on the brake. "How are you on this hot as hell morning?"

Maggie grinned. "Hot as hell."

"I like a plain-speaking woman." She was wearing well-worn denims, a man's shirt, and a large-brimmed man's hat. It suited her so well, Maggie wanted one for herself just like it.

Georgie got down from the wagon, and aided by a wooden cane slowly made her way to the porch.

"What happened to you?"

She waved off the concern in Maggie's voice. "Damn horse backed over my foot. Doc says it's not broken, but for me to take it easy."

"She wanted to drive herself here, but I told her no," said Little Dove. Maggie could see the mock scolding in her new friend's eyes.

"Yeah, yeah, yeah," Georgie said, and eased herself into one of the empty rockers. "Where's that handsome man of yours, Maggie?"

"Sleeping. He just got home a few hours ago. Can I offer you a cold drink of water? Charlie's made fresh lemonade."

"Sure."

Maggie went inside. She was placing the drink-filled tumblers on a tray when Charlie came in the back door.

"Who's here?"

"Little Dove and Georgie."

"Oh."

The way he uttered the one word made her look his way. She knew he thought the world of Little

Dove so she assumed whatever was going on with him had to do with Georgie. "Do you and Georgie not get along?"

He didn't respond at first, then confessed, "Got along real well until we got married."

Maggie almost dropped the tray. "You two were married?"

"Yep, for a couple years, then she divorced me."

"How long ago was this?"

"Forty years, give or take a few."

Maggie was stunned and speechless.

"Go give your guests their drinks, before the 'ade warms up." That said, he went back out the door.

For a moment she stood there rooted in place. A dozen questions clamored to be asked, but she shook them off and carried the tray outside.

"The patrols are a good idea," Georgie declared, taking a drink from the tray, while Little Dove did the same. "Whoever's behind all these fires, and we know who it is, needs to be stopped, one way or another."

Maggie agreed, but she wanted to ask about what she'd just heard in the kitchen.

"But I didn't come here to talk about Draper. Came to talk about the school Little Dove said you'd been expecting to find. Something wrong Maggie?"

She didn't know whether to ask her questions or not. "I'm not sure. Charlie just told me you were married to each other at one time?"

A bittersweet smile crossed her face and she sighed. "Yes, but he the loved the trapping and the wrangling and everything else more than he did me. It was like trying to keep a puma in a cage, so . . ."

"I'm sorry. It was rude of me to say anything."

"No apology needed, my dear. You live here now. You were bound to find out sooner or later. He and I had some grand times, and then it was over."

Little Dove had a noticeable sadness in her eyes.

"Anyway, back to what I was saying. Since Ian and the rest of the men are too busy chasing Draper to put up a building right now, I'd like to offer the old house on my property as a temporary solution. We dearly need a teacher now that Vivy's the mayor."

"Where'd she hold her class?"

"In my parlor mostly. The old house was occupied back then, but the family moved down to Denver and the place's empty. Might as well put it to good use."

The offer was a surprising and much welcome one. There was no way of knowing how long Ian and the men would be on patrol and Maggie knew personally how busy they were; she and Ian hadn't slept together in over a week. "Does the house need repairs of any kind?"

"No. It's in fine shape. If you want to ride to my ranch with us and see it, Little Dove can drop you back here on her way home."

The idea of seeing where she would be teaching was too tempting to turn down. "How soon can we leave?"

"Whenever you're ready," Little Dove replied.

"Let me go tell Charlie."

Georgie said, "I haven't seen him in a while. Tell him I send my love. That ought to shake him up."

Maggie wondered if Georgie could possibly be still in love with him. Realizing she'd probably never know the answer to the question, she went to find him to tell him she was leaving. There was no need to wake Ian for such a trivial reason. Charlie would tell him where she'd gone.

She found him in the stables tossing clean hay. "I'm going with them to Georgie's. She thinks the old house on her property would be a good place for the school."

"Okay. I'll let Ian know when he wakes up."

"She also said to tell you she sends her love."

He paused in mid-stroke. "Did she now? Tell her I send mine back. That ought to get her."

Wondering what the heck was going on, and if this was some type of game the two former lovers played, she shook her head in confusion and left the stable to rejoin the women on the porch. Maybe Little Dove could help her with the answer.

The house in question was a little over an hour away by wagon and Maggie found it to be perfect. It was a small, two-story structure trimmed in gingerbread and painted pink. There was a pot-bellied stove in the front parlor, along with a fireplace that would keep the children warm during the winter months. The kitchen was small but adequate. Georgie suggested that Maggie consider using the upstairs bedroom as an office, and after seeing it she agreed. There was a stable near the house where the children could house their horses, and Maggie wondered if Lightning would ever be tamed enough for Maggie to make the journey to school on her back.

"Well, what do you think, Maggie?" Georgie asked.

"I think I'd like to start as soon as possible."

"Then that's what we'll do."

After all the riding and touring the house, it was easy to see that Georgie had tired, so they drove the short distance to her large, sprawling ranch house. She tried to invite them in for sandwiches and cake, but Little Dove had to pick up her son from her neighbor's place where he'd spent the morning playing, and Maggie wanted to get back to share her news about the school with Ian. So after making sure Georgie was comfortable, the two friends set out for home.

"So tell me about Georgie and Charlie?" Maggie asked.

"From what I can see, she still loves him. Not sure how he feels about her, but they're both pretty stubborn."

"Do you think there's a chance they'll reconcile?"

"No idea. You heard her say they've been apart for forty years."

"That's a long time." Maggie wondered how she and Ian would be in forty years' time. Still very much in love, she imagined. She also wondered which of Charlie's many wives Georgie had been.

"Her first, his second, I believe," Little Dove answered in reply to the question. "He gave her all the land she owns when they parted. At one time, Charlie owned more land around here than anyone. She married twice more. Both passed away leaving her more and more wealthy. She said she had to stop taking husbands because the more she married, the richer she became and she had no way to spend it all."

Maggie was surprised to hear about Charlie's past and his wealth.

When they reached Maggie's home, she gave Little Dove a hug. "Thank you for today."

"You're welcome, schoolmarm."

Maggie grinned. She watched the wagon ramble back to the road and hurried inside.

She found Ian in the kitchen eating and she recapped the morning's exciting turn of events. "That's great news," Ian replied. "Make a list of the supplies you'll need and we'll see about getting them purchased."

She'd made a mental list the moment she left the old house. She'd jot it down later. For the moment, she was focused on her husband. He looked so weary. She wondered how much longer it might be before the Draper business came to a head so he could get a full night's sleep again.

"I'm glad Georgie stepped in," he told her, "because I've no idea when I'd be getting around to building the school I owe you."

"I'll get my pound of flesh some other way."

"I miss sleeping with you."

"I miss you as well."

He sat her on his lap and gave her a kiss, which she responded to warmly.

"We have the house to ourselves, you know," he murmured while his hands began slowly roaming. "Charlie's gone into town for supplies and I'm no longer a one-armed man."

She giggled and said, "Race you!" And took off at a run.

"Cheater!"

He ran after her and caught her before she reached their bedroom door. Scooping her up, he carried her inside and closed the door behind them.

For the next few days, Ian rode night watch and Maggie spent her days over at her school. The former tenants had left their furniture behind so there was ample seating at the large dining room table for the children. Georgie helped spread the word about the school's scheduled opening and let Maggie know that there would be at least four children attending.

When she wasn't at the school, she continued her work with Lightning, who'd finally accepted the blanket. Charlie said it was because Lightning watched Maggie drive off in the wagon every morning and probably wondered where she'd been spending her days. Maggie had seen the mare standing by the house in the mornings but she wasn't sure she agreed with Charlie's theory, but he knew horses better than she and so she didn't argue.

The first day of school, Maggie was so excited, she could barely contain herself. According to Georgie, the four children belonged to Sarah Green, the daughter of the cool-eyed Jolene that Maggie met the day of Henny's party. The gangly woman drove up with the children in the wagon.

"Good morning," Maggie said to the children as their mother escorted them inside. "I'm Maggie."

There were two boys: twelve-year-old Nathan and five-year-old William. The two little girls were eight-year-old twins Hester and Hannah. Hester had a strawberry birthmark on her cheek, which helped Maggie be able to tell them apart.

While the children took seats at the table, Maggie asked their mother about their educational abilities. Nathan and the twins could read, but five-year-old William could not. In the middle of the conversation, Little Dove arrived, and in the wagon with her were David and two little boys Maggie had yet to meet.

Sarah drew back. "You're letting Indian children in the school?"

"Yes." Maggie waited.

"I want them taught outside away from mine."

"Then you should probably take your children home because I won't be separating any of my students by race."

Maggie could see Sarah trying to decide what to do, so she let her think it over while she went to greet Little Dove.

In the end, Sarah Green's children stayed and the first day began.

Chapter 27

Ian rode into Osprey at a slow pace. The few buildings that made up the town's center stood as testament to how small it was. It had started out as a trading post patronized by trappers, Natives, and mountain men. As more and more men drifted into the county to work the mines and lay track for the railroads, a saloon was built and then a boardinghouse and then a few houses. It now sported a barbershop, a mercantile, and a telegraph office that doubled as the office of the sheriff and the mayor. He'd come to town to meet with Harper and to see if there had been any fires overnight. There hadn't been any in the past few days and everyone was hoping that Draper was giving up. Ian didn't believe it.

When he reached the office he saw Vivy rushing off to her carriage.

She called, "Tell Maggie, I'll be by the school soon as I can to see how things are going. You two should come have dinner with me sometime soon, too."

Ian had yet to meet a busier woman than

Vivian Palmer July. If she wasn't in town, she was in Casper or Cheyenne or Laramie or driving hell-bent across the countryside taking care of the needs of her constituents. She was a stellar mayor, but he understood why Harper had gone to the cathouse for someone to talk to. Getting her honor to sit still was like trying to catch the wind.

Inside the office with Harper was Tom Benton. There was also a man wearing a suit that Ian didn't know, so Tom made the introductions.

"Ian, this is Walt Clark. He works for the Pinkerton Detective Agency."

Ian shook his hand. "Pleased to meet you."

Clark said, "Same here. You look familiar."

Ian had done work for the Pinkertons a few times in the past but he didn't try and spark the detective's memory.

Harper said, "Walt's got good news. Take a look at this."

Ian studied the face on the poster Harper handed him. "This looks like Draper."

The detective said, "We're fairly sure it is, but he's changed his name."

The name on the wanted poster was Harold Mann and he was wanted in Ohio and Pennsylvania for embezzlement. Ian smiled. "Are you here to take him back?"

"Oh yes. He may be wanted in Indiana as well, but I'm waiting on verification from our Chicago office."

Tom said, "Maybe this will make my daughter come to her senses."

"Let's hope," Ian replied. "When are you going after him?"

"Just as soon as the sheriff, Mr. Benton, and I leave here."

Harper asked, "Do you want to go with us, Ian?"

"Can you handle him without me?"

"Yep."

"Any open warrants on Ketchum?"

"No," Harper said, "but once Draper's taken into custody he'll probably head for the hills."

Ian hoped so. "Then if you have everything under control, I'm going to stop in the mercantile, grab some things Maggie and Charlie asked me to bring home, and head home to spend the rest of my years catching up on my sleep and being with my wife."

Harp grinned. "Enjoy yourself."

"I plan to. Nice meeting you, Walt. Thanks, Tom."

"You're welcome."

Ian walked down to the mercantile. After purchasing the items on his list he rode home a happy man.

John Draper aka Harold Mann was arrested without incident a few hours later, and everyone breathed a long sigh of relief.

Maggie spent the rest of the month of June teaching her students and enjoying her husband's company, especially at night. Lightning finally relented to having Maggie on her back, but only after an entire day of bucking her off as if to emphasize that she was still in control.

But after much fussing and cussing by Maggie in response, along with applications of Charlie's liniment for all the bruises she sustained in the falls, she and the mare became horse and rider and spent their days galloping across the countryside.

Maggie was riding Lightning home from school one day when she saw Henny Benton approaching on the road ahead. To her surprise, riding with her was Pratt Ketchum. Maggie planned to ride on by but Henny stopped. Rather than be rude, Maggie stopped to be neighborly.

"Well if it isn't our little schoolmarm," Henny said.

Maggie hadn't heard anything about Henny since Draper's arrest and like everyone else assumed that Ketchum had left town. Apparently not. She wondered if Ian was aware that the gunslinger was still around. "How are you, Henny?"

"I'm well. Say hello to Mr. Ketchum. He's working for me now."

Maggie gave the cold-eyed man with his disfigured face a terse nod.

"Oh, you can do better than that, especially since you're going to be together for a while."

Maggie went still. When she looked back at Ketchum he had his gun drawn and pointed her way. She fought to keep her fear under control. "If I don't return home, Ian will come looking for me."

"But by then, you'll be long gone."

Maggie tightened her grip on the reins in anticipation of making a run for home only to have Ketchum threaten, "That's a fine mount you got there, be a pity to put a bullet in her."

Maggie relaxed her hands but not the hard set of her features.

Henny turned her horse and told Ketchum, "Thank you for your services."

"Anytime."

She rode away and as she did, he sighted and put two bullets in her back. Henny cried out, slumped over her horse, and then slid to the ground. Maggie turned stricken eyes his way. Henny managed to turn over for a moment and the surprise in her eyes as she stared back at Ketchum mirrored Maggie's.

"Nice working for you, Miss Benton."

Holding the gun on Maggie now, he waved her forward. "Let's go."

Maggie saw Henny collapse back onto the road and tried not to think about meeting the same fate.

When Maggie hadn't returned home by late afternoon, Ian figured she was engrossed in something at school and had lost track of time, but when Harp galloped onto the property a short while later to let him know Henny's dead body had been found on the road near the school, the hair on the back of his neck stood up.

"Someone shot her in the back."

"Good Lord." In spite of Henny's ways, no one would have wished her such a tragic end. "Any idea who might have killed her?"

"No. Old man Jeffers found the body. He said there were at least two other sets of hoofprints there."

"Maggie's late getting home."

"School door was closed when I passed by. Maybe she's at Georgie's."

"Maybe, but something's not right. I can feel it. I'm going over to the school and see if she's there. Hopefully she is with Georgie. Where are you going?"

"Back to the spot where Jeffers said he found Henny. I was at Tom's when he brought her body home."

"Okay. Let me get Charlie and we'll ride with you as far as the school."

Ian's heart was pounding. He hurried into the house to get his gun belt and on the way, he prayed.

Maggie was trying not to let her fear best her so she could think. She also needed to find out why she was being taken. "Did Henny pay you to get rid of me?"

Ketchum was riding beside her and they were heading south. "She did, but I don't work for her."

"Draper's in jail."

"Which is where he should be, but I'm not working for him, either."

"Then who?"

"An old friend of yours named Langley."

"What?"

"Yep. He must want you bad. Paid me a thousand dollars to find you and bring you back. Promised me a thousand more once he gets his hands on you."

"I thought Sheriff Wells had him in jail."

"Wells met with an accident, so to speak. Town gave him a real nice funeral."

Maggie was speechless. Here Ian had been thinking Ketchum showing up in Wyoming had been tied to revenge against him, but in reality the killer had been after her.

"Tried to get you the day I came to the house but you were ready for me."

I have to get away from this madman!

"I like my women feisty, maybe I'll get me a taste of what you've been giving the Preacher man before I turn you over."

She shuddered with revulsion. "When Ian finds us, and he will, you're going to pray for death."

The disfigured face smiled.

"How'd you find me?" Maggie wanted him to keep talking.

"Wasn't hard. Preacher man casts a big shadow. All I had to do was ask a few of the railroad agents if they'd seen you two. The sheriff in Abilene was particularly helpful."

"Granger."

"Yep."

She frantically searched her mind for what she might have in her saddlebag to aid her escape because she had no weapons. There was a primer, what was left of her lunch, a few quill pens. She paused on that. Quills weren't nearly as effective as a rifle might have been but . . . "So where are we going?"

"Denver, then we'll take the train east to Kansas."

Maggie prayed she'd be free long before then.

For the moment she only had herself to count on because she wasn't sure if Ian or anyone else knew she was missing.

Ian did. The hoofprints left in the dusty road were a bit covered by the wheels of Jeffers's wagon but Ian could tell by what was left that Lightning and Maggie had been there. Lightning's tracks were distinctive because being the prickly mare that she was, she'd only wear a special type of shoe, and that was what Ian was looking at. "They're heading south."

He and Charlie and Harp followed the tracks for about an hour.

Charlie said, "He doesn't know the area as well as he might, so he's keeping to the road."

Just as he said that, the prints of the two horses headed into the trees and disappeared. Ian cursed and looked around. They still had no idea who she was with but they assumed it to be the person who'd back shot Henny.

Harp said, "We'll find her. Let's just keep going."

As he rode, Ian let the fury he felt override his fear because if he didn't he'd not be clearheaded enough to keep on the trail. The parts of him that loved her more than his life wanted to go galloping off at full speed screaming her name, but that would only alert whoever had taken her to his presence behind them, and he wanted to come up on the person as silently as the angel of death. A verse from Lamentations rose up from inside: *And on the day of the anger of the Lord no one escaped or survived.*

As dusk rose, Maggie was certain Ian knew

she was missing because she could feel his presence somewhere behind them. She needed to slow down the man riding beside her. "I need to relieve myself."

"Soon as I find us a place to hole up for the night."

"I can't wait." She could tell by the way he was looking around that he wasn't certain as to where they were. Maggie didn't know, either, but Ian probably knew the area as well as he knew how much she loved him, so she kept her hopes high.

They rode for a short while longer and into a small cove surrounded by towering aspens. "We'll spend the night here."

"May I go now?"

"Yeah but not too far. Get back quick or I put a bullet in your mare's head."

Maggie dismounted and grabbed her saddlebag.

"Leave that here."

"I'm bleeding from my monthly. I need to make a change."

She could see him studying her in the descending gloom. She waited.

"Go on, but remember, make it quick."

"I will."

Maggie knew he wouldn't allow her to go far so she didn't. But once she was out of sight, she opened her bag and felt around inside until she found her two quill pens. She placed one in each pocket, took care of her needs, and headed back. She wasn't on her monthly. In fact, she hadn't had one since right after arriving at Night Hawk. She thought she might be carrying a child, but hadn't said anything to Ian as of yet because she'd wanted to be sure.

Maggie returned and threw the bag back over the saddle horn. She patted Lightning with sadness and affection. "He'll find us, don't worry."

"Move away and take a seat over there."

"Can I remove her saddle? She's had a long day."

"I'll do it. Sit over there."

She sat on a felled trunk. "How do you know Langley?"

"Met him through a friend of a friend."

He unsaddled Lightning. As he set the saddle on the ground, the mare reared high on her back legs, while he scrambled to get out of the way, Lightning galloped off into the dark. He drew his gun and fired. Maggie's heart leapt into her throat but when she didn't hear any equine cries of pain to indicate the bullets had found their mark, she relaxed and smiled. Too bad the mare hadn't kicked his brains out, but Lightning was free and undoubtedly headed home. Now Ketchum would have to make her walk or take her up on his mount. Maggie was fine with either choice because both would slow them down.

What she wasn't fine with was him stalking over to her and striking her with the back of his hand so forcefully her head rocked. She grabbed her throbbing cheek.

"Bitch, if you weren't worth so much alive I'd kill you right now."

The blow left her seeing stars, and hurt much more than the last time she'd been struck by

Carson Epps. He grabbed the front of her shirt and snatched her to her feet. In that same motion she swiftly drew the quills from her pockets and shoved one metal-tipped quill deep into his throat and the other into his eye.

His scream pierced the night and he stumbled back. Maggie had no time to gloat over her handiwork, she was too busy running.

The three men heard the scream and looked in that direction. Ian offered up a deadly smile. "I think my Maggie just struck back, boys. Come on."

But before they could ride off and investigate, they heard her calling Ian's name.

He hollered back, "We're here. Keep calling!"

A few minutes later, Lightning came crashing through the trees, making their mounts rear in fright.

Charlie cursed while trying to keep from being thrown. "Where the hell's your rider!" he snapped at the prima donna mare.

Gunfire peppered the night. Ian slapped Lightning's flank. "Home!"

The mare streaked off.

Charlie grumbled, "Useless!"

And the three riders set out.

They found Maggie a few minutes later. Ian grabbed her up and was so happy to see her his tears melted into hers. "Thank God, you're safe. You're not hurt?"

"No, no. I'm fine. I'm so happy to see you."

He knew his tight hug was probably hurting her but he couldn't help himself. "Who's back there?"

"Ketchum. He shot Henny! Langley sent him after me."

Ian stared. "Okay. Charlie. Harp. Take her home."

Now that he had her back it was time for him to teach Ketchum the error of his ways. Neither man balked.

Maggie said, "You shouldn't have any trouble finding him. He's probably blind from the quill I stabbed in his eye."

Charlie took Maggie up behind him and they rode north. Ian, more in love than ever with his fiery, take-no-prisoners wife, set out to hunt human prey for what he hoped would be the last time. Putting a lit match to a fallen tree branch, he used it as a torch to light the way.

Maggie was correct. Ketchum wasn't hard to find. He was sitting in a cove of trees on the ground. His coughing gave his position away.

Ketchum jumped to his feet and wiped the blood from his eye.

"Evening," Ian said easily, and dismounted. "How's the eye?"

Ketchum squinted and raised his gun.

Ian shot him in the leg. Ketchum fell to the ground.

"This isn't going to be you draw, I shoot back, you die. That's way too simple a way to kill you for what you tried to do."

Ketchum attempted to beg through his pain. "Look, Preacher man, I didn't hurt her." He wiped at the blood again.

"But you hurt me," Ian said quietly. "You took

my wife. Your brother took my Tilda. Do you not remember what happened to him?"

Ketchum coughed and spit blood. Ian could now see that he was also bleeding from somewhere near his throat. He silently cheered his wife for her spunk. "She said she got you in the eye. Did she get you in the throat as well?"

"Go to hell!"

"I probably will but you'll be there, too."

By the light of the torch he walked closer to Ketchum so he could see the man better. "You're bleeding pretty badly. Probably hurts a lot I'll bet. Eyes are real sensitive. Soft flesh doesn't stand up well to being pierced. You may as well toss your gun away. I counted how many shots your gun fired and you don't have any left."

Ian set about building a fire. "I suppose you can keep it. Won't make a difference."

Once the fire was going he placed his torch inside and hunkered down next to the shot and bleeding man who had tried to steal his wife. Ian pulled his handcuffs from his pocket.

"You taking me in?"

Ian smiled grimly at the hope he heard in Ketchum's voice. "Nope. Going to cuff you to a tree. Even leaving you the key."

Ketchum wiped away the blood that continued to pool in his eye.

"So stand up and let's get this done so I can go home and maybe you can, too."

Ketchum stood as best he could. "Always knew you were a fair man. Always knew that."

Ian didn't reply.

Ketchum dragged his hurt leg to the trees. Ian searched the branches, saw one at just the height he'd been looking for, and cuffed Ketchum's arm to it. It was about a foot above his head.

Ketchum had to stand on his toes. "You're still leaving me the key, right?"

"Said I would. Just didn't say where." Ian tossed the key into the fire.

Ketchum began to twist and pull. "You bastard!"

The branch was sturdy. There was no way Ketchum could free himself the way his arm was extended, not without pulling it from the socket. He tried to lash out at Ian with the fist of his free hand, but the hunting knife Ian now held made him still instantly. The tip of the razor-sharp blade glinted wickedly in the firelight.

Ian said, "I'm sure you don't know this, but I'm part Scottish and we can be as savage and bloodthirsty as any race of people on the earth, especially when it comes to family."

He scored the blade quickly down Ketchum's disfigured cheek and when the man screamed and tried to cover the wound, Ian calmly scored the back of his hand. He screamed again. By then Ketchum's eyes were filled with blood and absolute fear.

"Maybe you'll get lucky and someone will ride by and cut you down because bears can smell blood from an incredible distance away, and this area is filled with them. If you're alive in the morning, you'll be arrested for Henny's murder."

Ian walked away.

"No!"

Ian mounted Smoke. "Good-bye, Mr. Ketchum."

"No, you bastard! Come back here!"

As Ketchum cursed and screamed and tried to free himself from the branch of a hundred-year-old tree, Ian rode home.

Epilogue

February 25, 1890

Maggie gave birth to their first child in the middle of the night. Georgie and Little Dove were with her during the long labor while outside the bedroom the baby had been conceived in, Ian and Charlie paced the hallway worriedly.

Little Dove stepped out and said to Ian, "You can come in now if you want. Charlie, Maggie wants to see her husband first, then she said you're welcome to come in after."

Ian drew in a breath. They'd been waiting over fourteen hours for the child to make its appearance and now that it had he felt so light-headed he could barely put one foot in front of the other. He made it in, however, and Maggie's tired smile pierced him so completely he wiped at the water filling his eyes. Georgie and Little Dove tiptoed out quietly and left the new parents alone.

"Come and see your daughter, Ian."

He walked over to the bed, and the child wrapped up and sleeping peacefully after causing so much commotion made him light-headed again. "She's beautiful," he whispered. She had a head full of jet black hair and a little rosebud mouth. He stroked the tiny cheek. "Have you named her?"

"No, I wanted to talk with you about it first."

Ian leaned down and kissed his wife and the mother of their child. "I love you. Thank you for her."

She smiled weakly. "I love you, too. If it's okay, I thought we'd name her after our mothers."

"That would be wonderful."

She looked down at the sleeping beauty in her arms. "She'll be Colleen Morning Star Vance."

"Her name's as beautiful as both she and her mother."

"I don't feel particularly beautiful right now."

"You're always beautiful to me."

"Who knew such a lovely child would be the result of me making love to a one-armed man?"

Ian laughed and stroked her damp brow. Ian's life was now complete.

Maggie's was complete as well.

And because of that they knew their future would be as bright and as special as their love.

Author Note

Dear Readers,

After more than ten years of letters, e-mails, and personal pleas from readers at book signings, I've finally written the Preacher's story. He made his initial appearance in my 1999 Avon release *The Taming of Jessi Rose.* Many readers were intrigued by this gun-toting, Bible-quoting bounty hunter, and it increased with the small but vital role his character played in 2005's *Something Like Love.* I hope *Night Hawk* has been worth the wait.

Maggie's character grew out of a chance meeting at a book signing in Omaha, Nebraska, in 2010. A young woman introduced herself as Maggie Sherman and proceeded to humble me with her thanks for my work and her words of how much the books meant to her as a woman of mixed blood. Her mother's side of the family are members of the Kaw tribe. Maggie's grandfather, Joseph Mehojah, was the last pure-blood member of the Kaw Nation, and tribal president when he passed away on Easter Sunday in 2000 at age eighty-two. Maggie's African-American roots are from her father.

To be honest, I'd never heard of the Kaw tribe, but after working on *Night Hawk,* I now know about the Wind People and so do my readers. My deepest thanks to Maggie and her family for their help with my research. Without them the fictional Maggie would never have come to life, nor would I have learned that Charles Curtis, a member of the Kaw tribe, served as vice president to Herbert Hoover from 1929 to 1933.

Although Charlie's crazy story about the skin of Big Nose George Parrot being turned into a medical bag and a pair of shoes after his death by Dr. John Osborne may sound like a tall tale, this really did occur. Dr. Osborne went on to become the first Democratic governor of Wyoming and reportedly wore the shoes at his inaugural ball. Later, he became assistant secretary of state during President Woodrow Wilson's administration. Currently, the shoes, along with Big Nose's death mask and skull, are on display at the Carbon County Museum in Rawlins, Wyoming. Truth is stranger than fiction, folks!

The Chinese Exclusion Act was something else I knew nothing about until I began the research for this story. Sometimes we gain a greater respect for people when we know their history, so I hope the hard road the government forced the Chinese to walk was as much an eye-opener for my readers as it was for me.

Charlie's chronicling of Jim Beckworth is another true story. Beckworth was a mountain man in every sense of the word. Not only was he a Crow chief, but Beckworth Pass in Colorado is named after him. The next time your kids or grandkids have to do a report on the early days of the American West or for Black History month, Jim Beckworth is your man. Susie King Taylor, who paved the way for African-American nurses, is also worthy of further research.

Here are some of the resources I used to bring *Night Hawk* to life:

Taylor, Quintard, and Shirley Ann Wilson Moore, eds. *African American Women Confront the West, 1600–2000.* Norman: University of Oklahoma Press, 2003.

Unrau, William E. *The Kansa Indians: A History of the Wind People, 1673–1873.* Norman: University of Oklahoma Press, 1986.

In closing, I'd like to thank my readers for their tremendous support. I'd not have this amazing career without you.

Until next time,

B.

At Avon Books, we know your passion for romance—once you finish one of our novels, you find yourself wanting more.

May we tempt you with . . .

- **Excerpts** from our upcoming releases.
- Entertaining **extras**, including authors' personal photo albums and book lists.
- Behind-the-scenes **scoop** on your favorite characters and series.
- **Sweepstakes** for the chance to win free books, romantic getaways, and other fun prizes.
- Writing **tips** from our authors and editors.
- **Blog** with our authors and find out why they love to write romance.
- **Exclusive content** that's not contained within the pages of our novels.

Join us at
www.avonbooks.com

An Imprint of HarperCollins*Publishers*
www.avonromance.com

Available wherever books are sold or please call 1-800-331-3761 to order.

FTH 0708

978-0-06-200304-1

978-0-06-202719-1

978-0-06-206932-0

978-0-06-194638-7

978-0-06-199968-0

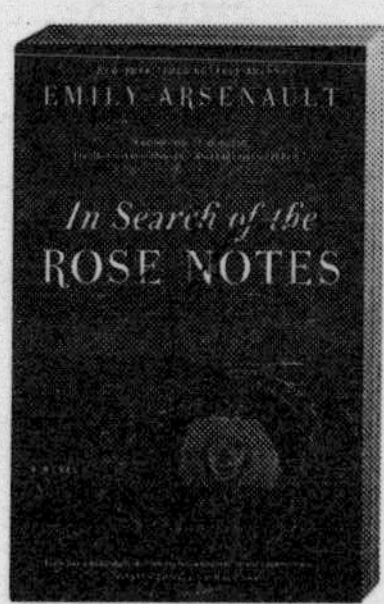

978-0-06-201232-6

Visit www.AuthorTracker.com for exclusive information on your favorite HarperCollins authors.

Available wherever books are sold, or call 1-800-331-3761 to order.

ATP 1111

Give in to Impulse . . .

and satisfy your every whim for romance!

Avon Impulse is

- Fresh, Fun, and Fabulous eBook Exclusives
- New Digital Titles Every Week

The best in romance fiction,
delivered digitally to today's savvy readers!

www.AvonImpulse.com

IMP 0711